哈福

哈福

哈福

— **English for Business Negotiations** —

商務談判英語
看這本就夠了

（AI時代第一本商務談判英語）
·成功談判·商場無敵·

關鍵100句談判英文，出奇制勝

附QR碼線上音檔
行動學習·即刷即聽

湯姆斯
張瑪麗 ◎合著

哈福

[前言]
AI時代的第一本
商務談判英語

●　●　●　●　●

　　商場局勢詭譎多變，如何在瞬息萬變的環境中，順利勝出，擁有流利的英語，及熟悉談判的技巧，是突危的重大關鍵。尤其在國際談判場合中，與多國人士打交道，能用道地的英語行話洽談，首次交鋒，便讓對方知難而退，為自己及所屬公司，謀取更多福利，打場漂亮的商場舌戰，順利達成任務。

　　美國作家湯姆斯先生，集結在多年的商場實戰經驗，費時一年寫出本著作，讓所有內行人看門道，提升英語談判能力；初階者，能在作者循循善誘及精心設計的內容中，快速一窺談判的殿堂，並用最道地、實用的美國行話進行會談，不論是在日常的會面場合，亦或是正式的談判桌前，您都能藉著湯姆斯的引導，輕鬆開啟談判成功之門。

　　書中內容深入淺出，每一頁、每一句都是專業人士的經驗結晶，在每個單元的開始處，都有中文及英文的「背景介紹」，完全以臨場實務為原則。搭配線上 MP3，讓您臨場會話一氣呵成，「背景介紹」則如同聽故事一般，搭配著宜人的輕音樂，輕鬆學習，快速進階。

一、For Your Information　背景介紹：融會作者十年商場經驗，為讀者做詳盡的談判戰略分析！

二、Dialog　範例對話：為了方便讀者的全面吸收，本書特別並將主要單字用有色字体標出，方便您記憶。同樣地，為了體貼生活分秒必爭的讀者們，對話部分也附上一針見血的中文譯解，增加您對談判用語、慣用語的印象與熟悉度。

三、Tips　談判停看聽：數十則最符合談判情境的解析，根據對話使用時機與實際臨場狀況，並將主要單字用有色字体標出，方便您記憶。最原汁原味的英語說明，除了為讀者補充談吐用詞，也是最方便的談判技巧秘訣！

四、Vocabulary　重要字彙：上百個最符合商務情境的單字，是您談判時最不可或缺的關鍵字彙，除了補充單字，也搭配幾個常用片語，談判大補帖絕對不能錯過！

有別於一般市面上的英語書籍，本書在字彙、對話及貼切中譯之外，更加上作者實際經驗談的「背景介紹」及拆招解招的「談判停看聽」。讀者只要一融會貫通，即能悠游於國際談判場合，從容談出新商機！

英語的表達方式豐富且多元，而這正是這個語言趣味的地方。藉由本書，相信您增加的不只是實用的字彙，更可以流暢談話，輕鬆融入外國商場的交際圈。不論是談判術語、事務研討、產品介紹或議價籌碼等等，讓您放眼國際，掌握全球趨勢，輕鬆駕御商務英語。

Part 2　商務談判贏家關鍵 100 句

英文會話本身重在了解對方意見、表達自身想法，有效達成溝通，完成意見交換。而商界常需使用到的談判英語，程度上則更進階，你必須在表達己意之外，還要說服對方、改變對方立場，這已經不是單純的禮貌性會話可以含括的，很多時候你可能需要強硬地堅定立場、以迂迴戰術旁敲側擊，或者展開瓦解對方防線的心理戰術。

你心裡或許會想：「這沒那麼容易吧！我的英文並沒有這麼厲害！」其實，真的沒有這麼難，面對一場談判桌上進行的英文會議，當然你一定要具備基本的會話能力，並且針對主題內容有充分的事前準備，除此之外，其實你只需要掌握一些關鍵的英文用語，不但完美的展現專業，並且只要用對時機，往往就能在談判過程中發揮推波助瀾的效果。

針對商界人士此一特殊需求，本書特別收錄超過 100 句談判桌上最常出現的慣用語，教你如何以純熟的技巧分析談判焦點，適時以退為進、以攻為守，或是轉換語氣、堅守立場，熟練這些談判桌上臨機應變的課題，就能輕鬆練就談判英文，活用籌碼出奇制勝！

在適當時刻巧妙發揮，不但能表現你的英語專業，更有為簡報或談判畫龍點睛之效。不論是何種規模或主題的會議進行，要達到說服對方的目的，自信的態度和深入人心的訴求為首要關鍵。面對外國客戶時，善用熟悉的慣用語，在表現自信之餘，更能迅速拉近彼此的距離，功效不容小覷。希望本書能加強充實您的英語會話功力，更讓每一場談判會議如魚得水，贏得商機！

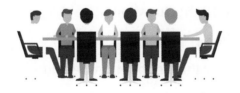

Contents

Part 2 商務談判贏家關鍵100句

Chapter 1

Daily Negotiations

日常談判

For Your Information
背景介紹

MP3-44

Negotiations aren't just for business; they lie at the heart of all human **interaction**. They make it possible for society to **function**. Unless you're a **hermit** living in a cave, you negotiate things every day from the time you get up, until you go to bed. At home, people **negotiate** the restaurant they go to, the movie they see, the TV program they watch, who showers first, and who goes to the market. At work, we negotiate who uses the **copy machine** first, and who watches the phone during lunch.

中譯 談判不只是為了做生意而已，它們根植於所有人類的溝通活動中，讓社會得以運作。除非你是一個住在洞穴裡的隱士，否則你每天從早上起床開始，到睡覺為止，都得談判。當人們在家中時，人們會為了要去哪家餐廳、看哪部電影、哪個電視節目、誰先洗澡、誰該去超市買東西而商量、決議。在工作上，我們得討論誰先用影印機、誰該在午餐時間留下來接電話……。

Our day is one continuous negotiation, and it's likely none of them **involve** money. We're so used to negotiating that we don't even think about it, it's how we live peacefully together. We learn in childhood that things are a value for value trade off.

中譯 我們每日的生活就是不斷的商議，而這些商議都和金錢無關。我們太習慣和他人商議，所以這樣的動作幾乎成了我們的反射動作，商議、談判正是人們得以和平相處的原因。我們在孩童時期就學到了每件事都有價值，都可以當作是談判籌碼。

To get what we want, we have to trade what we have, and we take that idea into adulthood. It's great if things stay like that your entire life. If all negotiations were performed with the honesty kids use in the playground, there'd be no need for this book. But, sometimes they don't. Things have been kicked up a few notches, and some negotiators don't play fair. This book will tell you what's going on, and how to handle it.

中譯 要得到自己想要的東西，我們就必須拿自己擁有的東西去交換，而我們也把這種思想模式帶到了成人階段。如果事情能夠一輩子都是這樣該多好。如果談判時，大家都秉持著孩提時代玩耍時的誠實態度，這本書就沒有寫的必要。但是有時候，人們並不會誠實相待。事情改觀了，有些談判人員並不會公平就事論事，而本書將會為你解析情況，並給你一些應對的參考。

There are no set pattern negotiations in English that you must follow. It's determined by the local customs and the players involved. I've seen minor points take days of hard talking, and once negotiated a three hundred thousand dollar contract during a two-hour lunch. We spent five minutes on the deal, the rest on other topics.

中譯 英語並沒有必得遵守的既定談判模式，全端看當地的規矩和相關人員而定。我曾為一些小事情，費盡唇舌商量；但也有一次，只花了兩個小時的午餐時間，便談成了總值三十萬美金的合約。真正在談生意只花了五分鐘，其他時間都在談其他的事。

The following are examples of day-to-day negations we perform without thinking. The first shows Jack and Mary as children at play working things out. In the second one, Jack and Mary are a couple planning an evening out. The third shows Jack and Mary as coworkers cooperating to keep things running smoothly.

中譯　下面這幾個對話，是我們不自覺中就會進行的日常生活談判。第一個對話是孩提時代的傑克和瑪莉，他們正想解決事情。第二個對話中，傑克和瑪莉是一對情侶，他們在商量晚上要去哪裡。在第三個對話中，傑克和瑪莉是同事，他們討論該如何把工作配合地盡善盡美。

Dialog 1　　　　　　　　　　　　　　　　MP3-2

This dialog is between Jack, who's pretty good at playing chess, and his friend and next-door neighbor Mary, a member of the school chess club. Jack promised to play chess with Mary on Monday after school, to help her get ready for a competition if she did the dishes for him on Sunday. Mary did the dishes and now Jack needs to keep his promises.

這個對話發生在傑克和瑪莉之間。傑克相當擅長西洋棋，他的隔壁鄰居瑪莉是學校西洋棋社的社員。傑克答應星期一放學後，要和瑪莉下西洋棋，幫助她準備競賽，條件是瑪莉星期天要幫他洗碗。瑪莉履行了她的承諾，現在傑克該實踐自己的諾言了。

Jack : I'm going to the park to play baseball with the guys.

我要去公園和大夥兒打棒球。

Mary : But you promised to play chess with me this afternoon.

可是你答應今天下午要和我一起下西洋棋。

Jack : Yeah, but that was before the guys asked me to join the team.

對啊，可是我之前不知他們會邀我加入球隊啊。

Mary : So what?

那又怎樣？

Jack : You know how much I want to be on the team, and now there's an opening for me.

你知道我多想要加入球隊，現在正好有一個名額可以給我。

If I don't go to practice today, they'll get someone else, and I'll miss my chance.

如果我今天不去練習的話，他們會去找別人，那我就會錯過這次機會。

Mary : I don't care about baseball, you know I need to practice for the chess championship, and you promised to help me if I washed the dishes for you last Sunday, and I did.

我才不管棒球，你知道我得為這次的西洋棋冠軍賽練習。你答應過，只要我上星期日幫你洗碗的話，你就會幫我，而我已經洗碗了。

Jack : I know, and I will.

我知道，我會幫你的。

Mary : When?

什麼時候？

Jack : After baseball practice.

棒球練習完以後。

Mary : By then, it will be dinnertime, then homework and then your TV show is on. You're going to break your promise.

可是那時候就是晚餐時間了，然後你又要做功課、看電視，你一定會不守信用。

Jack : No, I won't. I'm going to skip TV tonight and work on your chess game with you if that's okay with you?

我不會背信的。我今晚不看電視，和你一起下西洋棋，你說好不好？

Mary : Well, I'd rather do it the way we **set up**, but if you promise to give me your best game, it's okay with me.

我比較喜歡原來的約定，不過如果你保證會好好地陪我下棋，那就可以。

Jack : No problem. I'll play as hard as I can and give you an extra game to say thanks.

沒問題。我一定使出全力，再多陪你下一場，以示回報。

Dialog 2　　　　　　　　　　　　　　　　　MP3-3

Jack and Mary are now grown up and dating. Their friendship is as strong as ever and there's a strong bond between them, so their dialog is relaxed and flows pretty freely. It's more like a married couple than young adults dating to get to know each other.

傑克和瑪莉長大了，現在在他們是一對情侶。他們的友誼非常堅固，彼此有著深刻的默契。他們的談話也很自在、隨性，不像是約會中的年輕男女，反倒像一對恩愛的夫妻。

Mary : Let's have seafood tonight and then go see the new movie at the Mall Cinema.

我們今晚吃海鮮，然後再去「摩爾戲院」看最新上映的電影。

Betsy told me it's a beautiful love story and I shouldn't miss it.

貝希說那是一部唯美愛情文藝片，我絕對不能錯過。

Jack : Oh, Goodness, please not again. That's what we did last week.

噢，天啊，別又來了，我們上個星期也是這樣過的。

Mary : No, we didn't. Last week we went to see that

movie about a man's struggle against mental illness.

才沒有呢！上星期我們看的電影，是在講一個男人與心理病痛掙扎的過程。

Jack : Right, it was a **chick flick**, just like this one, so what's the difference?

沒錯，那是你們女生看的電影，這部也一樣。哪裡不同？

Besides, this is the last week for the third movie in the **Destroyer** series and I want to see that on a big screen.

再說，這是《毀滅者》第三部最後一週上演了，我希望能在大銀幕上看這部電影。

Action movies need to be seen in a theater on a big screen.

動作片就是要在電影院的大銀幕上看。

Mary : Oh, yeah, and I did promise to see it with you if we went to that movie last week. But you liked that movie, didn't you?

對啦，我的確答應過你，如果上週去看那部片子的話，就陪你去看這部電影。可是你應該很喜歡那部片吧？

Jack : Oh, sure, it was great. I had popcorn for dinner and paid the price of a movie ticket to get a two-hour nap.

喔，當然，真是棒透了。我的晚餐是爆米花，買了電影票卻睡了二個小時。

Mary : It wasn't that bad, and you're the one that **insisted on** skipping dinner. We went to an excellent restaurant.

沒那麼糟吧，是你自己說不要吃晚餐的；我們去的那家餐廳很棒啊。

Jack : That place doesn't have a single meat dish. Just fish and shellfish and you know I don't like fish that much.

那裡一道肉食都沒有，只有魚類和貝類，你知道我不是很喜歡吃魚。

Mary : And I don't like meat that much. The only meat I eat is chicken.

可是我不是很喜歡吃肉，我只吃雞肉而已。

Jack : But when I pick the restaurant, we go to a place that has both chicken and fish. I always respect your food **preferences**.

但是我選餐廳時，我都會選供應應雞肉和魚的餐廳。我一向都很尊重你對食物的喜好。

Mary : Well, I suppose that, to be fair, you should get to pick the movie and we can go to a restaurant that serves meat.

好吧，為了公平起見，還是你選電影，然後我們去有肉食料理的餐廳吃飯。

Jack : Now you're talking, we can see that love story next time.

你總算開竅了，我們可以下次再看愛情文藝片。

Dialog 3　　　　　　　　　　　　　　　MP3-4

In this dialog, Jack and Mary work at the same company, and remain good friends. They remain very **professional** and keep the dating part of their relationship to themselves and out of the work place. No one at work knows they're dating.

在下面的對話中，傑克和瑪莉是同事，也是好朋友。他們在工作上保持專業的態度，並公私分明。辦公室沒有人知道他們是情侶。

Jack : Hi, are you busy?

嗨，你在忙嗎？

Mary : Hi, I was just coming to see you. But since you made the **trek** to my office, you get to go first.

嗨，我正要過去找你，既然你都來了，有事你先說吧。

Jack : Okay, I'm putting together a report on the Allied Marketing Co. failure, and I seem to have **run into a stone wall**. Can you help me out?

好，我正在準備一份「聯合行銷公司」倒閉分析的報告。我遇到了瓶頸，你可以幫我一下嗎？

Mary : Well, I can try, what do you need?

我可以試試看，你需要什麼幫助？

Jack : You were there when the problem started. I was hoping you could **fill** me **in** on the details.

問題發生時，你在場，所以我希望能聽你說說當時的細節。

Mary : Sure, no problem. But I need something from you.

好啊，沒問題，但我也需要你的幫忙。

Jack : Name it.

儘管說。

Mary : I'm supposed to have this package ready for mailing out tomorrow morning and I'm **miles away from** being ready.

我得將這個套案整理好，明天一早發送出去，但我根本還沒有準備好。

Can you **edit** this product study I wrote while I do these?

你可以幫我編輯這份產品報告，好讓我準備這個套案嗎？

Jack : All right, I can do that, and as soon as we finish this, we can both work on my problem.

行，一旦這個部分做完了，我們就可以一起處理我的問題了。

Mary : That works for me.

當然沒問題。

Jack： Give me the study. I'll start as soon as I get back to my office.

把那份報告給我，我回到辦公室後，就會立刻開始做。

Mary： Here's a print out of the study, and this is a disc with the full report on it.

這是報告的影本，這張磁片裡有完整的報告檔案。

The *file* name is product study; this is an extra copy so you can do whatever you want with it.

檔案名稱是產品研究，這裡還有一份影本，你可以直接在上面作記號。

談判停看聽 The above are three **prime** examples of the kinds of negotiations we make with people in our everyday lives. There was no **formal** set up or **appointment** made first, they just happened **in the course of** doing the business of living. These are the sort of things we do every day.

中譯 上面這三個例子，是我們日常生活中常見的談判範例。這些自然而然發生的討論，並不須要事先制定或預約，而是我們每天都會經歷的。

Vocabulary 重要字彙	MP3-5
interaction	互動
function	運作
hermit	隱士
negotiate	談判
copy machine	影印機
involve	牽涉

trade off	交易
playground	遊樂場
kick up	引發
notch	鴻溝
play fair	公平行事
set pattern	固定模式
determined	堅定的
custom	慣例
minor point	次要點
hard talking	激烈談論
topic	主題
cooperate	合作
smoothly	順利地
chess	西洋棋
competition	競爭
do the dishes	洗碗
keep one's promise	守住承諾
so what?	又怎麼樣？
be on the team	成為隊員
opening	機會
championship	冠軍賽
break one's promise	背棄承諾
skip	略過
work on	工作
set up	訂下
bond	聯繫

mental	心理的
chick flick	女生愛看的電影
insist on	堅持
preference	偏好
remain	維持
professional	專業的
trek	艱難跋涉
run into a stone wall	遇到困難
fill in	提供最新消息
name it	直說
miles away from	很遠的
edit	編輯
file	檔案
prime	主要的
formal	正式的
appointment	約會
in the course of	在軌道上

Chapter 2

Sometimes
It's Fast and Easy

快速、簡單的談判

For Your Information
背景介紹

MP3-45

A fair and **equitable** deal can be reached quickly, with a **minimum** of **effort** on even the most **complex** issues. It depends on who the major players are, how **motivated** they feel and whether lawyers play an active role. If you think that's a little unfair to **attorneys**, you may be right. However, most of the lawyers I've worked with agree with me, **off the record**, of course.

中譯 公平、平等的交易，即使議題複雜，也可以輕鬆達成。這一切取決於主要談判人員是否積極，以及律師是否扮演了主動的角色。或許你認為這對代書來說有點不公平，但私下來說，大部分和我共事過的律師，都同意這點，當然是私底下囉。

There are businessmen and women out there who still do things the **old- fashioned** way. Their negotiating style is much the same as it was when they were kids. They know the rules, that to get value, they have to give value. All they want is a reasonable **profit**. When you **run across** a company like this, you should go out of your way to keep them happy.

中譯 商場上有些男女，仍然用傳統方法做事；他們的談判模式和孩提時代很像，遊戲規則就是：「想要什麼，就得拿東西來換。」既然他們要求的是「合理的利潤」，當你碰上這樣的公司時，應該盡量讓他們開心。

Dialog 1　MP3-6

In the following dialog, Mike is an honest old-fashioned businessman content to make an honest living. He wants to buy some big screen TV sets to distribute in the US. May has often contacted Mike and tried to sell him electronics, but this is the first time she's meeting Mike in person and she's hopeful Mike will actually buy from her.

在下面的會話中，麥可是一個誠實又傳統的商人，他喜歡安分地做生意。這次，他想要買一些大螢幕電視機，分銷到美國各地。梅常和麥可聯絡，想將電器賣給他。這是她第一次見到麥可本人，她希望麥可會和她下單。

Mike : Hello, come in, I've been waiting for you.

嗨，請進，我等你好久了。

May : Thank you, I'm not late, am I?

謝謝，我沒有遲到吧？

Mike : No, no, no, not at all. It's just that I've been looking forward to meeting you.

沒有，沒有。我只是很期待見到你，才會這麼説。

May : Well, thank you, but it's not all that hard to do, you know.

謝謝，不過你也知道，要見我並不難。

I've been calling your office and sending you proposals for about two years now, and you've never responded before.

我打電話、寄商業提案給你，前前後後也差不多二年了；你從來沒有回覆過。

Mike : Ha, ha, ha! Yes, I guess I deserved that. Let me explain, okay?

哈！看來我的確是不應該。聽我解釋，好嗎？

May : Please, I wish you would.

請，我正希望你這麼做。

Mike : Well, as you probably know I buy from a selected group of **suppliers** and don't, as a rule, deal with new people.

你應該知道我一向都和固定的供應商下單，照慣例，我不會和新人打交道。

May : Yes, I know that. It's why I've been trying to become one of those suppliers. I hear you're a good man to do business with.

是的，我知道。這也是為什麼，我一直想要打進那些供應商的圈子。我聽說和你做生意很不錯。

Mike : I'm very old-fashioned. I believe in **loyalty**. Once I start a sales relationship with someone, I stay with him or her, and we do most of our business on the phone.

我是個很傳統的人，我相信忠誠度。一旦建立了銷售關係，我就會延續下去，且大部分的生意都在電話上談。

I expect their absolute best price possible and don't **haggle**. But if I find out they **screwed** me **over**, then I find another supplier.

我希望得到最好的價格，不要討價還價。一旦發現有人欺騙我，我會立刻換廠商。

May : That's pretty much what I heard.

我也是這麼聽說。

Mike : Well, those are my terms. As long as you honor them, we do business.

這些是我的條件。只要你遵守這些規矩，我們就可以做生意。

If you break faith and try to **take advantage**, I'll find someone else to work with. Can you **live with** that?

若你背信或想佔便宜，我就會找別人。你可以接受這樣的條件嗎？

May： No problem at all, Mike. Just give me the chance.

沒問題，麥可。請給我一個機會。

Dialog 2　　　　　　　　　　　　　　　　　MP3-7

　　The meeting is going well for May. She's been offered a chance to work with Mike and become one of his suppliers. Next, they have to work out an understanding. Situations like this are not that uncommon, the buyer is in charge, and he gets to make the rules. That's the way it usually is. In the next part of the negotiation, May finds out Mike's ground rules and decides if she can live with them. Even though this sounds like instruction, it is a negotiation.

　　對梅而言，這次會面進行得很順利。麥可提供她一次合作的機會，讓她成為他的供應商。接下來，他們必須討論出一些共識。這類情形頗為常見，在這種情形中，買家會主導一切，訂定規則。通常情況都是這樣。在下面這種談判情形中，梅了解了麥可的基本原則，她得決定是否接受這些規則。雖然這聽起來像是指令，但還是談判。

Mike： Well, that's why you're here. My source for Big TV sets overcharged me on the last shipment, so I need someone new.

這就是我找你來的原因。我的大型電視供應商，上一次交貨時敲了我一筆，所以我現在要找新的供應商。

I wanted to meet you to see if we can work together. I think we can.

我跟你見面是想看看合作的可能性；我想應該沒問題。

May： I agree.

我同意。

Mike : Fine, but before you agree, don't you need to know what you're agreeing to?

很好，但在同意之前，你難道不想多了解一下，你到底同意了哪些條件嗎？

May : I guess you're right. But like you said, you called me here to check me out. I've been doing the same.

沒錯，但就像你說的，你打電話叫我過來，是想探探我的底細；當然，我也是一樣的。

Mike : Ha, ha, ha! That's fair. How did I do?

哈哈！這很公平，我表現得如何？

May : Quite good, actually. I'm pretty sure you're demanding, but fair and honest. I feel we can work together.

說真的，相當不錯。我確定你的要求很高，但是很公平、誠實。我想我們可以合作。

Mike : Good, well, here's what I need from you. Are you ready?

很好，我要說明需要你配合的地方了，準備好了嗎？

May : Shoot!

請說！

Mike : Well, I know you work for someone else, but as your client, please, we have to get this straight between us.

我知道你有老闆，但身為你的客戶，麻煩你，我們必須先把話說清楚。

I'm your client, not your company. As your client, I expect you to be square with me at all times. Can you do that?

我是你的客戶，不是你的公司。身為你的客戶，我希望你隨時對我坦誠，這點你做得到嗎？

May : I don't see a problem.

沒問題。

Mike : Good! Do you have any questions?

很好！你有問題想問嗎？

Dialog 3　　　　　　　　　　　　　MP3-8

　　Now that the basic ground rules are set and the details have to be cleared up. In the next stage of the negotiation, May learns what Mike needs and has to decide if she can do that.

　　既然現在這些基本的規則都訂好了，細節也都說清楚了，在下個階段的談判中，梅知道了麥可的需求後，得確定自己是否能達到要求。

May : What happens if we make a deal and thirty to sixty days after delivery the price goes down and you didn't get the best possible price?

如果我們達成了交易，但交貨的三十到六十天內，市面降價，導致你的價格不是最好的，該怎麼辦？

How do I handle that?

我要如何處理？

Mike : Well, these things happen, I know that. You just have to stay straight with me.

嗯，這是難免的，你只要誠實地告知我就可以了。

May : Right! So how do I do that? What will make you happy?

好！那我該如何配合，才是你最滿意的狀況？

Mike : Well, I suggest you just keep me posted. That should do it.

我建議你隨時跟我報告最新狀況，這樣就夠了。

That way the **burden** is on me to decide when to buy, not you.

那樣，我就能準確下單。畢竟決定的人是我，不是你。

May： Excuse me?

什麼？

Mike： Yeah, it really is that simple.

沒錯，就是這麼簡單。

Every time there's a change in the **items** we do business on, you let me know. That's all you need to do.

只要交易的項目有了改變，你就要讓我知道。這麼做就夠了。

May： What kind of change, just in prices?

什麼改變，只有價格嗎？

Mike： No, any change. I want you to keep me as informed as you are.

不，任何改變，我要你隨時提供最新發展給我。

I need to know as much as you do. If you hear about something that might happen, then tell me about it.

你知道的事，我也要知道。如果你聽到什麼風聲，你就要告訴我。

Tell me it's a **rumor**, what it's based on and your opinion on how likely it is.

就算是傳言，也要告訴我為什麼會有這種傳言，你認為其可信度怎樣。

May： You mean on product **availability**, **reliability** and price?

你是指產品的獲得性？可信度？還有價格？

Mike： No, everything. Those things for sure, but also labor problems, **raw materials**, new **subcontractors**, **mergers**, in short, anything and everything.

不只，是每件事。當然包含你剛剛說的那些項目，還有勞工問題、原料、新合約商、合併等。總而言之，每件事我都要知道。

So I can make a fully informed decision.

這樣我的決定才不會下錯。

May : So it's like you want me to be your eyes and ears into the industry.

也就是說，你要我當你在業界的眼線。

I can do that, provided the company I'm working for isn't hurt.

可以是可以，只要不影響我的公司就好。

Mike : I think we'll get along fine.

我想我們會合作愉快的。

Vocabulary　重要字彙

MP3-9

equitable	公平的
minimum	最小的
effort	努力
complex	複雜的
motivate	激發
attorney	律師；代書
off the record	私下來說；沒有記載的
old-fashioned	老式的；傳統的
profit	利潤
run across	審視
content	高興的
make a living	謀生

distribute	供應
electronics	電器
proposal	企劃；提案
respond	回應
supplier	供應商
loyalty	忠誠度
haggle	討價還價
screw over	欺騙
take advantage	利用；佔便宜
live with	（勉強）接受
ground rule	基本原則
instruction	指令
overcharged	索價過高
shipment	運貨
shoot	直說
square	正直的
burden	重擔；負擔
item	貨物；項目
rumor	謠傳
availability	可得度
reliability	可信度
raw material	原料
subcontractor	承包商
merger	合併

Chapter 3

Playing Fair
公平交易

For Your Information
背景介紹

MP3-46

I did my best for my clients, but I never screwed a contractor to gain my client an unfair advantage, and that earned me a **reputation** for being fair. It made it easier for me to do business and get good deals for my clients. I was more effective with less effort than the other managers in the office. I got things done faster and the company's board was able to handle business more easily, especially when it came to getting competitive bids.

中譯　我一向盡全力服務客戶，但我也不會因此壓榨承包商，藉此為客戶獲取額外的利益，而這也為我贏得了公平的美譽。跟客戶做生意時，我比其他經理更有效率，也花費較少精力。我辦事快速，因此董事會可以更輕鬆地處理公務，尤其是在爭取競爭激烈的標價時。

Thankfully, there were a lot of businessmen and women out there who were the same way and bidding out work was one of the easier parts of my job. Being fair and easy to deal with got me the bids on time with a minimum of effort. Once a bid was accepted, working out the details was friendly and quick.

中譯　幸好，商場上有許多男女也持相同的做事態度，所以對外競標是我工作上最簡單的一部分。「公平」和「親和力」這兩項特質，讓我花最少的力氣，就能準時得到報價。報價一旦得手，談細節就會友善又快速。

When I asked for a bid, the contractor knew I was serious and the work would be done. I wasn't just getting data for a curious board that might not do the work for another year or two. What I'm getting at is that no matter how large the town where you do business is, not everyone in the town is in the same business. The people in your field are competitors and they may not share trade secrets but they do talk and from time to time you get to be the topic of the day. It's a small town, and everybody knows everybody else.

中譯　當我要求標價時，合約商知道我是認真的，就會準時出價。因為我不是在幫一、兩年內都不打算動工的董事會，蒐集滿足他們好奇心的資料而已。我的重點是，不管你在多大的城市做生意，遇到的不可能都是同行。同行的人都是競爭者，當然不會把商業機密談開來。但是大家還是會討論，甚至有時候，你也會是大家的談論主題。業界是個小地方，每個人都知道對方的底細。

Remember there's no such thing as a free lunch. Everything has a price and somebody pays for it. A free estimate isn't free. It's called free because you don't have to pay for it but it cost time and materials for the vendor to prepare. They are part of the game and every proposal doesn't get accepted, but if a vendor has a choice of doing one for someone who only asks when he's serious or someone who is only testing the waters for a sale that's still months down the road, and the job will have to be bid for again, who gets priority?

中譯　要記住，「天下沒有白吃的午餐」，每樣東西都有價碼，總有人要付出代價。「免費估價」不是真的免費，之所以稱為免費，是指你不用付費，但它是需要賣方花功夫或材料準備的。這是遊戲的一部分，並不是每個提案都會被接受。然而如果廠商能選擇為誰估價，一方是很認真詢問的人；另一方只是試探的要一些資料，好幾個月後才會動工,且到時又要再報一次價。你認為廠商會以誰為優先考量?

If it's for information only, I tell them so. Then, the vendor knows how much research he needs and it will take him or her a tenth of the time it takes to put a formal bid. After you're asked for a bid, stay in contact with your contacts. If they lose the bid, you should call them and tell them the details about why they lost it, so they know all their work wasn't for nothing.

中譯 如果我的目的只是為了獲取資料,我會坦白告訴對方,讓賣方知道自己該出多少力:通常只需正式報價的十分之一準備即可。在招標時,你也該和對方的窗口保持聯絡,若對方競標失敗,你也該致電對方,解釋原因,讓他們知道自己的努力不是白費。

Dialog 1 　　　　　　　　　　　　　　MP3-10

The following dialogs are phone conversations. The first dialog is about asking for bid information only, just to find out what prices are like. The second is about asking for a real bid, and a contract will be awarded. In the third dialog, a loser is called to inform him how the bidding went. Marsha is the manager and Bill the contractor.

下面的都是電話對談。第一個會話是關於探聽行情時的報價資料索取。第二個對話是關於須簽訂合約的正式招標。第三個對話是沒有得標的商家,接到競標結果的通知電話。瑪莎是經理,比爾是廠商。

Marsha : Hi, Bill. It's Marsha Black at MPPM Ltd. How are you?

嗨,比爾。我是 MPPM 公司的瑪莎・布萊克,你好嗎?

Bill : Hello, Marsha, I haven't heard from you in a long time. I'm great, and you?

嗨，瑪莎，好久沒有你的消息了。我很好，你呢？

Marsha : Not too bad at all. Do you have a minute?

還不錯。你有空嗎？

Bill : Sure, what can I do for you?

當然，有什麼需要我效勞的？

Marsha : We're getting ready to place our Christmas orders and we need to know about how much it's going to run this year. You know, so we can have the funds put aside.

我們正準備要下聖誕節的訂單，因此想先探探行情是多少。你也知道，這樣我們才能撥出適當的經費。

Bill : I'm really busy right now. I got a lot on my plate. So this isn't an actual bid you want but just a **ballpark** figure?

我現在真的很忙，有很多事得處理。你要的不是正式報價，只是大概的估計數字嗎？

Marsha : Right, a ballpark figure is fine, and **slant** it a little high if you have to.

對，約略數字就可以了。必要的話，價格可以估高一點。

Bill : Well, I can give you those figures now over the phone, is that okay? Or do you need them in writing?

直接在電話上跟你說，還是你要書面估價？

Marsha : It's going to be shown to the Board so I need it in writing.

這是董事會要看的，所以我要書面估價。

Make all the prices subject to confirmation so you can't be held to them. How soon can I have it?

每個數值都要再確認，免得人家挑你毛病。什麼時候可以給我？

Bill : Is this another rush, dear? Did you forget and wait until the last minute again?

親愛的，又是急件？你又壓到最後一刻才處理啊？

Marsha : Yeah, I'm afraid so. I really need your help here.

是啊，恐怕是，我真的需要你的幫忙。

Bill : Well, just because it's you. Tomorrow, say around noon.

好吧，就為了你，大概明天中午吧。

Dialog 2

MP3-11

In the above dialog, Marsha is very honest about what she needs and gets it as a favor from a busy vendor. In this dialog, she's ready to buy and gets good service.

在上面的對話中，瑪莎誠實地說明自己索取資料的目的，所以即使對方很忙，還是願意幫忙。這個對話中，瑪莎決定正式採購，因此也得到很配合的回應。

Marsha : Hi, Bill. It's Marsha Black at MPPM Ltd. How are you?

嗨，比爾。我是 MPPM 的瑪莎·布萊克，你好嗎？

Bill : Hello, Marsha. I'm great, and you?

嗨，瑪莎。我很好，你呢？

Marsha : Not too bad at all. Do you have a minute?

還好，你有空嗎？

Bill : Sure, what can I do for you?

當然，有什麼需要我效勞的？

Marsha : We're ready to place our Christmas order and we need a formal bid.

我們準備好要下聖誕節的訂單，所以需要正式的標價。

Bill : So this is the real thing?

這次來真的了？

Marsha : Right, this is not a **drill**. This is for all the **marbles**.

沒錯，這可不是演習，而是真槍實彈的。

Bill : When do you need it?

你什麼時候要？

Marsha : ASAP, in writing of course.

越快越好，當然是書面的。

Bill : Sure, who am I bidding against?

沒問題，我的競標對手是誰？

Marsha : The usual guys, so you better use a sharp pencil.

老面孔，所以你的價格要特別注意。

Bill : Okay, give me a week and I'll have time to get my pencil real sharp. I should have some new figures from Malaysia by then.

好，給我一個禮拜，我會把價錢算得服服貼貼的。那時候，馬來西亞也該有新價格了。

Dialog 3 MP3-12

Telling a vendor who they're bidding against is acceptable. How much they bid is a secret until after the winner is selected. In this dialog, Bill's bid lost and Marsha discusses it with him.

競標對手不算機密，因此可以告知賣方。而在得標者出爐前，各廠商的競標價格才是機密。在這個對話中，比爾沒有得標，瑪莎和他討論這件事。

Bill : So how did I do?

我表現得怎樣？

Marsha : Not too good, I'm sorry.

很遺憾，沒有預期中那麼好。

Bill : I lost?

我沒得標？

Marsha : It was close. To be honest, you had the lowest price by three cents per unit, but they didn't like your delivery date.

差一點。老實説，你的價格是最低的，平均單價便宜了三分錢，但他們不滿意你的交貨期。

Acme promised them almost a full month sooner.

「艾可盟公司」打包票説可以早一個月交貨。

Bill : So the price was good?

那就不是價格的問題？

Marsha : Yes, they loved the price; the delivery date was the problem. They just didn't want to cut the **delivery** date that close.

嗯，他們喜歡你的價格，問題是交期；他們不想把交期押的這麼急。

If something went wrong and you didn't deliver, we might not be able to get **stock** in time for Christmas.

萬一出問題，你交不出貨，我們可能就趕不上聖誕節舖貨了。

If you could have been two or three weeks faster on delivery, they might have gone with you.

如果你能快個二到三個星期交貨，他們可能就會選你。

Bill : So I didn't miss by much then.

那麼我沒有輸很多？

Marsha : No. It was very close and they argued over the bid for a long time. Better luck next time.

沒有，你們的標很接近，他們為這個討論了很久，祝你下次好運囉。

Bill : I knew the delivery was slow but I figured the price would win it for me.

我知道交期比較晚，但我以為可以靠價格取勝。

Marsha : That's possible, Bill, but the price would have to have been a lot lower, like around fifty cents per unit.

是有可能，比爾。但這樣的話，可能要比原來的更便宜，大概單價只能報五十分而已。

Vocabulary　重要字彙	MP3-13
reputation	聲譽
estimate	估計；衡量
vendor	賣方
test the waters	市場測試
priority	優先
awarded	給予
ballpark	相近的；估算的
drill	演習
marble	籌碼
delivery	運送
stock	存貨；現貨

Chapter 4

Honesty is the Best Policy
誠實是上策

For Your Information
背景介紹

MP3-47

Having a reputation for honesty is important in doing business and following the advice above will go a long way, but that's not everything.

中譯 做生意時，「信譽」是很重要的。遵循前面提到的忠告，可以帶來很大的幫助，但還是不夠。

I was offered **bribes**, but never took them. Without making an issue out of it, I thanked them for the offer, declined and rarely called them again. I feel if a man needs bribes to sell his product, it can't be very good, and I don't want to defend a poor product **purchased** at my **recommendation**. After a few months, the offers stopped. Also, because I was honest, I got things from clients and suppliers the other **executives** couldn't, or found difficult. Having a reputation for honesty helps.

中譯 我不接受任何賄賂：我不會大驚小怪，只是簡單地答謝、予以拒絕，並減少電話往來。我覺得如果要靠賄賂，才能把產品賣出去，那麼這個產品就有問題。我不希望推薦某個產品，然後再為不好的產品辯解。幾個月後，這種送紅包的行為就停止了。再者，因為我很誠實，我可以得到客戶與供應商的獨家消息。信譽良好對生意上的幫助是很大的。

Dialog

MP3-14

The following is an example of just how easy it can be. It could be face to face or over the phone. Jack is selling speakers made in Taiwan, and Donna works for an American

distributor.

下面這個對話告訴你，不論透過電話或面對面進行，談判都可以很簡單。對話中，傑克在銷售台灣製的喇叭，唐娜則為美國批發商工作。

Jack : Donna! How are you? It's good to hear your voice.

唐娜，你好嗎？很高興聽到你的聲音。

Donna : Thank you, Jack, it's always a pleasure doing business with you.

謝謝你，傑克，和你做生意向來都是很愉快的事。

Jack : So how are things in the land of the free and the home of the brave?

你那充滿自由與勇氣的美國，最近還好吧？

Donna : Great! And, how are things in your neck of the woods?

好極了！那你的地盤呢？

Jack : Things are so great here. I almost smiled myself to death last week. One of my coworkers had to give me CPR.

好到不能再好了。上週我差點高興得笑死，其中一個同事還幫我做心肺復甦術。

Donna : Oh, Jack, I have missed your sense of humor. Ha, ha, ha! Nobody else sees things quite like you do. It's your gift.

喔，傑克，我真想念你的幽默感。哈哈，沒有人像你這樣看待事物，這是你的天份。

Jack : Or a curse.

是詛咒吧。

Donna : Nope, it's a gift. Anyway, we need some more of those **mid-range** speakers you tricked me into buying last time.

不，這是天份。言歸正傳，我需要中程喇叭，你上次騙我買的那種。

Jack : That, my dear, was classic sales technique delivered by a professional.

親愛的，那是由專業人士操刀的經典銷售技巧。

Donna : Are you still **gouging** your customers the same price per unit?

你還是用這個價格去騙客戶嗎？

Jack : Heck no, we doubled the price, but because it's you, I'll let you have 'em at 50 % off. Heh, heh, heh! How does that sound?

當然不是，我們漲了一倍，但看在你的份上，我會給你五折。嘿！嘿！你覺得怎樣？

Donna : You **silver-tongued** devil. Can't you ever just answer a question with a simple yes or no?

你這耍嘴皮子的惡魔，你回答問題時，難道不能簡單地回答「好」或「不好」嗎？

Jack : I could, but where's the fun in that?

可以啊，但這就不好玩了吧？

Vocabulary 重要字彙		MP3-14
bribe	賄賂；買通	
purchase	採購	
recommendation	推薦；建議	
executives	執行主管	
distribution	分配	
mid-range	中程	
gouge	詐欺；勒索	
silver-tongued	很會說話的	

Chapter 5

Motivation

動機

For Your Information
背景介紹

`MP3-48`

It's no secret that it's easier dealing with the highly motivated than someone who doesn't care. When I was the principal broker for one of the largest management companies in the US, we went looking for new accounting software, and the company we chose was very cooperative. They returned calls promptly and called often to ask how we were doing. When I opened my own company, I went to the same people and got nothing but trouble, because my new company was too small to matter.

中譯 　很明顯的，跟積極的人談生意比跟一臉無所謂的人談，容易得多。我曾是美國最大管理公司之一的首要經紀人，當時我們在找新的會計軟體，而入選的公司非常配合。他們總是快速回電，且常常來電詢問我們的使用狀況。當我自己開公司找他們合作時，卻換來一堆麻煩；因為我的公司很小。

So I made my company matter. I reminded them who I was, and that I had contacts around the country from attending the annual international conferences. I reminded them that I still got calls from around the country from people who knew me when I was the principal broker for that other company, asking about their product.

中譯 　為此，我讓公司的身價提升。我提醒對方我以前的工作；告訴他們，我以前常參加年度的國際會議，因此在國內到處都有人脈；很多人還記得我以前是那家公司的首要經紀人，因此還是會打電話問我一些產品上的事情。

After that things got a lot better, maybe not as good as when I was ordering over a hundred thousand dollars in extras, but good enough to get the job done. So the message here is that if the other side isn't that interested in doing business, then you have to inspire them.

中譯 後來事情就順利多了。或許當你聽說我得多付十萬元,並不會這麼覺得,但至少工作得以順利發展。而這裡的重點就是:若對方意興闌珊,不想跟你做生意,你就得激發他們的意願。

Dialog 1 MP3-15

There are lots of ways to get the other guy motivated. The following is an example of inspiring a supplier to do right by you. Lucy works for a computer hardware supplier, and Hal for a small company just starting out that is only going to buy one unit.

要增加動機的方法很多,以下就是激發供應商,幫你服務到家的範例。露西是電腦硬體公司的員工,哈爾在一家剛起步不久的公司工作,他的公司想買一組電腦。

Lucy : Ace Computers, this is Lucy.

「艾斯電腦」,我是露西。

Hal : Hi, Lucy, my name is Hal and I'm looking to buy a new machine. I understand you guys build to order.

嗨,露西。我是哈爾,我想買一台新機種。我知道你們公司有接受訂貨。

Lucy : Yes, we do. What kind of machine are you looking for?

是的,沒錯,你需要哪樣的機種?

Hal : Well, this is for a business and it won't be connected to the net, nor will it be used to play games.

呃，商業用的，不必連接網路，也不會用來玩遊戲。

I want one to be as fast as possible while staying in the **sweet spot**. Do you know what I mean?

我想要能穩穩地運作、速度快就好。你懂我的意思嗎？

Lucy : Sure, you want fast but you don't need the top of the line.

當然，你想要速度快的，但不需要最高檔的機種。

You want fast but what was just **superseded** in favor of something faster, and **reduced** in price.

你需要速度比平常更快的，然後價錢不要太貴的。

Hal : Right, that's it. Fast enough to do business and handle software **upgrades** for the next few years.

對，沒錯。快到可以做生意就好，能配合幾年後的軟體升級。

Lucy : And, you only want one?

你只要一台嗎？

Hal : For right now, I only need one. Before I commit myself to replacing all my machines, I want to see how yours performs.

目前，我只需要一台。在電腦全部換新前，我得先測試一下你們的。

Lucy : So then, you will eventually want more?

這麼說，你以後會再跟我們買？

Hal : Yes, definitely. Do you offer phone support and training classes for my employees?

當然，你們有提供電話牽線、員工訓練課程嗎？

Lucy : Yes, we do, for an **additional fee**.

有，但須額外收費。

Hal : Good. I'm looking for a full service place to do business with.

好，我正在找有提供全面服務的公司來合作。

Could you fax me a proposal for the computer as well as a list of all the extra services you provide.

你能否傳真一份電腦的估價單，跟額外服務的項目清單給我。

Lucy : When do you want that?

你什麼時候要這些資料？

Hal : ASAP, but maybe you should reflect a discount if all the machines are purchased at one time, say all five machines I need.

越快越好。你也可以註明，如果我一次全買，應該總共五台，你們公司能否提供折扣？

Lucy : I can do that. You say you need five machines in all?

好的，你是說貴公司總共需要五台電腦？

Hal : Yes.

是的。

Dialog 2　　　　　　　　　　　　　　　　　MP3-16

Here, Lucy works for an electronics subcontractor and Hal only needs two thousand CD motors from a company that usually deals in the tens of thousands. Lucy was supposed to call Hal two days ago but didn't because she was busy with bigger customers.

這個例子中，露西為一家電器轉包商工作。哈爾需要兩千個光碟馬達，但是露西的公司向來處理的都是千萬筆的訂單。露西兩天前就應該要打電話給哈爾，但因為忙於和較大的客戶聯絡，她疏忽了。

Lucy : Hello, Hal, I was just going to call you.

嗨，哈爾，我正要打電話給你。

Hal : Oh! Really? Great minds think alike.

噢！真的？真是「英雄所見略同」。

Lucy : Heh, heh, heh! I suppose they do. How did the test units I sent you work out?

嘿嘿！大概吧。我寄給你的那些機種，測試結果如何？

Hal : They did just fine. We figured they would, but we had to test to make sure.

還不錯，跟預期的一樣，但還是必須做測試，來確定一下。

Lucy : Of course. So what else can I do for you today?

當然，那還有什麼事需要我幫忙的？

Hal : Well, we like your unit but really think the price is way too steep. We tested the units from several companies and yours had the best overall performance, but frankly because of the price I was told to make a deal with Brooks and Son Their price is more reasonable.

我們喜歡你的機種，但真的太貴了。我們測試了好幾家公司的機種，你們的性能最好，但老實說，因為價錢的關係，上面交代我跟「布氏公司」買，他們的價錢比較合理。

Lucy : Well, I'm sorry to hear that, but for the volume you're talking about, I really can't do much better.

真的很遺憾，但是就你的數量而言，我只能提供這樣的價格。

Hal : Let me lay my cards on the table. This order is small because it's a production line test.

我坦白講了，這個訂單很小，因為這是生產線測試用的。

If things do well here, then we'll properly get all our motors from you and that means a lot more volume for you.

如果一切順利的話，我們或許全部都跟你們買，這樣的數量就會比較大。

Lucy : Are we still talking about the same numbers you mentioned during our first conversation?

我們現在討論的數量，和第一次談的數量一樣嗎？

Hal : Yes, there about. But that'll only happen if you meet or beat the price of the bidder I was supposed to call.

對，差不多。但前提是你們的價格，要比我預定的那一家還要好。

Lucy : If you fax me a copy of that price, I'll take it to my boss.

如果你把那個價格傳真給我，我會呈給老闆看。

We usually don't do this for such a small order, but I'm pretty sure I can get you a yes.

對於這麼小的訂單，我們通常不會這樣做，但我很確定我能幫你調價。

Hal : Okay, you'll have it this afternoon.

好，今天下午你就可以收到了。

談判停看聽 All the above dialogs were handled over the phone. The people are easy to deal with, and are the kind of people you want to continue doing business with. They were easy to motivate, and highly cooperative. If a difference comes up, they look for a reasonable compromise. However, not all honest negotiators are this easy to do business with. Next, we'll discuss the difficult to deal with types. Some can be quite difficult, but no matter how bad they get, they're still just looking for a deal they can live with.

中譯 上面所有的對話，都是在電話中進行。這些人都很好相處，讓人想要繼續合作下去。他們很容易被說動且非常合作，如果有爭議出

Chapter 5

55

現，他們會搜尋合理的配套。但是，並不是所有的誠實談判者，都這麼好做生意。接下來，我們要討論難相處的類型。有些人很難溝通，即使他們的狀況不佳，他們也想得到一個最好的生意。

Vocabulary　重要字彙

MP3-17

sweet spot	安穩的地方
superseded	代替；取代
reduce	減少
upgrade	升級
additional fee	附加費用
provide	提供
revenue	收益
volunteer	自動提供
steep	過份的；不合理的
volume	數量

Chapter 6

Lawyers As Professional Negotiators

談判專家──律師

For Your Information
背景介紹

MP3-49

Usually, almost every one at the negotiating table earns their living by making and selling, or buying and selling a product. Negotiating sales is the least of what they do. The lawyers are the **exception**. Their work begins and ends at the meeting.

中譯　通常上談判桌的人，本業都是製造零售、買賣產品，談判並不是他們的本行。律師則例外，他們的工作在會議中開始，也在會議中結束。

They're looking for something for free, and act like there's no tomorrow. To win, they will **humiliate** the other side as if they won't ever have to do business with them again. A judge once joked, it's best to consider lawyers as **amoral**. Regardless of whether it's you or the other side who hires a lawyer, it won't hurt to know what makes them tick.

中譯　律師總是一付「沒有明天」的樣子；為了求勝，他們不惜侮辱對方，好像以後都不會碰頭似的。一位法官曾開玩笑道：「不論律師是你請的，還是對方請的，最好都把他們當作沒良心的人，盡其所能地找出他們的弱點。」

Lawyers are paid by the hour. The best example I've seen of how being paid by the hour affects their work involves a client whose building was on **leased** land. The landowner required my client to draw up the papers for review by his own attorney.

中譯 律師是按時數收費的。我舉個最好的例子，說明按時數收費對律師的工作效率影響之大。那次案子是，一位客戶的建築物建在一塊租賃土地上。土地所有人要求我的客戶找律師起草一份文件，以做檢閱之用。

I later learned the client's firm wrote several contracts for this landowner, but the attorney always required a rewrite of one or two certain sections. To avoid the cost of a rewrite, they put together a contract made up completely of approved provisions from other contracts. But, the landowner's attorney wanted a section rewritten. The regular firm replied that the bad language was approved on another contract and asked why was it not okay now.

中譯 我後來才知道，客戶的事務所寫了好幾份合約給土地所有人，但對方律師總是要求他們重寫其中一、兩個章節的條文。為了要避免重新草擬合約的費用，他們用其他合格合約作範本，擬了一份新的合約。但是土地所有人的律師，還是要求更改其中一個章節。於是這間事務所詢問對方說，既然這份合約是以另一份合格合約為範本的，為什麼還要更改。

The attorney apologized and approved the contract. However, every future offers the landowner made specifically stated my client's firm may not represent the building owner.

中譯 那位律師立刻道歉，並核准了那份合約。但是土地所有人之後所簽的合約，都特別規定，此事務所代書不能代表屋主。

To practice law in the U.S., an attorney must belong to the local Bar Association. The Bar requires its members be absolutely honest, reasonably competent and act as zealous advocates for their client. The Bar is a self-policing agency, and they strictly enforce their code of ethics.

中譯 要在美國法律界執業，律師必須要加入律師協會。律師協會要求其成員必須全然誠實、理性且熱切地勝任客戶的代言者。律師協會是一個自我管理的機構，他們嚴格地推動自身的職業法規。

A lawyer won't lie, but you have to ask the right questions, not accept answers with more than one interpretation and never assume anything. Never use pronouns, or nicknames instead of the subject's proper name. If this sounds like you're playing a word game, you are.

中譯 律師不會說謊，但你要問對問題。不要接受任何模稜兩可的回應，也別做任何假設。提問時，不要用代名詞或暱稱，而要用主題的適切名稱。假如你的言論聽起來像在玩文字遊戲，別人就會這麼以為。

Today, all legal documents are written in a precise way and lawyers earn their living either writing things so there can be no misunderstanding, or by deliberately creating misunderstanding to negate documents. The legal profession came into being through the clever use of words. Today's lawyers use that talent to their clients' advantage and their own.

中譯 現在，所有的法律文件都是用精準的文字所擬出。律師靠擬稿子吃飯，不論是毫無誤差的文件，或故意加入爭議點使合約失效的寫法。法律專業者擅於利用文字來取巧，現今的律師也運用這個優勢，替客戶與自己爭取利益。

Everyone intends to make the best deal possible. The attorney is there to protect the client, but he's also there to make a buck. They will protect the client, but at the same time they'll stretch out the time at the negotiating table, and increase the workload so they can bill more. They will also interrupt things and kick up a fuss just to make sure the client sees them doing their job.

中譯 　每個人都想要達成最好的交易。律師的確是要保護客戶，但他也要賺錢。他們會保護客戶，但同時，他們會盡量延長談判時間，這樣才能增加工作量，並向客戶收取更多的費用。他們也會打斷事情的進展、小題大作，只為了讓客戶看到，他們真的有在做事。

At one negotiation, the other side demanded something **prohibited** in the by-laws, my client simply couldn't do. The other lawyer told his client it was possible, because he reasoned anything is possible. Instead of pointing out why we couldn't **comply**, our lawyer started yelling and screaming that we would see them in court.

中譯 　有一次談判，對方要求在細則中不要列出某些條文，我方客戶就是不能照辦，但對方的律師卻說沒有不可能的事，因為他認為什麼都是可能的。我方律師沒有解釋原因，卻開始大吼說：「咱們法院見吧！」

The meeting had turned to **chaos** so I stood and explained the law, and how every time this question was tried in the past the court ruled in favor of my client's position. Then, I asked their attorney to show the board and their client a case where the court agreed with his client's position. He couldn't and the argument was over.

中譯 　會議變得一團亂，因此我站起來解釋條文，告知對方過去這種情形法院受理過幾次，但裁決結果都偏向我方客戶所持的立場。然後，我要求對方的律師在董事會與客戶面前，舉出法院曾贊同他客戶所持立場的記錄。對方律師舉不出來這樣的案例，所以爭執就算告終。

Their lawyer told his clients what they wanted to hear, not the facts. He gave his opinion on their request and a court ruling, and agreed to represent them in court. But he left out how small their chance of winning was, didn't cite case law, and my client's limited ability to comply. Our lawyer did the same. Both were zealous advocates for their client, doing exactly what the client wanted, which earned them the most possible.

中譯 他們的律師只是說客戶想聽的話，而不是事實。律師針對客戶的要求、法院的判決提出他的看法，並同意代表客戶在法院出庭。但是律師沒有提及客戶的獲勝機率很小，他沒有引用過去的案例法則，也沒有告訴對方，我的客戶沒有權限照他們的要求去做，我方律師也是一樣。兩方都一片赤誠，為自己的客戶發言，他們所做的事都是客戶想要看的，這樣才能為他們賺取最大利益。

Dialog　　　　　　　　　　　　　　　MP3-18

Lawyers are trained to phrase things in such a way that their clients or they themselves benefit. This is a little hard to explain, but it's much easier to give you examples. The following dialog illustrates how clever manipulation of the language can be very rewarding. An analysis of what happened and why immediately follows.

律師所受的訓練，就是把事情說得好像客戶（或是他們自己）會是受益者。這有點難解釋，但是看範例就清楚的多。下面這個對話清楚顯示，懂得如何操控語言，是很有利的。下面例子我們可以看出。

Brenda : That's what happened. Do you think we have a

case?

這就是事情發生的經過。你覺得這案子可以成立嗎？

Lawyer : Okay, let me see if I've got this straight.

好，我看看是不是這樣。

You want to **install** a large air conditioning unit in your home, put the motor on the roof, and run conduit across the outside of the building. Is that it?

你想要在家裡裝設一個大型冷氣機，將馬達放在頂樓，管線繞過大樓的外面。對吧？

Brenda : Well, actually we already installed it, and the board of directors says it's not allowed, and they want us to remove it. We think they're just picking on us.

呃，其實我們已經裝了。管委會説不可以，並要我們把它拆了。我們覺得他們只是在找我們麻煩。

I mean, it's twenty-five floors up. Hardly anyone will see it. And it makes too much noise to put it in the living room, or on the **balcony**.

再説，裝在二十五樓，根本不會有人看到。如果把馬達裝在我們客廳或陽台的話，會造成很大噪音。

I ask you, does that seem fair?

我問你，這公平嗎？

Lawyer : It sounds like a reasonable request to me.

我覺得這是蠻合理的要求。

Brenda : That's what we think too, but they say they'll take us to court if we don't remove it.

我們也這樣想，但是他們説如果我們不拆的話，他們要把這件事鬧上法院。

So we need your help to represent us in court and make the property manager let us **mount** the unit on the building's **ledge**.

所以我們需要你的協助，代表我們出庭，讓房地產經理人同意將馬達裝在大樓的外架上。

Lawyer : The law says you're entitled to the quiet enjoyment of your property, and using that as justification for your position, I think we can win.

法律條文說，你們有權在自家中享受安靜，以這一點來進行爭辯的話，我想我們可以贏。

Brenda : So you really think we have a chance?

那，你真的認為我們有機會贏？

Lawyer : Definitely, there's always a chance. But, you realize anything can happen in court. It could go either way.

當然，機會總是有的。但你要知道，在法院裡什麼事都可能，所以也可能會有出乎意料的發展。

Brenda : Yes, of course we know that, but the important thing is you believe in the case and think we can win.

是的，我們了解這種情況，但重點是你相信我們的案子可以成立，我們會贏。

Lawyer : Like I said, anything can happen in open court. However, I hope you understand this isn't an open and shut thing.

就像我之前說的，在法院中，任何事情都有可能發生。我希望你們了解，這件事沒有這麼單純。

To win, we have to line up our ducks. We've got to be ready. This case is going to require a lot of preparation.

想贏，我們就必須拿出全力，我們必須要準備好。這個案子需要許多準備。

Brenda : But, don't you think we can ask the judge to give us court costs?

我們不能要求法官補助訴訟費用嗎？

Lawyer : Of course, we can ask.

當然，我們可以這樣要求。

談判停看聽 The above is a possible consultation between a lawyer and prospective clients. Please note the lawyer never says they'll win, he only says 'it's possible', and 'it's going to require a lot of preparation', that's lawyer talk for 'this is going to be expensive'. Then, he discounts the **potential** cost by saying they may be able to recover court costs.

中譯 這個例子顯示了未來客戶和律師之間的諮詢過程。請注意，律師從來都沒說他們會贏。他只說：「可能會贏。」、「這個案子需要許多準備。」這時候，律師是在告訴客戶：「這將會很花錢。」然後，他又告訴客戶，他們或許可以要求賠償補助。

Vocabulary 重要字彙   MP3-18

exception	例外
humiliate	使蒙羞
amoral	道德觀念的
leased	出租的
section	段落；範圍
provision	條款
zealous	熱心的
code	法規；範例
ethics	（職業）道德；原理
interpretation	解釋
assume	假定；認為
pronoun	代名詞
intend	意圖要……

prohibit	禁止
comply	服從；遵照
chaos	大混亂
illustrate	說明；闡述
manipulation	巧妙地使用
install	裝置；安裝
balcony	陽台
ledge	棚架
mount	裝置；安裝
justification	辯護；正當化
potential	可能性；潛力

Chapter 7

Asking the Right Questions

要問對問題

For Your Information
背景介紹

MP3-50

The previous chapter covered how lawyers manipulate the language to mislead people. This chapter centers on how to prevent that from happening. If you apply the lesson here, you should be in charge of the attorney and get the most for your money.

中譯 　上一章談到，律師如何巧妙利用文字來誤導他人。這章著重在告訴您如何預防這樣的事發生。如果你運用這章的內容，你就可以主導律師，不花冤枉錢。

Dialog 1

MP3-19

Brenda was being very hopeful in the above dialog. In the next one, she is a lot more practical and asking the right questions. Much of the dialog remains the same but, by pinning the attorney down with precise language, she gets a very different result. By asking the right questions, they find out what their chances really are.

布蘭達在上段對話中非常樂觀，在下面的對話中，她比較實際，並問出確切的問題。這個對話大部分內容都沒有改變，但是布蘭達用比較精準的語言文字，針對律師發問，這樣一來，她得到了非常不同的結果。藉由正確的發問，他們知道自己獲勝的機率到底有多少。

Brenda : That's what happened. Do you think we have a case?

這就是事情發生的經過。你覺得這案子可以成立嗎？

Lawyer : Okay, let me see if I've got this straight.

好的,我看看是不是這樣。

You want to install a large air conditioning unit in your home and put the main motor on the roof, and run **conduit** across the outside of the building. Is that it?

你想要在家中裝設一台大型冷氣機,馬達放在樓頂,並將管線繞過大樓的外面。對吧?

Brenda : Yes, and the board of directors say it's not allowed. We think they're just picking on us.

雖然管委會說這是不可以的,但我們覺得他們只是在挑剔我們。

I mean, it's twenty-five floors up. Hardly anyone will see it. And it makes too much noise for us to put it in our living room.

我是說,裝在二十五樓,根本不會有人看到。如果把馬達裝在家裡客廳或陽台的話,會造成很大的噪音。

I ask you, does that seem fair?

我問你,這公平嗎?

Lawyer : It sounds like a reasonable request to me.

我覺得這是蠻合理的要求。

Brenda : Well, we know it seems reasonable, to us at least. But, what about in court, what is a judge likely to do?

至少對我們而言,這似乎是合理的。但是法庭上呢?法官會怎麼判?

Lawyer : Anything can happen in court. It's possible we could win. It could go either way.

法庭上,任何事情都有可能發生。我們可能會贏,事情也可能有完全不同的發展。

Brenda : We already know that in this country anybody can sue anyone for anything.

在這個民主法治國家，每個人都有控告權；這點我們早就知道了。

I want to know if this is a winnable case, or is it a loser. What's the case law on this?

我想知道的是，這案子會贏？還是穩輸的？過去的案例法則情況如何？

Lawyer : Well, to be honest, the case law is not in our favor. Lots of owners have sought relief in the courts for similar requests. Not many of them have won.

老實說，過去的案例法則對我們不利，類似訴求的屋主很多，但很少人能勝訴。

Brenda : How many have won?

有幾個成功案例？

Lawyer : I'm not really sure of the exact number. I'd have to do some research.

我不清楚確實的數字，這得找個資料才知道。

Brenda : Okay, but **offhand** how many do you know of?

好，但是就你現在所知道的，有多少人贏過？

Lawyer : Actually, I don't know of any but that doesn't mean we couldn't win.

實際上，據我所知，沒人贏過。但這並不代表我們不會贏。

Brenda : Fine, I understand that. I want to know what our chances really are.

那好，我了解了。我想知道我們有多少勝算。

Lawyer : To know that, I'd have to do some research.

這個嘛，我得找資料分析才知道。

Brenda : Have you ever been a party to a similar lawsuit, representing either side? I assume you have. You're supposed to be experienced in this field of law.

你有代表過其中一方，參與類似的法律訴訟案嗎？我想有吧，你在法律界應該經驗豐富才對。

Lawyer : Yes I am, and I've been involved in several cases like this one. But, I was usually on the other side.

沒錯，我參與過這類案子好幾次，但我通常都是另一方的律師。

Brenda : And in how many of those cases did the unit owner win?

在這些案子中，住戶到底贏過幾次？

Lawyer : Well, actually, none. But that doesn't mean we couldn't be the first.

呃，說真的，完全沒有，但這並不代表我們不能首開先例。

談判停看聽 The above dialogs don't have much to do with negotiations but they do clearly illustrate how a lawyer hungry for work could evade the bad news and tell the client what they wanted to hear. Their aim is to fire up the client with the hope that they could win and open up their purse to fund the attempt. I was involved with a case very similar to this one. However, unlike the above dialogs, the aim from the start was always to get the board to negotiate a settlement.

中譯 上列對話和談判沒有什麼關係，但它們正清楚顯示，一個想要接案的律師是多麼擅於規避壞消息，只告訴客戶他們想要聽的事。他們的目標是燃起客戶的希望，讓他們以為自己能贏，然後乖乖打開錢包支援律師的每個行動。我曾經參與一個案子，它和這個案子很類似。但不同於上列對話，這種案子通常一開始的目標，就是要和董事會達成協議。

What actually happened was that the owners asked for permission to mount the unit on the roof, out of sight from the street and wanted to penetrate the roof with conduit. But, after the property manager said no, they apparently came up with the plan to do what was clearly unacceptable and allowed themselves to be negotiated back to what they wanted in the first place.

中譯 真實情況中住戶要求大樓，准許他在樓頂（街道視野以外的地方）裝冷氣，並打通屋頂，把管線接進來。當房地產經理人拒絕之後，他們想出一個計畫，要做一些違反大樓規定的事，好讓對方來和自己談判，藉以得到自己原來想要的東西。

Dialog 2 <kbd>MP3-20</kbd>

In this dialog, Brenda deliberately installed the air conditioning unit in open defiance of the property manager. Brenda's lawyer meets with the board's lawyer, and suggests that, in order to avoid expensive litigation, the board should accept the original plan and allow installation on the roof. Brenda's lawyer is Bob, and the board's lawyer is Gail.

在這個對話中，布蘭達故意將冷氣機裝起來，公然違背房地產經理人的命令。布蘭達的律師和董事會的律師碰面，建議為了避免昂貴的訴訟費用，董事會應該接受原來的計畫，准許住戶將冷氣機裝在頂樓。布蘭達的律師是鮑伯，董事會的律師是嘉兒。

Bob : That was a good lunch. It really hit the spot. Did you enjoy yours?

午餐真棒，我很喜歡。你呢？

Gail : Very good, thank you. Shall we get to the matter at hand?

很好吃，謝謝。談正事了，好嗎？

Bob : Yes, of course. I think I have an alternative that may solve everyone's problem.

好的，當然。我想提出一個應變之道，也許可以解決大家的問題。

Gail : What's that?

說來聽聽。

Bob : My client believes the present instillation is fine as it is but she wants to avoid expensive litigation, so in order to appease everyone, she'll move the unit to the roof at her own cost.

我的客戶認為現在的裝法沒有什麼問題，但她想要避免昂貴的訴訟費用，所以為了息事寧人，她會自掏腰包，將冷氣機移到頂樓去。

To prevent the conduit from being visible from the street, she is willing to pay to have it penetrate the roof.

為避免管線暴露在外，影響美觀，她很樂意花錢，將屋頂打通、引進管線。

Gail : You know the board can't allow that. The building's documents don't give them the authority.

你知道董事會不會允許這樣的事。大樓文件中沒有賦予他們這樣的權限。

Bob : I've reviewed the documents. I think they do.

我仔細看過這些文件。我想他們有這權限。

Gail : I don't know how you can say that. That's a major change to the building's common area, the roof.

我真搞不懂你哪兒來的道理。屋頂工程可是大樓公共區域的重大異動。

Not only is it against the documents, it's contrary to state law.

這樣做不只是有違文件規定，更是違反了州法。

Bob : Well, I don't see how you can call that a major

change to the common elements.

我不認同你說的「對大樓公共區域的重大改變」。

We believe it's a minor change, and that it really affects no one but my client. Therefore, it is within the board's authority to **grant** my client's request.

我們認為這是個小改變；除了我的客戶，沒有影響到任何人。因此，董事會有權限，批准我客戶的請求。

Gail : Well, you may be right except for one thing: penetrating the roof will **compromise** its **integrity**, and that is a major issue.

你說的對，不過有一件事錯了：打通頂樓會影響大樓的整體性，這樣就會構成重大改變。

That definitely moves it beyond the scope of the board's authority.

而這點，董事會是絕對沒有權限批准的。

談判停看聽 In the above, both sides **maneuver** for position. Gale's client, the board, is against allowing Brenda to install an A/C unit on the roof. Their attorney has strongly warned them that would likely be beyond their authority. Penetrating the roof would create a **maintenance** problem, increase the maintenance costs and could seriously damage the roof by creating **leaks** in many units. The additional maintenance costs would be paid from general funds. In short, people who won't benefit will pay the bill. Granting permission creates only a gain for Brenda, while it creates a loss for everyone else.

中譯 在上列的對話中，雙方都想達到自己的預設立場。嘉兒的客戶是董事會，其立場是不准布蘭達在屋頂裝設冷氣機。他們的律師強烈警告，這樣的事情遠超過他們的權限。打穿屋頂會造成維護上的問題，增加保固成本，也可能會嚴重地損害屋頂，導致許多住戶漏水的問題。額外的保固費用要從管理費來支出。簡言之，沒有受益的人還是要付費。准許這樣的要求只有對布蘭達有利，但卻造成他人的損失。

MP3-21

This dialog is a continuation of the above. Bob, Brenda's attorney tries to argue Gail into agreeing a compromise is possible.

此對話是上一個對話的延伸。鮑伯是布蘭達的律師，他試著要說服嘉兒妥協。

Bob : Huh! You know that just isn't true. A roof penetration won't mean anything.

哈！你也知道根本沒那一事；屋頂鑽洞工程根本不算什麼。

Gail : Roof penetrations aren't cut after the roof is poured. They're carefully planned before the roof is poured.

屋頂的鑽洞工程，不是等屋頂蓋好才開鑽，那是蓋屋頂前就仔細規畫過的。

A Styrofoam plug is placed where the hole is needed to avoid doing what you're proposing.

每個洞都用聚苯乙烯封起來，就是不希望發生你這樣的案例。

Using a jackhammer to create the hole will cause cracking radiating from the penetration and that will require additional maintenance. There's no way to calculate the additional expense.

用手提鑽來鑽洞，會導致洞口外裂，並造成額外的保固費用。這樣額外的開銷是沒辦法衡量的。

Bob : That's not true and you know it.

你知道，根本不是這樣。

Gail : You don't have to take my word for it. Check

Chapter 7

with a professional.

你可以不用聽我的，去問專家吧。

Bob : We did and they said it wouldn't be a problem. Brenda did her homework here.

我們已經問過了，他們說這不會影響；布蘭達有做一些研究。

She checked all these potential problems out, and the roofer said it would be no problem.

她檢查過所有可能的潛在危機，屋頂工人說不會有問題的。

Gail : A roofer is a professional for waterproofing systems, not the structural integrity of **concrete**.

屋頂工人是水電專家，但不是水泥建築專家。

You need to check with an architect or a structural engineer.

你應該再問問建築師或結構工程師。

Bob : That's not necessary.

沒有這個必要。

Gail : We checked it out with an architect and he gave us a written opinion that says we shouldn't do it.

我們問過建築師，他用書面文件向我們解釋，這為何不可行。

In a court of law, his opinion would **prevail** over that of a roofer.

在法院裡，他的意見應該比屋頂工人有效才對。

Bob : You just bought a hired gun to write a **conservative** opinion.

你只是雇了個槍手，幫你寫這些保守派的意見。

We could do the same thing, hire an architect to write an opinion that supports our position.

我們也可以這麼做，雇個建築師寫些支持我方的論點。

Gail : So why didn't you?

那你為什麼不這麼做？

Bob : My client wants to settle this in a friendly way.

那是因為，我的客戶想用友善的方式解決這個問題。

Gail : Well, that's just not going to happen. The board can't abandon its position.

這是不可能的，董事會不會放棄他們的立場。

If they did, they would be opening a real can of worms.

如果他們這樣做的話，會給自己帶來一大堆麻煩。

Bob : I disagree on that point. But I will tell you that if the board takes my client to court, she's prepared to fight it all the way. And that'll be **a real can of worms**.

我不同意這一點，但我可以告訴你：如果董事會和我的客戶鬧上了法庭，她已經做好準備，要抗爭到底，這樣才會導致一大堆的問題。

Gail : Your client can do whatever she wants. The board won't back down on this point.

你的客戶愛怎麼樣是她的事，董事會不可能讓步的。

And, unless you've got something else to offer, something we haven't already heard today, then I think this lunch is over.

還有，除非你能提出新的論點，不然我想午餐就進行到這裡吧。

談判停看聽 The above was an attempt by someone with a really poor position to **bluff** the party in the strong position into backing down. It didn't work. After the meeting, Brenda's lawyer told her the **strategy** failed. She left the offending unit in place until the board got a court order requiring her to remove it at her expense, and to pay court costs. Only then did she comply.

中譯　　上面對話是處於劣勢的人，想要唬弄強勢的一方讓步，但這沒有用。在會面結束後，布蘭達的律師告訴她，他們的計策失敗了。她把違規的冷氣機放著，直到董事會拿到法令，叫她自費把冷氣機拆了，另外還叫她支付訴訟費用。這下子，她才照做。

The above case illustrates two important points. Lawyers may not lie to their clients, but they are willing to avoid telling the truth. This attorney knew he was unlikely to win but instead of telling his client that, he told her what she wanted hear.

中譯　　上面這個案子説明了兩個重點：律師或許不會對客戶説謊，但他們也會避免説實話。這位律師知道他不太可能會贏，但他並沒有直接告知客戶，反而，只告訴客戶她想要聽的話。

Secondly, it shows how the negotiation process can be misused. Here, the **plaintiff**, Brenda, did her best to get what she wanted. Her strategy was to do something really unacceptable and allow herself to be negotiated into what she wanted in the first place.

中譯　　第二，上面這個例子也顯示了，談判過程是極可能被濫用的。在上面的對話中，布蘭達是原告，她極力爭取自己想要的東西。她的計策是去做一些違規的事，好讓對方來和自己談判，藉以換取自己原先想要的東西。

pin	釘著
conduit	管線
offhand	立刻地
evade	避開；躲開
fund	基金
attempt	企圖；試圖
settlement	協議；和解
aim	目標要……
penetrate	貫穿
defiance	反抗
litigation	訴訟
instillation	設立；安裝
appease	安撫；平息
authority	權限
be contrary to	違反
grant	允許；答應
compromise	危害
integrity	整體性
maneuver	操擬
maintenance	維修管理
leak	漏水
continuation	繼續
jackhammer	手提鑽
concrete	水泥

Chapter 7

prevail	佔優勢
conservative	保守的
a can of worms	大麻煩
bluff	虛張聲勢
strategy	策略
plaintiff	原告

Chapter 8

The Non-Dealer
談判傀儡

For Your Information
背景介紹

If negotiations are a part of your job, you'll definitely run into these guys from time to time. These are people who attend or even set up negotiation sessions just to make it appear as if they're willing to bargain, when they really aren't. Their idea of give and take is you give and I take.

中譯 如果談判是你工作的一部分，你一定不時地會碰到這種人，這種人會參加或籌畫談判過程，但只是想讓別人以為他們願意溝通，其實他們並不想要談判。他們心目中對施與受的看法是：「你給，我拿。」

They're easy to **spot**. In most situations, the parties state what they're willing to do to make the deal, then make adjustments, moving closer to the other's position until they match. The non-dealer spends his time talking about everything except the deal, or why his offer is already so good you'd be a fool not to accept it.

中譯 這些人很好認。在大多數情況下，談判各方都會表明自己為了達成交易，願意做何種程度的讓步，然後大家會調整自己的立場，越來越靠近對方的立場，直到大家達成共識為止。這些不願意談交易的人，把時間花在討論除了交易之外的每件事情，他會告訴你，他提供的條件已經很棒，所以你不接受的話，就是傻瓜一個。

I've negotiated with a non-dealer several times and it's always been the same. Sometimes, he listened to everything I said and repeated his offer. Other times, he'd say our two offers were very close anyway, and suggest I give a little and accept his offer. He would tell me how nice a guy he is and I should take his offer for that reason, or that he might have made an even worse offer so I should be happy with what I got.

中譯 我曾經和一個談判傀儡談判過好幾次。每次結果都是一樣。有時他會聽我說完每件事，然後又將他的提議重複一次。其他時候，他則是說我們的提議實在很接近，會建議我再讓步一點，接受他的提議。他會跟我說，他是個好人，我應該要接受他的提議，要不然他會提出更差的提議，這樣我就會知道他之前提出的建議還真不錯。

Non-dealers aren't fools; they're actually very clever. The strategy is to wear you down to the point you just give up and agree to his terms, and it works. Most people are fair and assume others are too. They come to the table to make a deal and expect everyone is trying to play fair. As the talks go on, their desire to make the deal work becomes stronger and they become so frustrated that they're willing to do anything to make a deal.

中譯 談判傀儡不是傻瓜，實際上他們非常聰明。他們的計策就是要一直磨你，讓你吃不消，就會放棄，同意他們的條件，這種作法常常奏效。大多數的人都很公平，他們認為別人也是這樣。他們來到談判桌談交易，希望每個人都會遵守公平的原則。隨著談話的進展，他們想要交易成功的希望會越來越強烈。一碰上了這種談判傀儡，他們會很有挫折感，常常會為了達成交易，而願意做出一切讓步。

That's when the non-dealer makes a concession, usually it's something he already has to do anyway or a hollow gesture that doesn't mean anything. But it's a concession, and the other side is eager to end the talks so they jump on it and walk away happy that they got something. Later, when they examine the deal they made, they may realize they got nothing. Or, they just give in or walk away empty handed.

> **中譯** 　在這個時候，談判傀儡就會提出讓步，通常這些都是他早已準備好要做的讓步，有時他只是做個幌子，根本沒有什麼實質的讓步。但當他這麼做時，對方會因為等不及要結束談判，然後一口就答應，離開時還很高興，以為自己賺到了一些東西。稍後，等到他們再細細檢閱交易內容時，他們會發現自己什麼也沒得到。另一種可能是他們就這樣放棄了，然後空手而回。

Thankfully, few people negotiate like this. They're usually well known and unpopular. A simple background check should tell you if you're going up against one. They're tough to beat. Countering them with a better offer sends a signal to the non-dealer that they are winning. The only way to beat a non-dealer is to use his own game against him.

> **中譯** 　值得慶幸的是，很少人是這樣談判的，這種人通常都臭名遠播、不受人歡迎。簡單的背景調查，就可以知道你碰上的人是不是這樣的人。要打贏這種人很難。再提供更好的提議，就等於告訴談判傀儡，他們贏了。要打敗這種人唯一的方式，就是「以其人之道，還治其人之身。」

Once I had a client who was in a bad way with no room to maneuver. I made our best offer and remained as firm as the non-dealer. After two hours of no movement, the non-dealer made a counter offer. It wasn't what I was supposed to get but it was a lot more than anyone else ever got. If you're representing someone else, you should tell that client about this situation so he can accept the counter. If it comes, he's unlikely to leave it on the table for long. If he looks at his counter offer too closely, he'll see it as a defeat and take it back. Any concession from a non-dealer is a win. I recommend taking the offer just for the bragging rights.

中譯 有一次我的客戶處於劣勢，一點談判的空間都沒有。我們提出了最好的提議，並跟對方一樣毫不妥協。在僵持了兩個小時以後，那個談判傀儡提出了一個相對提議。內容不是我預想的那樣，但是和別人相比，那結果已經好太多了。如果你代表他人，就應該據實以告，這樣他才會接受這個相對提議。一旦對方開出新條件，他不會等你很久。因為他可能再仔細評估後，他就會發現這是一個敗筆，而收回提議。凡是談判傀儡所做出的讓步，對另一方來說都算贏了。我的建議是接受那個相對提議，之後再慢慢收回權益。

Dialog 1

MP3-23

It's frustrating to try to deal with a non-dealer. Regardless of what you offer, the non-dealer won't change their tune. It's like talking to a stone wall. Sometimes, this situation occurs when you're dealing with someone ordered to negotiate with you, but without the authority to change the offer. The following dialog is typical of trying to deal with a non-dearer. Peter is the non-dealer, and Paula tries to get a better deal.

和談判傀儡溝通會讓人很有挫折感：不管你提供什麼條件，這種人都不會改變他們的語調；和他們說話就像和石頭牆壁講話一樣。有時候這種情況會發生，是因為你的談判對手是上面派來的，而他並沒有什麼更改條件的權限。下面這個對話是個典型的例子，例子裡的人盡了全力，要改變那個談判傀儡的立場。彼得是個談判傀儡，寶拉嘗試著要獲取更好的交易。

Peter : This is an excellent offer. I don't know why you

don't just accept it.

這是個很好的提議，我不知道你為什麼不接受。

Paula : It's not even close to reasonable, and you know it.

這根本談不上算是合理，你心裡應該很明白。

Peter : I know no such thing. Our selling price is within the **appraised** value.

我不懂你在說什麼。我們的售價在估價範圍之內。

Paula : Appraised by who? You? The owner?

是誰的估價？你的？還是老闆的？

Peter : That's correct. We studied the issue and determined the old value was far less than fair. The new value is much more **realistic**.

估價是正確的，我們研究過這個議題，決定舊價格非常的不公平，新價格比較實際。

Paula : But there is not one single appraisal firm in town that agrees with you. And none of them say they understand your **formula**.

但是整區的估價中心都不同意你們的價格，沒半個人了解你們的計算公式。

Peter : Look, I'm not here to **debate** the formula that we use to set the price.

我不是來這裡辯論我們計價的公式。

Our offer is what it is. If you think it's too much, then you don't have to buy.

我們的提議就是這樣。如果你認為太貴，就不要買。

Paula : It's not like we can just walk away from the property. We already have a serious investment in it.

這不是買不買的問題，我們已經投資很多了。

Peter : Then, I suggest you accept our offer. Lots of people have.

那麼，我建議你接受我們的提議，很多人都已經接受了。

Paula : The offer we made was ten times the old appraised value.

我們提供的價格，已經比原先的高出十倍了。

We figure that's more than fair. Why won't you accept that?

我們認為這已經非常划算了，為什麼你們不接受呢？

Peter : Because we don't think it's fair. We set a price according to our formula and we're going to **stick by** it.

因為我們覺得這不合理。我們要堅守公式算出來的價格。

Paula : That's ridiculous. No one can afford your price. Not even God has enough money to pay your price.

這真是太可笑了。沒有人可以付得起你們的價格，就算是老天爺也不夠錢付你們。

In this dialog, Peter, the non-dealer, is talking with Paula, he remained firm. Peter needs the deal as much as Paula and after several hours of **stalled talks**, he sees Paula won't give any more, so he makes a counter offer.

接下來這個對話中，彼得這個談判傀儡正在和寶拉溝通，寶拉在做了許多努力之後，決定堅守自己的立場。彼得需要這個交易的程度不下寶拉，在幾個小時的僵持之後，彼得了解到寶拉是不會再做任何讓步，所以他提出了一個相對提議。

Peter : I still don't see why you don't just accept the deal. It's a good one.

我還是不懂你幹嘛不接受，這條件不錯啊。

Paula： I don't think so.

我不認為。

Our counter offer is more than generous and I don't know why you insist on this ridiculous price your formula gives you.

我們的提議比較好，我不懂你何必要堅持公式算出來的愚蠢價格。

Peter： It's not ridiculous; it's fair.

這不是愚蠢，這是公正。

Paula： I don't think so. My client is firm on this point. If that's your best offer, we'll take the matter to **arbitration**.

我不同意。我的客戶對這點很堅持，如果這是你最好的提議，我們只好把這件事交付仲裁。

Peter： There's no reason why we would agree to arbitration.

我們沒必要走到仲裁這一步吧。

Paula： Whatever, then, we'll wait until you come down to a more reasonable price. All I know is this price is not going to fly.

隨你怎麼說，反正我們會等到你降價為止，我確定你這個價錢是不會有人要的。

Peter： Very well, I'll tell you what I'll do.

好，不如這樣吧。

You can have the property for 20% off our asking price. That's my best price.

按照這個價格，可以打八折賣給你們，這已經是最好的價碼了。

Paula： All right, I'll talk to my client and get back to you.

好的。我會回報我的客戶，再和你聯絡。

In the above dialog, Paula won her concession and she should have taken it there and then, but didn't. She went back to her client and got an okay to take the offer but when she called Peter, it was late Friday afternoon and he had already gone home. The following dialog takes place Monday morning over the phone, Peter had the whole weekend to look at what happened and decides he may have made a mistake.

在上面的對話中，寶拉贏得了對方的讓步，她應該當場就接受這個讓步才對，但她當時並沒有接受。她回報客戶，得到了首肯，才接受這個價格。當她星期五下午打電話給彼得時，彼得已經回家了。下面這個電話對話發生時間是星期一上午。彼得有整個週末的時間去考慮這整件事，最後他發現讓步是錯誤的。

Paula : Hi, Peter, how was your weekend?

嗨，彼得，週末過得如何？

Peter : Not bad, took the family to the beach, it was nice. How about you?

不錯，全家一起去海邊，挺棒的。你呢？

Paula : My husband and I went out for dinner and a movie, that's about it. But it was good. We saw the new Mel Gibson movie. I recommend it.

外子和我出外用餐，還去看了電影，只有這樣而已，但蠻不錯的。我們看了梅爾·吉伯遜演的電影，我建議你可以看看。

Peter : Thanks, I'll keep that in mind. So, what can I do for you?

謝謝，我會記住的。有什麼事情嗎？

Paula : Well, I tried to call you Friday afternoon but you had already left the office.

我上禮拜五下午有打電話給你，但是你下班了。

Peter : I waited for your call, but by five I figured it was **a no go** so that's what I told the owner.

我等你的電話等到五點，後來我想或許是談不攏，所以就這樣呈報上去了。

Paula : I had a little trouble getting a hold of my client and it was pretty late when we finally connected. He said to accept the offer.

我的客戶有點難聯絡。等我聯絡上時，已經很晚了；他說他接受那個提議。

Peter : I'm sorry, Paula, but that offer is no longer on the table.

寶拉，很抱歉，但那個提議已經無效了。

Paula : I told you I'd get back to you, and I'm doing that now.

我說過我會打電話給你，所以我現在回電了啊。

Peter : That offer was only good for the day. That was Friday and this is Monday. I'm sorry but it's too late.

那個提議只有當天有效，而那是禮拜五的事了，現在是星期一。很抱歉，太遲了。

Paula : Are you serious?

你不是當真的吧？

Peter : Sorry, but I've already talked to my client.

抱歉，但是我已經跟客戶談好了。

spot	察覺；認出
frustrating	累人的；受挫的
appraised	評估的
realistic	實際的
formula	公式
debate	辯論
concession	讓步
hollow gesture	空洞的姿態
bragging	蓄勢待發的
stalled talk	固定的說話模式
arbitration	仲裁；調停
a no go	拒絕提案

Chapter 8

Chapter 9

Preparing for the
Negotiation Session

準備談判

For Your Information
背景介紹

MP3-52

Negotiations require preparation. You have to do your homework. Both sides need to know all they can about the other, just to know what to expect. The buyer needs to know all he can about the product, what else is available, the properties it must possess, the cost of parts acquired from subcontractors, and production costs. Basically, he must know everything the manufacturer knows. The seller has to know who the buyer will sell it to, and the price range it has to meet to be competitive.

中譯 談判須要事前準備，你得做功課。雙方都應盡可能地了解對方，才能快速進入狀況。買家對他想買的產品，需要全盤了解，知道還有其他什麼樣的選擇、產品屬性、承包商的零件成本和生產成本。基本上，買方必須知道製造商所知道的一切資訊。賣方則必須知道買方要將產品賣給誰，這樣價格範圍才會有競爭性。

If you're buying **components**, check with your production staff for special packaging, manufacturing or assembly changes the source can do cheaper than you. You should look for things that would reduce your production cost more than it would increase theirs. Then, compute exactly how much that would reduce your overhead on a per unit basis, and the total projected savings for this purchase.

中譯 如果你要買零件，要先和生產人員商量，知道特殊的包裝要求、製造或拼裝改變，還要知道什麼樣的來源可以提供比你更低的價格。你所找尋的東西，應該是要減低，而非增加你的生產成本。然後，計算這樣可以實際降低多少的單位成本價格，這項購買預計可以為你節省多少總額。

There are two ways to introduce these cost cutting steps. You can include them in the bid specification. This is clearly the best way to go in most cases. If you know the supplier is difficult and sometimes unreasonable on price, it may be better to not include them in the contract. Don't put them on the table at the start of negotiations. Use them as **bargaining chips** during the talks. For example, let's say you've worked out the problems and it's a matter of price. You need a certain price to make the deal work, but your supplier refuses to come down to something you can afford. This is where you put the bargaining chips into play.

中譯　有兩種方式可以介紹這些減低成本的步驟，你可以將它們包括在估價單中，這也是多數情況都適用的處理方式。如果你知道供應商不好溝通，價格不合理，那就不要把他們列入合約考量。不要一談判，就讓對方知道他們的存在。你可以在談判時，把他們當作議價的籌碼。舉例來說，你解決了其他的問題，只剩下價格。你需要某一個價格，來達成交易，但你的供應商拒絕將價格降低到你可以負擔的價格。這時，你就可以拿籌碼來議價。

If you know how much these extras reduce your overhead, factor it into the price and increase your offer accordingly. If you have discussed all this before you left home, there's nothing to figure at the table; you know right where you stand. Of course, you don't offer the entire savings at the start, but let the other side negotiate you to a higher amount. They'll feel like they've gained something and who knows, maybe they'll accept your first price.

Almost any trade off can be used as a bargaining chip. A trade-off is when one side offers something valuable to the other side. There are several frequently used types we'll cover here, and this isn't a complete list.

中譯　如果你知道這些額外品，可以減低你多少經常性成本，就把這個列入價格考量，然後提高你的估價。如果你在離開公司之前，已經和內部的人討論過這個細節，在談判桌上就沒有什麼需要額外思考的了，你知道自己的立場為何。當然，你不會在一開始就把最好的價格提供給對方，相反的，你要讓對方幫你把價格哄抬的高一點。他們會以為自己得到了好處，所以誰知道呢？也許他們會接受你提的第一個提議也說不定。幾乎所有的交換都可以來拿做談判籌碼。所謂的交換是指其中一方，提供一個有價值的東西給另外一方。我們在這裡會提到幾個常用的交換方式，當然這不是全部內容。

Dialog　　　　　　　　　　　　　　　MP3-27

　　The dialog below shows a negotiation stalled on price, neither side will compromise. This is the perfect time to play a bargaining chip. Mel represents an electronic control **panel** manufacturer. Bill works for a stereo maker that manufactures most of its own parts. They want to buy a large quantity of Mel's control panels. Because new design is **superior** to what Bill's company is currently making retooling will take a lot of time.

　　下面這個對話，因價格而呈現僵局，雙方都不願讓步。所以這是使出議價技巧的好時機。梅兒代表一個電子控制儀表板公司。比爾為一家音響公司做事，其大部分的零件都由製造商所製造。他們想要向梅兒購買大量的控制儀表。因為新的設計比比爾公司現有生產的機種優良，而更換機械設備需要花上很大的時間。

Mel : I'm sorry, Bill, but I can't help you.

比爾，很抱歉，我幫不上你的忙。

US$6.37 per unit delivered to your factory in Taiwan is the best I can do.

我能提供的最好價格是，每單位 6.37 美元，貨送到台灣。

I'm only willing to let them go this cheap because you're buying so many of them.

因為你買的數量多，所以我才願意降到這麼低價。

My normal price is US$6.45 plus shipping. I'm offering you a heck of a discount.

我通常的定價是美國境內 6.45 美元，外加運費。我已經給你很多折扣了。

Bill : I understand that, Mel. It's a good price, but we have to remain competitive.

梅兒，我知道。價格很好，但我們必須保持競爭性。

We're already one of the most expensive units on the market.

我們現在已經是市場中最貴的供應商之一。

The only reason we get that much is because of our reputation for quality.

我們之所以得到這麼高的訂貨量，是因為我們的品質保證。

And, the only reason we're thinking about buying your control panels, instead of making them, is your reputation for quality.

之所以考慮買你們的控制儀表板，不自己製造，是因為你們的品質評價不錯。

Mel : Bill, quality costs money.

比爾，品質需要靠錢維持。

Bill : We understand that. But, at that unit cost, we would have to significantly increase our consumer price.

那我們也知道，但如果單位價格是這樣，我們就得大幅提高客戶價格。

And that would definitely cost us a piece of our market share. This is something we want to avoid.

這一定會讓我們損失部分的市場佔有率，而我們就不希望這樣。

Mel : I understand completely, but if I drop the price even 2 cents I'll be swimming in red ink.

我完全可以了解，但就算我只降個二分錢，我也會虧大錢的。

Bill : This could be a deal breaker. My instructions from the boss are very clear. I can't go over US$6.30.

那就可能讓大家談判破裂了。老闆給我的指示很清楚，我不能讓價格超過美金 6.30 元。

I hate to see this deal fall apart for a lousy seven cents.

我很不希望為了該死的七分錢，就讓生意吹了。

Mel : Me too, but my hands are tied. A seven-cent loss times two hundred and fifty thousand units is more than I can afford.

我也是，但真的沒辦法。每單位損失七分錢，乘上二十五萬的數量，總合起來我可負擔不起。

That works out to around twenty grand if you factor in the operating losses.

如果再加上運作損失的話，總和將近是兩萬元。

Bill : Stop the presses, Mel. There's more than one way to skin a cat, and I might just have an idea.

梅兒，別再爭了，解決問題的方法不只一種，我剛想到一個主意。

Mel : Well, let's hear it. I'm all ears.

好，說說看，我洗耳恭聽。

Bill : My production people mentioned a few modifications you could make that would be a negligible cost to you but would save us a production step.

我的生產人員提到一些你可以做的變更，也許這些成本對你而言不算什麼，但卻可以為我們省下一個生產程序。

Mel : I don't know, Bill. We usually charge at least set up fees to deviate from the standard production model.

比爾，我不確定，若是要有異於標準的生產模子，我們通常會向客戶收取裝配調試費用。

Bill : I know. That's why I didn't mention them before.

我知道，所以之前沒提到這個。

I realized pretty quick that money was a problem and we can't afford your usual set up fees.

我發現，錢是一個問題——我們負擔不起你們一貫的裝配費用。

But, if you're willing to work with me, we may be able to pull the fat out of the fire.

但如果你願意配合，我們也許可以拯救這個交易。

Mel : I'm still listening.

我還在聽。

Bill : What if we ship the panel housings to you and instead of you placing each unit in a shipping box, you permanently crimp the units into place on the housing and ship it back to us ready to install.

如果我們將控制表的外罩運給你，這樣你就不用把外罩裝入運貨箱，只要把東西大致位置固定在外罩上，再運回來，我們自己裝配。

Mel : I don't know.

我不知道……

Bill : Look, the crimping process isn't even an extra step.

嘿，放一下根本不算額外的手續。

You could do it at the same time you crimp the back and front plates together.

而且正面、反面可以一次放好。

Then, you save the expense of loading each unit into an individual packing box.

這樣就可以省下個別包裝的箱子成本。

Just lay a couple of slotted Styrofoam bars in the bottom of the crate to keep the units separated in shipping and you save the cost of the packing box.

只要將幾個有溝槽的聚苯乙烯放入板箱隔開，讓運輸過程中，東西不會碰撞即可，這就可以省下箱子的錢了。

Mel : We could do that, but the cost of a packing box is only 2.5 cents. We would still be losing money.

可以是可以，但裝箱的成本只有二分半，我們還是會虧錢。

Bill : What about the savings on packing, both labor and materials? That's got to be worth seven cents a unit.

相關費用像是工錢和材料費呢？每單位應該可以省下七分錢。

Mel : Actually, it's more like three or four.

實際上，應該只有三、四分。

Bill : Ha, ha, ha! Okay, Mel, I'll tell you what I'm going to do.

哈哈，好吧，梅兒，不如這樣吧。

If you agree to do everything I covered so far, plus mount the knobs on the units instead of sending them in a separate box for us to mount, I'll up our offer four cents to US\$6.34.

如果你同意採取我目前的所有提議，再加上將每單位上的旋鈕一起裝上，不另外分箱運送，我會把價格提高到美金 6.34 元。

But this is only because I want to put this deal and myself to bed as soon as possible.

但這只是因為我想要趕快談成這筆交易，好好地休息一下。

Mel : Okay, I'm tired too. Let's shake on $6.34 and I'll buy the drinks. We'll work out the details tomorrow.

好吧，我也累了，就決定 6.34 美元這個價格了。我請大家喝飲料，其他的細節明天再談。

Bill : Let's go.

走吧。

談判停看聽 The above is a win-win situation. Mel is giving up the set-up fee, but to be honest, the changes required are minor. The savings on the packing are a bit more than he admitted to. Once you add the savings of getting the knobs mounted, Bill is saving almost ten cents a unit. So everybody is happy.

中譯 上面這個情況是雙贏局面，梅兒放棄了裝配費用，但老實說，這些改變都是小改變。包裝省下的成本其實比他說的還要多：一旦省了安裝旋鈕的成本，比爾一個單位幾乎可以省下十分錢，所以當然大家都高興。

Vocabulary 重要字彙	MP3-27
competitive	有競爭力的
component	零件
bargaining chip	議價籌碼
panel	儀器板

superior	勝過於
consumer	消費者
swim in red ink	被赤字淹沒
go over	超過
lousy	差勁的
skin a cat	解決問題
modification	變更
negligible	微不足道的
deviate	脫離（常軌）
permanently	持久地
crimp	使捲起
slotted	鑽鑿的
crate	板條箱
knob	旋鈕

Chapter 10

Increase the Quantity

增加採購量

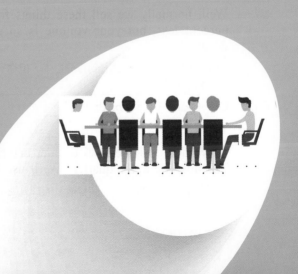

背景介紹

MP3-53

Please listen to the dialog directly.

中譯 從對話中，見真章。

MP3-28

Dialog

Another bargaining chip could be increasing the quantity. Buying in volume often gets the buyer a significant savings. The following dialog discusses that possibility.

另外一個可用來議價的籌碼是增加採購量。購買的數量龐大，常為買方省下許多錢。下面這個對話討論到這個可能性。

Mel : I'm sorry, but that's my best price.

抱歉，但這是我可以提供的最好價格。

Bill : Isn't there any way you could sharpen your pencil and get that figure down a bit more?

你難道沒有辦法再精打細算，多降價一點？

Mel : Well, normally we sell these things for five to ten percent less, but your volume is so small I can't do that.

通常我們會降個百分之五到百分之十，但你買的數量太少，我沒辦法這麼做。

Bill : Oh! Okay, I can fix that.

喔，好，這點我可以改善。

How about if I promise to order another batch just like this one every quarter? We'll use them.

如果我們每季都跟你們下同樣數量的訂單呢？我們以後的確

需要。

Mel : That won't help. We can give the discount if we don't have to retool and set up so often. That's where we save money and we pass that on to you.

沒什麼用。若可以省掉重新設置、安裝的功夫，就能降價。我們通常都是透過這些步驟，來省錢回饋給客戶群。

If you double your order, we can give you a 5% discount, and if you double that to four times your order, I can give you a 10 % discount.

如果你將訂單數量加倍，我們就可提供百分之五的折扣，如果你將數量增到四倍，就可以有百分之十的折扣。

Bill : I don't understand.

我不懂。

Mel : We sell a lot of these things but not enough to keep a production line going full time.

我們雖然產量很多，但卻還沒到可以全天候開機生產的地步。

We have to set up our shop to make these things and that takes about a day to set up and another half day to tear down when we finish.

這些產品在工廠生產時，光裝置就要花一天；在生產完畢後，又要花半天時間拆除。

By saving me three set up days and 1.5 tear down days, that's the salary of three men four and a half days.

如果你的數量多的話，你可以幫我節省三天安裝、一天半拆裝的時間，這相當於三個工人，工作四天半的工資。

I'm willing to let you save that money.

如果是這樣，我會很樂意幫你省錢。

Bill : I'd love to but I got no place to put them.

我也想，可是我沒地方存貨。

Mel : If **storage** is your only worry, I can help you there.

如果庫存是你唯一的顧慮，我可以幫你。

Bill : How?

怎麼幫？

Mel : If you sign a contract for a year's **supply**, I'll make them all in one run.

如果你簽署合約，購買一年的供應量，我會一次把它們生產好。

And you qualify for the discount. But, you have to pay me in full for the whole run as soon as you take delivery of the first of four shipments.

你也可以得到折扣。但你必須在收到第一季的貨後，盡快把全額貨款付清，總共會有四次出貨。

I can store the rest for you for nine months for free. How does that **grab** you?

我可以免費幫你保管商品九個月，這條件你覺得怎麼樣？

Bill : You have a deal. Not only do I get the discount, but today's price is locked in for a year. I can't lose.

成交。我不只有了折扣，這一年的價格也不會再漲，我一點都不吃虧。

Mel : I'll have the contract ready for your signature tomorrow.

我明天會準備合約，給你簽名。

Bill : Great.

太好了。

Vocabulary 重要字彙

significant saving	重大的節省
sharpen one's pencil	審價削款
figure	數字
salary	薪水
storage	存貨處
supply	供應
grab	抓住

Chapter 11

Modify the Delivery Date

修改交貨日期

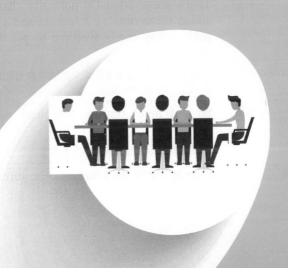

MP3-54

Please listen to the dialog directly.

中譯 從對話中，一探究竟。

Dialog

MP3-29

A third bargaining chip is modifying the delivery date to allow more time for the manufacturer to produce the required units.

第三個可用來議價的籌碼是修改交貨日期，這給製造商更充裕的時間來製造你所訂的數量。

Mel : And that's the **bottom line**. Not too bad, even if I do say so myself.

這是最後價格了，我自己看都覺得很不錯了。

Bill : Well, to be honest, I was figuring on something about 10 % lower.

老實說，我還希望能再打九折。

Mel : That's about what I'd normally charge, but you added these time **restrictions** and I'm going to have to pay some overtime to get it in **under the wire**.

其實我平常不是這個價碼，但因為你有時間限制，我得請工人加班，才能準時交貨。

Bill : So how much time do you need to lower the price?

時間要往後延多久，我才能有折扣？

Mel : Usually there isn't any time requirement.

我通常都不押時間限制的。

Bill : I know that, but I'm not going to do that. I want this finished quickly with no breaks in between, so the time limit stays.

我知道，但我不要這樣。我希望這批貨盡快完成，完全沒有延誤，所以時間限制不能變。

Mel : I won't do that to you.

我不會害你開天窗的。

Bill : Right, not with this **penalty** in the contract.

沒錯，因為這次遲交會有罰款。

Mel : Okay. Give me fifteen working days from start to finish and I'll lower the price 10%.

好吧。開工後，給我十五個工作天，我就再降個百分之十。

Bill : How about ten days?

十天如何？

Mel : I need 12 or no deal.

我要十二天，否則免談。

Bill : Done!

成交。

Vocabulary	重要字彙	MP3-29

bottom line	總帳底線
restriction	限制
under the wire	順利運作
penalty	罰款

Chapter 12

Alter the Point of Delivery
改變交貨地點

For Your Information
背景介紹

MP3-55

Please listen to the dialog directly.

中譯 從對話中，窺其巧妙。

Dialog

MP3-30

A fourth bargaining chip is altering the point of delivery. Usually the terms require the seller to deliver the goods to a location specified by the buyer, so the cost of transportation is almost always carried by the seller. The contract price could be reduced if a closer, more convenient location was used. The point of delivery could be the seller's shipping dock. That would completely eliminate transportation costs as the buyer would take possession of the goods as soon as they were on the truck.

第四個可以用來議價的籌碼是改變交貨地點。通常賣主的交貨地點，當然是送到買主指定的地方，所以運輸費用多是由賣主消化。若送貨地點改在買主和賣主之間的中點，或是交貨點直接改在賣主的卸貨站，就可以儉省不少運輸費。甚至有時候雙方合約的運費，可以完全省掉，這是因為一旦買方把貨收到自己的卡車時，就算交貨完結了。

Mel : We just finished running the numbers and I think we came up with a pretty good price.

我們已經算過價錢了，現在給你的價碼應該算是很好了。

Bill : Great, let's see.

太好了，讓我看看。

Mel : Here you go. As you can see, this assumes delivery anywhere within the **metropolitan** area. If we go outside the area, we have to use a different transportation company and the expense may increase dramatically. We can keep the price that low because we're using the company truck to deliver your goods.

這裡。你看到的是都市的送貨基準,假如是郊區,運輸系統又不同,所以價碼可能會提高很多。我們可以給你低價,是因為我們用自己的貨車幫你送貨。

Bill : We did have something come up at our local plant and we won't be able to use the goods there. The delivery point's been changed to a place about a hundred miles outside of the metropolitan area.

呃,可是我們的場地出了點狀況,所以用不到那些貨。送貨地點正好改到離都市一百哩外的地方了。

Mel : That's going to screw up our transportation figures, we'll need another day to figure out the new delivery point and all the other costs.

這樣所有運送數據就全都沒用了,我們還要再花一天才能針對新地點估價。

Bill : I don't think so. Not if you have the transportation costs **computed** separately like I asked.

不會吧,如果你已經像我要求的那樣,將運輸成本另計,就不用花上那麼多的時間了。

Mel : We do. Look, on the bottom of page eight.

我們的確是這樣做的,你看看第八頁最下面就知道了。

Bill : Right, here it is. And this figure includes all transportation costs. Is that right?

對,這就是了。那麼這個數字是總共運輸花費囉?

Mel : Right.

是的。

Bill : Good, then, here's the deal. We draw a line through page eight and eliminate it and all the transportation costs from the contract.

好，乾脆這樣吧。我們把第八頁總花費的地方劃掉。

We assume responsibility for the goods as soon as you load them on to the truck we provide.

我們會派車去收貨，你們只要幫我們裝好貨，就算交易結束。

Mel : So we load your trucks for free?

你要我們免費幫你裝貨？

Bill : It's no different than if your truck were delayed a day and you had to store the goods until it was free.

這只不過是佔用你們貨櫃一天時間罷了，再說你們的貨櫃不清空，也沒辦法再裝新貨啊。

Mel : Right, we can do that.

說的也對，就這樣做吧。

Bill : Then, if you're agreed, we have a deal.

那麼如果你同意的話，我們就成交了。

Mel : One last point, Bill.

比爾，還有一件事。

We need you to park a trailer at our dock one week prior to the shipping date so we can load it as the goods come off the production line.

我希望你們在交貨前一週就派輛拖車過來我們的貨站，這樣貨一出廠，我們就可以馬上移裝。

Bill : Okay, but you're responsible for security until the truck is driven off the lot.

可以，不過卡車在你們貨站的那段時間，你們要全權負責。

Mel : No problem. It will stay at the dock locked up indoors.

沒問題，我們的貨站會緊緊地反鎖好。

Bill : Sounds like a bell ringer to me.

看來我們可以成交散會囉。

Vocabulary　　重要字彙	MP3-30
altering	改變
transportation	交通運輸
eliminate	除去
possession	擁有
metropolitan	都市的
computed	估算過的
trailer	拖車
prior	先前的
bell ringer	敲鐘（指事情結束）

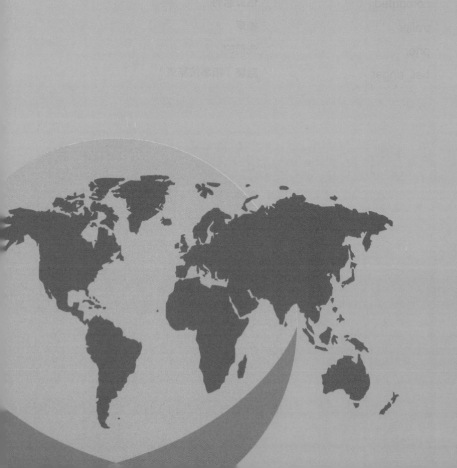

Chapter 13

Alter the Schedule of Payments

改變原訂的付款日期

背景介紹

MP3-56

Please listen to the dialog directly.

中譯 請直接研讀對話內容。

MP3-31

Dialog

A fifth bargaining chip could be to alter the schedule of payments. Because this is frequently done in construction contracts, I changed the scene to that type of job for this dialog.

第五個可以用來議價的籌碼是改變原訂的付款日期。因為在工程合約中這種情況常常發生，所以我在這個對話中，稍微將工作場景修改了一下。

Mel : There you go. Everything just like you requested, except the price.

好了，一切都合你的意了，除了價格以外。

Bill : Why not the price?

為什麼價格不行？

Mel : Well, your terms require me to carry the cost of everything and wait for my payment until 30 days after the work is completed.

這個嘛，你的條件是要我全額負擔開銷，直到完工後一個月才能取款。

Bill : That's right.

沒錯。

I want to be sure everything is done right before I pay you off, otherwise you might not respond to my call back to complete the punch list.

我想確定全部完善後才付錢，不然，一出問題你可能就不會回覆了。

Mel : I can understand that, but in the meantime I have to cover the cost of materials and **payroll** for your job.

我了解你的顧慮，但是我還要負擔你的材料費和工人的薪資。

The increase is to cover the cost of a short-term loan I have to get to stay in business while you wait and make sure.

為了等你那一個月，我可能要週轉貸款，打平經營費用；所以反應給你的就是漲價。

Bill : How about if I **alter** the deal to 50% upon substantial completion and 50% within 30 days,

那我改成大致完工就後付一半，完工一個月再付一半呢？

Mel : Still the same.

還是一樣。

I've got to have some **front money** to buy supplies, and no more than 10% retained pending final inspection.

我一定要有前置費去買原料、補給品，所以在你檢查確定前，頂多可以扣押百分之十的尾款。

Bill : Then, how do I know you'll come back and finish the job?

那我怎麼知道你會不會把工作做完？

Mel : You have my word. That's enough for most people.

我跟你保證。通常大家聽我這麼說就夠了。

Bill : Okay, then, how's this. I buy the materials and have them delivered here, and I retain 15% for up to 30 days after the punch list.

好，這樣吧。我負責買材料，並運送到這裡；完工後，我會先扣百分之十五的尾款,一個月後付清。

I'll give you the rest upon substantial completion, so you can make your payroll.

只要大部分完工,我就先付百分之八十五,這樣你就可以付工人薪水了。

Mel : All right, I'll do it for nothing up front, but you buy the supplies, and pay me everything except the 15% retainage, upon substantial completion.

好吧,這樣沒頭期款我也可以動工,但你得負責購買材料,在工作大致完成後,你要支付百分之八十五的貨款,扣押款不得超過百分之十五。

Bill : Done!

成交!

Vocabulary　　重要字彙

MP3-31

punch list	後續表單
payroll	薪資總額
alter	改變
front money	預付之訂金
retainage	尾款

Chapter 14

Alter the Time Frame
改變時間日程

背景介紹

MP3-57

A sixth bargaining chip could be made by altering the job's time frame. A common problem with roofers, asphalt workers or any contractor that travels to a work site is they make promises to start by a certain date and do, but then disappear for anywhere from a day to two weeks. Presumably they return to the job they abandoned to start yours on time, or perhaps to start another job on time as per that agreement. If you want to avoid it, write penalties into the contract, it works. In most cases, simply having those restrictions prevents the problem so this generally won't be an issue, but it could be.

中譯 第六個能夠用來議價的籌碼，是改變合約所需的工作日程。蓋屋頂的人、舖柏油路的人或任何必須通勤到達工作場所的人，都有一個共同的問題。那就是他們常常答應你在某一時間開始工作，他們也的確都做得到，但之後，他們常會無故消失一天到兩個星期。他們可能會回到工作崗位上，讓你的工程準時開工，或準時開始別人的工作。如果你想避免這種情況，合約中註明罰款是有效的制止方式。在大多數的案例中，只要有了這些限制，就可以預防問題的產生，但這並不表示就不用談判。

Dialog

MP3-32

Making it into a bargaining chip is a good idea. Several things could be done such as altering the start date, the time each day that has to be spent on the job, or the size of the crew assigned to the job. Any of these items could be altered or there could be a combination of the restrictions allowed. Several factors could be called into play, just discuss it and find out what works.

拿這個來當議價籌碼是個不錯的做法。有好幾件事可以做，像是改變工作開始日期、每天的工作時數、工作人員總數……這些條件都可以改變，或是你可以設定組合式的條件，將多項因素列入考量，並和他人討論，找出可行的方式。

Mel : Your provisions in the scope of work section are very restrictive. They don't give me much room to work.

你在工作內容部分的條款很嚴格，沒有給我很大的空間。

Bill : That's why they're there. My client wants to hold the disruption of activity on the site to a minimum.

這就是為什麼要將它們列出來的原因；我的客戶想要將工作地點可能發生的問題減到最低。

These restrictions will avoid the most common problems.

這些限制可以避免最普遍的問題。

But I do have some room to work with you. What do you need?

不過我也還有商量的空間，你有什麼需要嗎？

Mel : I'd like a day off two days after start up to go to another site.

開工二天後，我得休假一天，到另一個工地去。

They have a start date I have to honor.

我必須遵守他們的開工日期。

Bill : Can't do it. But I'll tell you what I could do.

不行，不過有折衷辦法。

Mel : What's that?

什麼辦法？

Bill : We can push back our start date to give you time to finish that one.

我們可以把開工日延後，等你先完成另一個工作。

Our start and completion dates are wide open. I can move them to any date you like.

我們的開工和完工日都很有彈性，可以配合你的時間。

I won't give you any time off in the middle except for weekends, holidays and weather delays.

但是一旦工程開始，除了週末、國定假日、天候造成的延誤，就不准有任何的休假。

Mel : Will you let me cut the crew size for a few of those days?

那我工作期間可以刪減工作人數嗎？

Bill : Nope, can't do it. That would lengthen the **disruption**.

不可以，那會延長工程不便。

Mel : I don't see how.

我不懂。

Bill : Your truck takes up three parking stalls and vehicles in the lot have to be moved away from the building to prevent damage. That's the kind of disruption I mean.

你的卡車佔了三個停車位，停車場的車輛必須離開建築物，以免造成損壞，那就是我所謂的不便。

Mel : So if I **avoid** that, I can reduce the size of the crew?

如果能避免這種情況，我可以減少人數嗎？

Bill : That would be okay.

可以。

Mel : If you allow me that, and let me push back the start date one week. Then, we can go with this contract.

若你同意這點，並讓開工日延後一週。我們就可以簽定這個合約。

Bill : Great, let's do it.

太好了，就這樣。

Vocabulary 重要字彙	MP3-32
factor	因素
provision	供應
in the scope of	在 …… 範圍
disruption	混亂
avoid	避免

Chapter 15

Dream Chips or Give-Away Chips

虛張聲勢的談判籌碼

For Your Information
背景介紹

MP3-58

Thus far, all the bargaining chips have been real items that actually meant something. I mean the side that asked really thought the requests were reasonable, and expected to get them. Thus far, the parties bargained in good faith, and every request was made in earnest. To understand the next section, you need a little background.

中譯 到目前為止，所有的議價籌碼都是一些實際項目，都有自身的意義。我的意思是說，提出籌碼的一方，真的認為他們的要求是合理的，並希望得到他們想要的東西。截至目前為止，雙方都以誠信來議價，每個要求都很真誠。要了解下面這個章節，你需要一些背景資料。

The way negotiations work is you give up something for every point you win, and all the issues on the table are credible. The next step is asking for more than you need and allowing yourself to be pushed back to what you wanted in the first place. It's called puffing, and it's an old tactic, tried and true. The idea of puffing up demands to the point they became ridiculous had been tried from time to time but it never works. The other side sees right through the scheme, calls you on it and it's over.

中譯 談判進行的方式，是你每贏一次就要放棄一些東西，會議桌上的每個議題都有其可信度。下一步，提出要求的內容比你所需的更多，讓對方要求你讓步，這樣一來，你可得到原來想要的東西。這也叫做「虛張聲勢」，它是個老技巧，屢試不爽。有人不時會嘗試，把要求誇大到讓人覺得可笑的程度，但通常都不奏效。對方一眼就看穿了你的把戲，將你逮個正著，遊戲便結束了。

For unrealistic puffing to work, you have to do more than just act as if the issues were valuable. You have to make them valuable. You have to convince the other side you're telling the truth. The problem is how do you do that when the other team knows the playing field as well as you do? To make it work, you need some convincing play-acting and you have to do your homework. If the other side tries to run this tactic, you can expect some very convincing arguments to justify their ridiculous demands. So convincing that you may even start to believe it. Well, that's what the cover story was designed to do. Don't fall for it.

中譯 想要將不切實際的唬人技巧發揮作用,你所要做的不只是演戲而已,還要真正把這些議題視為很重要。你得讓議題變得有價值,並要讓對方相信你說的是實話。問題是:當對方跟你一樣了解遊戲規則,你要怎麼做呢?要使你的計策奏效,你需要一些讓人信服的演戲技巧,還必須做點功課才行。如果對方嘗試將這計策用在你身上,你可以用一些非常有說服力的論點,使對方相信他們的要求是不合理、可笑的,你的演技必須逼真到連自己都想相信。當然,這就是封面故事的作用,別上當了。

The first time they tried this ploy; okay it worked. The other side dismissed the demands as false and without merit. They said okay to stop wasting time and tried to move on to serious discussion. But, instead of letting it go and moving on, they came up with credible arguments supporting their requests, for which their opponents had no reply. The other side was caught flat-footed; they'd been blindsided by the ploy, and won big time.

中譯 第一次用這計策時,也許有用。對方會撤回要求,以為自己的條件不合理。他們決定不再浪費時間,應該去討論一些更重大的議題,但也有可能不是這樣；他們會想出其他有可信度的論據，來支持他們的要求，若對手沒有預期到這一步，就會當場破功，慘遭滑鐵盧，使對方大獲全勝。

Now, nearly all big league negotiations use them, and weeks, even months are wasted **peeling** away the false demands. Now, it's a standard time waster at the start of negotiations where you trade your dream chips for theirs. This tactic is most effective when the two sides have no place to go, like in a labor negotiation where the two sides have no choice but to work with each other. Okay, fall for the deception. When I mentioned this to my Business English students, they became very interested. The tactic was used on them, and they didn't understand what was going on, nor did they know what to do. It never occurred to them the points were give-away — points made up to be traded — because there were justifying arguments. They negotiated them just like they were valid points.

中譯　　現在，幾乎所有大型談判都會用這些計策，雙方常常花上數週、甚至是數月的時間，一一揭開對方的不實要求。在談判開始時，雙方通常都得先拿這些假籌碼禮尚往來一番。通常當雙方沒有其他選擇，一定要和對方合作時，像是勞資雙方的談判，這個技巧會比較有效。這時，就會有人掉入這種陷阱中。當我向商用英語的學生提到這點時，他們都對此相當有興趣。但當他們被這招設計時，他們完全不知道怎麼回事，也不知道該如何應對。他們從沒遇過「虛幌籌碼（等著跟對方交換用的條件）」的攻勢；因此在談判中，他們用認真的心態來議論這些條件。

There's a simple defense for this tactic that works like a charm in a sales negotiation. All you have to do is say

"Okay, we'll go elsewhere", and start to leave. If they don't offer a large concession, I suggest you walk away. A friend once said to me, "I can afford to walk away from a lot of good deals and I lose nothing, but a potential profit. True, I won't make anything, but I still have what I need to do other deals. However, if I make one bad deal I can lose it all, and that I can't afford."

中譯　有一個很簡單的辦法,可以防禦這個計策,在銷售談判中,這個辦法就像魔咒一樣有效。你只要說:「算了,我們去找別人。」講完後,起身準備離開,如果他們不提供更多讓步,我建議你最好離開。有個朋友跟過我說:「我可以從很多不錯的交易上抽身,畢竟我損失的,不過是一些潛在可能的利潤。的確,從這當中我沒賺到什麼,但我還保有跟其他人談生意的籌碼。可是,若談到一筆爛生意,我可能全盤皆輸。這個,我就承擔不起。」

Dialog 1

MP3-33

The two dialogs below show how to handle the dream chip tactic. A Taiwanese could find him or herself on either side of the sale, so I did it both ways, one as the buyer and one as the seller. In both cases, Bob is the American. In the first dialog, Jane tried to sell DVD players to Bob.

下面兩個對話告訴你,如何面對虛幌的談判條件。台灣人可能會是買賣雙方中的一方,所以我兩種情況都會提到,一次當買方,一次當賣方。在兩個案例中,鮑伯是個美國人,在第一個對話中,珍試著要將DVD放影機賣給鮑伯。

Bob : It's good to meet you, Jane. Is this your first visit to the States?

珍,很高興見到你。這是你第一次到美國嗎?

Jane : It's nice to meet you too, Bob. No, I've been here a few times in the past.

鮑伯，我也很高興見到你；我已經來過美國幾次了。

Bob : Oh, really, on business or pleasure?

真的嗎？是出差還是休息？

Jane : Both.

都有。

Bob : Great, so you know your way around then.

太好了，那你對環境應該很熟了。

But if there's anything we can do to make your stay more comfortable, don't **hesitate** to ask.

如果有任何我們可以協助的地方，儘管開口。

Jane : Thank you, Bob, I will. That's very kind of you.

謝謝你，鮑伯，我會的。你人真好。

Bob : No problem. Now, shall we get down to business?

別客氣，現在來談正事吧。

Jane : Please.

請說。

Bob : I think we can handle this pretty quickly.

我想應該很就可以談完的。

We've studied the market pretty closely and I think we can make you a very attractive offer.

我們仔細研究過市場，應該可以提供你很好的價碼。

We're prepared to give you $12.42 per unit delivered to L.A. That's U.S. dollars of course.

報價是 12.42 元，並將貨送到洛杉磯。當然是指美金。

Jane : That's a lot less than we were expecting.

這比我們預期的價格低了很多。

It's not even close to what we were talking about over the phone.

跟我們在電話中提到的，也差很多。

Bob : I know, but there's nothing I can do, Jane.

我知道，珍，但我也無能為力。

My hands are tied. The Koreans are **dumping** tons of DVD players on the market, and we have to compete.

沒辦法，因為韓國人傾銷很多 DVD 放影機到市面上來，我們得跟他們競爭。

Jane : But still, if we take that price, my company won't even be able to pay for my trip here.

這種價錢，根本連這次的出差費都不夠本。

The discussion continued for another hour but Bob never **budged**, and showed no signs of weakening. When Jane was sure Bob was going to hang tough at $12.42, she played her **trump card**.

討論又進行了一個鐘頭，鮑伯完全不改價，一點讓步的跡象都沒有。當珍確信鮑伯死守12.42元單價時，她使出了王牌。

Jane : Bob, we've been here for over two hours and you paint a very **bleak** picture of business here in the U.S.

鮑伯，我們已經僵持了兩個小時，你一直拿美國的經濟狀況來壓我。

I guess you really are serious about your $12.42 offer.

或許你對 12.42 元這個價碼是當真的。

Bob : I wish I could offer you more, Jane, but I just can't.

珍，我也想提供你更高的價格，但真的沒辦法。

If I pay more than that, they'll just sit in my warehouse.

如果我把價格抬高，這些東西會堆在倉庫裡，賣不出去的。

Jane : We can't afford to sell for that, not if we want to stay in business, so I really don't see where there's anything to be gained by continuing this negotiation.

公司要營運，不可能這樣子賣東西，我想再談下去也沒用了。

Let's say goodbye and part, friend.

乾脆說再見，咱們分道揚鑣吧。

Bob : Oh! Well, I don't think things are at a stand-still.

噢！呃，我想應該還有轉圜餘地。

Tell me what your bottom line is. What do you need to get per unit?

告訴我你的底限吧，你需要的單價是多少？

Jane : Well, we can shave a little off the price we discussed over the phone.

電話裡談的價格，我們可以再降低一點。

Dialog 2 MP3-34

Sometimes, it works and sometimes it doesn't. In the above dialog, it broke things loose and got the talks moving again. In the second dialog, Beth is trying to buy computer chips for use in Taiwan.

有時，這個技巧很有用，但有時則不然。在上面的對話中，這個技巧使事情有了轉機，讓雙方又開始溝通。在第二個對話中，貝絲嘗試要購買在台灣可以使用的電腦晶片。

Bob : It's good to see you again, Beth. How was your trip?

貝絲，很高興再見到你。飛行還順利嗎？

Beth : Good to see you too, Bob. The trip was okay, a little long but otherwise it was fine.

鮑伯，很高興見到你。旅程很順利，有點久，但還不錯。

Bob : Is there anything we can do to help make you more comfortable?

需要什麼額外的幫忙嗎？

Beth : Not really, I'm fine

不用了，我很好。

Bob : Good, then, shall we get right to business?

好，那我們就談正事吧。

Beth : Yes, of course.

當然。

Bob : We can let you have the chips for just a little above the price we discussed over the phone.

我們在電話裡談的價格，只要再提高一點，就可以成交了。

Beth : How much is that?

那是多少呢？

Bob : How does $8.07 per unit sound?

單位價 8.07 元如何？

Beth : It sounds very high. That's an increase of more than 18%. I don't think we can go that high.

太高了，已經超過百分之十八的漲額，我們不能提高這麼多。

Bob : I'm sorry to hear that.

那真是太遺憾了。

We were looking forward to doing business with you. But that's the best price I can offer.

我們很期待和貴公司做生意，但這是我可以提供的最好價格。

After we last talked on the phone, one of our suppliers raised his prices for the next **batch** of materials we buy and so did several others. So the **price hike** is pretty much industry wide.

上次通完電話後，其中一家供應商的材料費漲價，其他幾家也是，所以整個業界都在漲價。

Beth : We heard about the price hike before I left Taiwan, but our information says the **impact** should not be this bad.

我在離開台灣前就聽說過漲價的事，但根據我們的資料顯示，這個影響應該沒有這麼大。

Bob and Beth continue to bargain for over an hour and Bob won't compromise. In fact, he refuses to budge at all. Beth can see the **writing on the wall** and decides to pull the plug on the negotiation.

鮑伯和貝絲繼續談判了一個小時，但鮑伯不願讓步。事實上，他完全拒絕讓步，貝絲可以感覺出結果已經很明顯了，所以她決定終結這個談判。

Bob : Beth, I wish I could cut my price, even as a personal favor for you, but my hands are tied. My money people tell me this is our bottom line.

貝絲，就算幫你個忙，我也希望能夠降價，但我無能為力。財務人員告訴我這是底價。

It's only because you're such a good customer that I'm willing to offer you this price.

因為你是這麼好的客戶，我才願意提供你這個價格。

Beth : Thank you, Bob. I really appreciate that. It's just more than I'm authorized to pay.

謝謝你，鮑伯，我真的很感謝，不過這個價格超過了我的權限。

I guess the only thing to do now is call a **halt** to this negotiation and part, friend.

我想現在唯一能做的就是喊停，然後分道揚鑣吧。

Bob : What do you mean?

什麼意思？

Beth : Well, we have a budget we have to stay under, so we'll have to shop around some more.

我們有一定的預算限制，所以我只好去別家問問看。

True, everyone raised his / her prices but you seem to be at the high end of the scale. So we're going to shop around a bit.

沒錯，每一家廠商都提高了價格，但你們似乎是最貴的，所以我們要去找別家看看。

Bob : I sure hate to see you go across the street. We've had a good relationship for a lot of years.

我很不希望看你去找別家，我們的良好合作關係已經維持多年了。

Beth : **These things happen.**

這種事是難免的。

I have some other suppliers I can visit on this trip, so I have to get moving.

我這次來，也可以順路去拜訪其他廠商，所以我該走了。

Give me a call if you can come down on the price.

等你們降價，再打個電話給我。

談判停看聽 That's the easy way, and it works. But what if you have to do business with them because there's no place else to go? When that happens, there are two things you can do. You can play it dumb, the easy way, or play it smart, and that requires a lot of homework. They both offer advantages, so I suggest you consider the personalities involved.

中譯 這是比較簡單的做法，也很有用。但如果你一定要和他們做生意，沒有其他選擇時，要怎麼做呢？當這種情況發生時，你有兩種做法。你可以裝傻，這是比較簡單的做法；你也可以裝聰明，而這需要許多的準備。這兩種方法都有好處，所以我建議你考慮談判的關係人員，再選擇要用哪一種應對方式。

Dialog 3　　　　　　　　　　　　　　　MP3-35

The following dialog is based on the above, using the same characters. There's a break in the dialog where Jane sees the talks are pointless. When she returns, she tries walking away. In the dialog, the section prior to the break remains unchanged. However, this time Jane has to work with this company, so she can't walk away. She has to find a way to make the deal work, so she tries the stupid response. The dialog below picks up after the break.

下面這個對話，以上面情況為背景，主角都一樣。當他們的談判出現裂痕，珍覺得沒必要再談下去，打算一走了之。在這段對話中，決裂前的部分都大同小異；不同的是，這次珍一定得跟對方做生意，所以不能說走就走。為了想辦法談成交易，她試著裝傻；以下對話從上面的裂痕處開始。

Bob : Well, it's the best I can do. If you want to sell me your DVD players, you need to accept my offer. Do we have a deal?

這是我最好的價格了，如果你想要把你們的 DVD 放影機賣給我們，你就得接受我的提議，可以成交了嗎？

Jane : I'm afraid not, Bob. I really don't have any more room to maneuver.

恐怕不行，鮑伯，我真的沒辦法再降了。

You're going to have to up the price some more, a lot more.

你得將價格提高點，甚至要提高很多。

Bob : Jane, I told you, with business the way it is, the Koreans dumping units in our market, the down economy, our decreased market share in the last three quarters.

珍，我告訴過你，現在業界的狀況是，韓國人傾銷大量的 DVD 放影機到市場上、經濟又不景氣，我們的市場佔有率已經跌了三季。

We can't compete if we pay your price.

付你們這個價碼，我們就沒競爭力了。

Jane : Bob, you're breaking my heart, but my hands are also tied.

鮑伯，你真是傷我的心，但是我也沒辦法啊。

My boss told me not to sell these units for less than it costs to make them. I can't go any lower.

老闆有指示，售價不可以比造價低，我真的不能降。

I already made two counter offers to yours and you haven't budged.

我已經改了兩次價，而你一點都不配合。

Now I've demonstrated I'm willing to work with you, and all you can say is 'take my offer'.

我展現出我們的合作誠意，但你還是那句老話，叫我「接受你的價格」。

Bob : It's a good offer, the best we can do.

這條件很好，是我們所能提供的最好價格。

Jane : Look, this is getting us nowhere.

我們這樣是談不出結果來的。

We've been here for more than seven hours and we're no closer to a deal than when we started.

已經談了七個多小時，卻一點進展都沒有。

I suggest we call it a day, and try again tomorrow.

我看今天就談到這裡吧，明天再繼續。

That is if you think we have anything to talk about tomorrow.

當然前提是——我們明天還有東西好談。

Bob : Maybe you're right.

也許你説的對。

Look, this isn't an official offer, I'm not authorized to go any higher, but during the evening I'll check with my people and see if we can sweeten our offer a bit.

這並不是正式報價，我沒有權限可以再提高價格。晚上我會和內部的人談談，看看能不能再提出更好的價格。

Like I said, this isn't official but maybe I can come up a little. Maybe as much as twenty-five cents per unit.

就像我説的，這個報價不算正式，也許我可以再多給一點，大概平均提高二十五分錢。

Jane : Bob, you know I need something more like two and a half dollars. That's still way too low.

鮑伯，你也知道多個二塊半才是我要的；二十五分還是太少。

Bob : I know, but don't forget that wasn't an offer. I'm not authorized to offer any more.

我知道，但別忘了，那不是報價，我沒有權限，可以提供更好的價格。

I'm just sort of thinking out loud that maybe my people will allow me to come up that much.

我只是把自己的想法說出來而已，也許公司的人可以做到這個。

Jane : When you talk to them, I suggest you discuss some larger numbers, and I'll call Taiwan.

當你和他們討論時，我希望你談大筆一點的數字。我會打電話回台灣。

談判停看聽 In the above dialog, Bob and Jane spent the day repeating themselves. In a gesture of good faith, Jane lowered the asking price twice and Bob didn't budge. That means either he can't bid higher and is serious about the bid being the best he can do, or he's really going for a **windfall** profit. Then, at the end of the day he **blinked**. He hinted a lower price might be possible.

中譯 在上面的對話中，鮑伯和珍花了一天的時間，重述自己的立場。為了表示自己的誠意，珍把價格降了兩次，但鮑伯仍不肯讓步。可能他真的沒辦法將價格提高，不然就是他真的認為這是最好的價碼，也有可能是他想賺個甜頭。但最後，他動搖了，他暗示也許可以把價格降低一點，也許可以成交。

There's no point to my showing you more dialog because the key to this kind of tactic is: talk but say nothing new. You and the other side stated your position in the first five minutes. The rest of the day is spent repeating yourself, not losing your temper, and listening to your counterpart **recite** a string of fairy tales.

中譯 我不必再舉更多的例子來做解釋，因為這個技巧的秘訣是：說些了無新意的話。你和對方在開始的前五分鐘，就各自把自己的立場闡述，剩下的時間都用來重複自己說過的話；並控制脾氣，聆聽對方重複那些天方夜譚。

Vocabulary　重要字彙　　　　　　　MP3-36

bargain in good faith	善意的談判
credible	可信的；可靠的
puffing	誇張不實的
tactic	手段；策略
merit	值得；好處
opponent	對手
flat-footed	笨拙的
peel	消除
hesitate	猶豫
dump	傾倒
budge	改變意見
trump card	王牌
bleak	黯淡的
batch	一批（貨）
price hike	價格上揚
impact	衝擊
writing on the wall	註定的事
halt	停止
these things happen.	難免的
quarter	一季
demonstrate	指示；示範
windfall	意外的收穫
blink	動搖；眨眼
recite	背誦；朗誦

Chapter 16

Countering Give-Away Chips

回應虛張型籌碼

For Your Information
背景介紹

MP3-59

When you're locked in a room with someone determined to win a price concession, you have to wait him out. Don't forget his plan is to wait you out, so this tactic could easily last days, with no **guarantee** of success. It all depends on how badly the guys playing the dream chips want to do business with you.

中譯 和一個堅決要贏得談價的對手對峙時,你得把他的耐性磨光;別忘了,對方也想用同一個招數來整你。因此,這種情況下來,有時候會有好幾天僵局,而且不保證你就能獲勝。這得端看談判對手多想跟你做生意了。

The dumb counter tactic works, but it's not the best way to win a dream chip session. The dumb reply can be done by a negotiator working alone or by a staff that hasn't done their homework. It's all you can do if you haven't prepared a smart reply.

中譯 裝傻的應變策略有效,但並不是贏得好條件的最佳方式。裝傻通常是單打獨鬥的談判者,或準備不足的組員使用,因為當你準備不足時,這是唯一的上策。

Dialog 1

MP3-37

The dialog below is an example of a dumb reply. As in the previous chapter, this is about DVD player negotiations, and Bob and Jane are still the principals. In this scenario, Jane expected an easy time of it and got a nasty surprise. She uses the dumb method, as follows.

下面這個對話，就是一個裝傻的回應。前一章是關於DVD
放影機談判的例子，鮑伯和珍仍然是主角。在這次的故事中，
珍以為談判過程會很簡單，卻碰了一鼻子灰。於是她用了下面
這個裝傻的方式。

Bob : Well, it's the best I can do. If you want to sell me
your DVD players, you need to accept my offer.
Do we have a deal?

我已經盡力了，如果你想把你們的 DVD 放影機賣給我，就
得接受我們的價格，可以成交嗎？

Jane : I'm afraid not, Bob. I really don't have room to
maneuver. You're going to have to come up to
what we discussed on the phone.

恐怕不行，鮑伯。我真的沒辦法動。你的價格要比我們在電
話裡談的，再高一些才行。

Bob : Jane, I told you how it is, the Koreans are
dumping units in our market, the bad economy,
our decreased market share, we can't compete at
your price.

珍，我已經告訴過你了，韓國人傾銷 DVD 放影機到我們的
市場中，經濟又不景氣，市場佔有率日漸減少，你們的價格
沒有競爭性。

Jane : That isn't my problem, Bob. You said my coming
here was just a **formality** to sign the contract. We
spoke on the phone Friday and you said nothing
about this. As far as I'm concerned, we had a
deal.

這不是我的問題，鮑伯，你說我這次只是來簽個約而已。星
期五通電話時，你卻完全沒有提到這個，我以為我們那時候
就成交了。

Bob : But that wasn't an offer. I'm not authorized to go
higher.

但那並不是報價，我沒有權限提高價格。

Jane : Then, you should have said something.

那你應該早點告訴我。

Bob : Well, we really didn't know we had to adjust the offer until this weekend.

這個嘛，到這個週末我們才知道要調價。

Jane : I have a lot of trouble believing that.

我很難再相信你的話了。

Bob : It's the truth.

這是真的。

Jane : I'm not even going to debate that issue. Now, let's stop this foolishness and do what we agreed to.

我不管真的假的。不要再說這些沒用的話，我們照原先同意的來辦吧。

Bob : That price was never an official offer, and it's not on the table now.

那個價格根本不是正式報價，也不在我們的談價範圍內。

Jane : You can't **renege** on what you represented over the phone. I thought you were straight shooters.

你不能否決電話上的提議。虧我還以為你們是有信用的生意人。

談判停看聽　　And so it goes on and on into the night. Remember this may take a while and don't **waiver**. **Stick to your guns**.

中譯　　就這樣，情況一直僵持到晚上。記住，這可能會耗上好一陣子，千萬別動搖，堅持你的立場。

The smart method is demonstrated below. I call it the smart reply because it requires a lot of research on every facet of the deal. You have to be ready with your and their market data. You need their performance for the last year, or as far back as you can go. Your own technical product data, performance studies etc. are also necessary. You really don't know what the other side is going to use so you have to be ready for anything. This is why high power negotiators show up with a team. Each member knows one facet of the deal and the principle lets the expert talk on his or her subject.

中譯　聰明的做法是下面這個方式。我稱之為聰明的回覆方式，因為這麼做的當事人，需要下很多功夫準備，了解交易的每個部分。你必須要準備好，雙方的市場資料、對方去年的營業表現，或盡可能找到以前的資料。你的技術產品資料和營運表現，也都是有必要的。你不知道對方會用哪些資料，所以你必須做好萬全準備。這就是為什麼權位較高的談判者，會帶著一群人的緣故。每個人都擅長交易的某一部分，主導著會讓專家們視情況發言。

Dialog 2　　　　　　　　　　　　　MP3-38

As in the previous chapter, this dialog is about DVD player negotiations, Bob and Jane are still the principals. In this scenario, Jane uses the smart method. She heads up a team who did their homework and they're ready for anything. She'll introduce team members to defend or attack, as needed. The dialog picks up after the introductions.

在前一章節中，其對話是關於DVD放影機的談判。鮑伯和珍仍然是主角，在這次的故事中，珍用了聰明的對應方式，她帶領一組人員，每個人都做了準備，可以處理任何狀況，她會視情況而定，指示小組要攻、還是要守。對話在彼此介紹後開始。

Bob : Well, let's get to it, shall we? My **numbers people** tell me we can afford to offer $12.42 per unit delivered to L.A.

好了，開始辦正事了吧。我的財務人員告訴我，我方可以提供的價格是單位價 12.42 美元，洛杉磯交貨。

Jane : That's a lot less than we were expecting.

這比我們所期望的價格低了很多。

Bob : That's true, Jane, but we have a little crisis going on over here.

沒錯，珍，但我們這裡發生了一些狀況。

The Koreans are dumping units in the southern California market and we need a lower price to be competitive.

韓國人傾銷了許多產品到南加州市場，我們需要低一點的價格，才能和別人競爭。

Otherwise, the units will just sit in the warehouse. Bill made a study of the market and he's prepared a report for us. Bill, would you please?

要不然，所有產品就只能放在倉庫裡了。比爾做了市場調查，為我們準備了一份報告。比爾，可以開始嗎？

Bill : That's right. A manufacturer **headquartered** in Seoul is assembling units in Malaysia and shipping them directly to L.A.

好的。有一家首爾的製造商，正在馬來西亞做產品組裝，將成品直接運送到洛杉磯。

They goosed their exports fifteen percent and it's all landing in our territory.

他們增加了百分之十五的出口量，全部都到了美國來。

They've nearly doubled their market share and we**'re on the ropes**.

最近他們的市佔率更是成長了一倍，我們的情況很不利。

Jane : We heard about the Koreans and Joseph did some checking for me. I'll let him tell you what he found out. Joe?

我們聽說了韓國人這回事，喬瑟夫幫我查了一下情況。我會讓他向大家報告一下他所知道的情況，喬？

Joe : Yes. We were also worried about the Koreans and found that they did increase output by fifteen percent.

好的。我們也很擔心韓國人這次的傾銷舉動，發現他們的確增加了百分之十五的產量。

However, they increased distribution throughout the west coast, and only about five percent, at most, is getting to your market in southern California.

但他們的鋪貨量是平均分散到整個美國西岸，最多也只有百分之五是銷售到你們南加州的市場中。

Further, the price is low but the quality sucks.

再說，他們的價格雖然低，但品質很差。

We have reports of about an eighteen percent return and exchange rate, and sales fell off dramatically once word of that got out.

我們接到的報告顯示，他們大約有百分之十八的退貨率和換貨率。消息流出去後，他們的銷售業績就大幅下滑。

The overall impact in Northern California is at worst, minimal.

即使受到最大衝擊的北加州，也只有些微影響。

In fact, there's evidence the poor quality is lowering their market share on not just comparable units, but all their lines--everything they sell under that brand name across the boards. Gentleman, I think you're worried about nothing.

事實上，證據顯示，因為他們的品質不良，不只 DVD 放影機，幾乎所有同廠牌的產品線都受到波及，市佔率都下滑。各位，我想你們的煩惱是多餘的。

Bob : Well, that's certainly nice to know. But, it doesn't alter the **depressed economy**. If we're going to move those units, we have to offer them at a damn good price.

知道那種情況，的確讓人安心不少。但經濟還是不景氣。如果我們要把這些產品銷售出去，我們必須要能提供一個非常好的價格。

Jane : We agree. Louis prepared a study on that aspect of your market and… Well, I'll let him tell you what he found.

沒錯，路易斯準備了一份有關你們市場景氣的報告，讓他來說明一下結果。

談判停看聽 For every made-up excuse, you have the truth; perhaps it's puffed up a little, but the important thing is you counter their claim. You might shame them into paying full price, but I doubt it. This should **coax** them into a realistic offer. If they don't, then perhaps they have a financial problem they've hidden that prevents them from making prompt payment, whatever the price.

中譯 他們每給一個藉口，你都有應變的答辯事實，也許你的答案某一程度來說，是誇大了一點，但重點是你能反駁對方的論點。你也許會讓他們覺得很不好意思，而同意你想要的價格，但我想這不太可能發生。這可以勸誘他們提出一個比較實際的價格。如果對方不這麼做的話，可能是有財務問題，並想要掩飾付不出錢的事實。

I've noticed the way business is done in Taiwan is like it was in the U.S. back in the 50's and 60's, when honesty and integrity meant something. All I can say is not everyone in the U.S. does business the way it's shown in the above dialog, and as for myself, I try to avoid people who operate like that. But sometimes you have to deal with the devil, and when you do, you should play to win.

中譯 我發現台灣人做生意的方式，很像五〇、六〇年代的美國商人。那時候，誠實、正直是很重要的。我只能說，不是所有美國人都像對話中的角色這樣談生意。就我而言，我也盡量避開他們。但有時候還是會碰上這種人，建議你，以必勝的決心來面對。

Vocabulary 重要字彙	MP3-39
formality	制式
renege	食言
waiver	放棄者
stick to one's guns	堅持立場
facet	一面
headquarter	總公司
be on the ropes	在邊緣
output	產量
depressed economy	經濟不景氣
coax	勸誘

Chapter 17

Negotiations Staff who to Bring

談判組員的篩選

For Your Information
背景介紹

MP3-60

The reason you go to a negotiation is because you're unwilling to accept the price asked, and you believe it's possible to do better. That means you're there to win. Never go to a negotiation before you learn everything you can about who you're dealing with. Only then will you know who to bring.

中譯 通常需要談判是因為你不願意接受對方提出的價格,你認為價格應該可以更好。也就是說,你去談判是為了要贏。在你去談判之前,一定要確定你詳知自己對手的所有資料,只有這樣,你才會知道該帶什麼樣的人一起去。

If you're meeting with a new buyer or source, you should call around to your competitor and ask them if they've ever had dealings with them. The odds are someone in the area you know has dealt with them before, and they are usually happy to fill you in on what they're like.

中譯 如果你和新買主或供應商會面,你應該打電話給競爭同業,詢問他們是否和這些人打過交道。很可能在你周遭就有人曾經和他們做過生意,這些人通常會很樂意告訴你,這些新買主或供應商是怎樣的人。

If you can't find out what they're like from someone in the area, you can try checking with old contacts in the same area as your new one. It's very seldom you can't find out anything about a new business contact, if you put a little effort into it. It's also a bad sign about the contact if you can't find out anything about them, unless they're a new company.

中譯　如果在你當地打聽不出來這些人的底細，你可以試著聯絡一些和對方在同地區的老客戶。通常只要你稍微努力一下，應該都可以找到一些關於這個新買主或供應商的資料。如果你找不到任何與他們有關的資料，這通常不是個好現象，除非對方是一家新公司。

If the word is they're sweethearts to work with, you should be okay with a minimal team, maybe a single representative is enough. However, if the word is bad, or if you can't find out anything on the new company, the safest thing is to prepare for the worst. Show up at the meeting loaded for bear, but how much you wring is up to you and your budget.

中譯　如果你打聽到他們是很好的合作對象，你只要帶一些人去參加議價談判就夠了，甚至只要帶一個代表去就可以了。但若你聽說對方挺難纏的，或找不到任何有關這家新公司的資料，那麼最保險的做法是：預先想好最糟的情況，做好萬全的準備，嚴陣以待，但要做多少讓步端看你自己和你的預算。

When the negotiation is a deal between old friends, you don't need any coaching from me, aside from the idiom definitions in the companion volume to this book, which should come in handy. However, if you're expecting things to get hot, you'll need the information in here.

中譯　當議價談判發生在老朋友之間時，你不需要我的教導，你只要讀讀本系列的成語解說即可，就能夠派上用場。但若談判相當激烈，你就需要這裡的資訊。

That's about as bad as it can get. If you choose the

smart defense, you should bring the right people. You're going to need a world of information at your fingertips, but you're also going to have to pay to get and keep them there. If the meeting is across town, then the expenses are no big deal. If it's across the ocean, then you want to get the best **bang** for your buck. You need the most information you can get **crammed** into the fewest people possible. True, these are give-away chips the other side doesn't expect to win, but that's not the point. You're being tested, and how well you do will determine how they treat you, later on.

中譯 事情應該不會比這個更糟。如果你選擇以聰明的方式回應對方，你應該要帶適當的人一起去。你會需要許多即時資訊，但帶這些人一起去是需要花錢的。如果談判會議是在同一個城市，那麼花費就不會很大。但若談判會議需要漂洋過海，你就必須確定花下去的錢，可以達到最大功效。你帶的人數需要精簡，但資料卻要很多。的確，你會有一些虛幌用的籌碼，讓對方招架不住，但這不是重點。重點是對方會試探你，你的應對方式如何，將決定他們之後對待你的方式。

If you stand your ground in the meeting, you'll greatly increase their opinion of you, and they'll be less likely to try to trick you. If you check with your office for answers to most questions, they won't respect you or the company that sent you. If you show up with the answers, in yourself or a team of experts ready to answer every demand with solid information, they'll respect you and your company.

中譯 如果你在會議中堅定立場，對方會加深對你的印象，他們比較不會想和你玩花招。如果你大部分的問題，都要向公司請示才能回答，對方就不會尊重你或你的公司。反之若你能提供對方答案，你或你所帶領的專業人士，可以應付對方提出的問題，並給予詳細資料，他們就會尊重你和你的公司。

If you're attending a sales meeting, it doesn't matter which side of the deal you're on. You'll need the background information on both companies and the product. You'll need to know about other similar products, their reliability, availability and price. Also, you need to have reasons for why you're dealing with them, and not the others. Remember, it doesn't have to be true, just believable. If you're selling them a product, the most important information you'll need is a comprehensive market study for the ware they sell and what they will buy from you.

中譯　參加銷售會議時，你代表哪一方並不是很重要。因為你都需要兩家公司的背景，包括產品資料；你需要知道其他類似的產品、可靠性、可得性及價格。同時，你必須清楚你為什麼要和對方打交道，而不和其他商家做生意。記住，這些原因不見得要是真的原因，只要聽起來讓人信服就夠了。如果你要把產品賣給對方，你需要的最重要資訊，就是一個全面性的市場報告：知道他們賣哪些產品、他們可能跟你買什麼產品。

If one properly prepared man or woman is enough, then there's no reason to send more. I suggest assigning a team to gather the information and brief your representative before he or she leaves the office.

中譯　若一位準備周全的代表出席就夠了，那就不必多派人手。我建議事先指派一小組負責收集資料，再請他們向指定代表報告，讓代表知道所有細節資料後，再赴談判場。

Showing up with a team of people is mostly an intimidation tactic. It's unnecessary, unless your intention is to impress or intimidate the other side. The team method is usually reserved for union contracts and political negotiations. For a sales meeting, two or three people are more than enough. The steamroller from a high power team is ineffective against a well prepared, confident, man or woman.

中譯 帶一組人員參加談判會議，通常是向對方施壓的計策。除非你就是要嚇唬對方，讓他們印象深刻，否則這是沒有必要的。小組談判通常都留到工會合約，或政治談判時才用。對銷售會議來說，兩三個人就綽綽有餘了。想要拿高階小組的聲勢，來壓倒一個準備周全、有自信的男士或女士，這種作法並不會奏效。

Dialog 1

MP3-40

The first dialog shows a well-prepared woman, Lilly, at a sales meeting selling computer sound cards. She's up against a team, led by Hank representing the buyer. This is the first time these companies are dealing with each other, so the buyer is going to try to overwhelm Lilly to get a better deal. Lilly is alone and all other characters at the meeting work for the potential buyer.

第一個對話中，莉莉是一個準備周全的女性，她參加了電腦音效卡的銷售會議。她的談判對象，是以漢克為首的買方小組。這是兩家公司第一次做生意，因此買方想用一組成員來壓制莉莉，以得到更好的條件。莉莉單獨出席這次會議，其他與會人士都屬買方陣營。

Hank :All right, Lilly, we've been getting a good product and excellent service from our regular supplier. Why should we buy from you?

莉莉，我們的供應商提供我們很好的產品和服務。請你說明
一下，為什麼我們應該向你下訂單？

Lilly : Our sound cards are just as good; in fact, they're
made by the same company that makes the unit
you're using now. My service is just as good,
maybe better. Give me a chance, and I'll prove it.
I'll give you the service like…

我們的音效卡品質也很好，事實上，這些音效卡的製造商，
正是生產你現在所用產品的製造商。我們的服務也很好，
甚至比你現在合作的廠商更好，給我一次機會，我會證明給
你看。我可以提供的服務有……

Hank : Service is the least of our concerns. Because of
the volume we deal in, we've always gotten the
best service.

我們最不擔心的就是服務。因為我們的量夠大，所以得到的
服務總是最好的。

Lilly : I can do better. I can get you the same sound
card you're buying now for less than 50% of
your current price if you don't mind using the
manufacturer's own brand name.

我可以做得更好。如果你不介意使用製造商的品牌名稱，只
要半價，我就能提供一樣的音效卡。

Jack : We can get that from our old people as well. We
prefer using the well-known brand name. Our
customers like it.

原來的廠商也可以提供這個；我們比較喜歡有名的品牌，因
為客戶也喜歡。

Lilly : Okay, I've got two answers for you. First, I can
give you the name brand for two or three percent
less than you're currently paying.

關於這個，我有兩點回應。第一，我能提供你相同的品牌名
稱，價格比你現在支付的價格，少上百分之二到三。

Second, a recent market study in the U.S. shows
most end users don't care whose sound card you

use so long as it works.

第二，美國一份最新市場調查顯示：大部分的使用者，並不在乎使用哪一家的音效卡，只要能用就好。

And these cards work. You know that. I sent you five units for testing, and if they didn't perform I wouldn't be standing here.

我們的音效卡可以用，你們很清楚這點。我之前寄了五組音效卡給你們測試，如果這些音效卡不好，我現在也不會站在這裡了，不是嗎？

Jane : Who did this study you just referred to, and when?

你剛剛說的那份報告是誰做的？什麼時候做的？

Lilly : Just a minute, I have it right here.

等一下，我有帶來。

Lilly opens an **indexed** file, pulls out a group of **stapled** papers and hands them to the person seated next to her.

莉莉打開她的檔案夾，拿出一份裝訂好的資料，並交給坐在她旁邊的人。

These are copies of the study. I have one for everyone. Take one and pass on the rest please.

這是那份報告的影本，我幫大家都準備了一份，麻煩一人一份傳下去。

As you can see, it was done by a well-known professional market research company.

你們可以看得出來，這份報告是由一家知名的專業市場研究公司所做的。

If you have questions, I'll do my best to answer them.

如果大家有任何問題，我會盡力回答。

But I recommend you go to the source and call

the people that did the study. Their name and contact person are on the last page.

但我建議大家可以打電話給做這份研究報告的人，他們的名字和聯絡人都在最後一頁上面。

Sam : Look! We've got a winner right now. Why should we drop them and go with you?

聽著！我們已經有合作對象了，為什麼應該要捨他們而就你們呢？

Lilly : Because I can deliver you the service. Jimmy Lee at World Components is a good man, I know him well, but he's gotten fat off of customers like you, and he doesn't work as hard as he used to.

因為我能提供給你們的服務。「世界零件公司」的李吉米先生是個好人，我跟他很熟，但他從你們這種公司身上，得到太多利益，他現在已經不像以往那般努力工作了。

Sam : Why do you say that?

此話怎說？

Lilly : We're in the same business, buying from the same source, but my prices are better.

我們在同一行競爭，向同一位供應商購買產品，但我的價格比較好。

A customer like you should get the best price right off the bat. You shouldn't have to call him and ask what happened here.

你們這種好顧客值得最好的價格，甚至你根本不必打電話問他，市面上的情況才對。

Why is my price better than his? He's not really trying any more. If you give me an order today, I'll deliver them at the price in my proposal, not a cent more.

為什麼我的條件比較好？因為他已經失去衝勁了。如果你們今天向我下單，我會照提出的價格送貨，絕對不多收一毛。

Dialog 2

MP3-41

This dialog is a continuation of the first except now Lilly answers questions she can't look up the answers to.

這個對話是上一個的延續，唯一不同點是，莉莉被問到的問題，她並不打算回答。

Hank : Well, Lilly, before we even think about making an order, I have some more questions for you.

莉莉，在我們考慮下單之前，我有一些問題想請教你。

Lilly : Fire away.

儘管問。

Hank : There's no doubt you did your homework. If anything, you seem to have done it a little too well.

無疑地，你事前做過準備。可是你好像準備太充分了一點。

Lilly : What do you mean, Hank?

什麼意思？

Hank : Where the heck did you get all this data on us? Why do you know what we're paying to another supplier? Do we have a leak in our company?

你到底是從哪裡得到這些相關資料的？你怎麼知道我們付多少錢給供應商？我們公司有人洩密嗎？

Lilly : I'm not prepared to name my source, but I can assure you it wasn't from anyone in your company.

我不打算告訴你我的消息來源，但我可以向你保證，這些資料不是來自貴公司。

Hank : So you have a source at World?

那麼，你的消息來源在「世界零件」？

Lilly : That is a good guess, but I'm not going to confirm

---

or deny it. I'm only going to say the leak isn't here, in your company.

猜的好，但我不予置評。我只是要告訴你，我的消息來源不是來自貴公司。

Jane : I have a question. Why did you know about this study when Jimmy didn't?

我想請問，你為什麼會有這份報告，而吉米卻沒提過？

Lilly : I'm pretty sure Jimmy knew about it.

我很確定吉米也知道這份報告的事。

My guess is his **commission** is based on gross sales and he makes more if you stay with the name brand.

我猜他的佣金是以銷售總額為基準，如果你們繼續使用這個品牌的話，他應該可以抽比較多的佣金。

But that's just a guess, I really don't know the answer.

但這只是我的猜想，我也不知道他為什麼不告訴你們。

Hank : Very well done, Lilly. Thank you for your time.

很好，莉莉。謝謝你今天過來一趟。

We have some talking to do and we'll give you a call at the hotel tonight or tomorrow morning.

我們內部必須商量一下，今晚或明早會打電話到旅館給你。

Lilly : Okay, I'll stay available if you have any questions. You have my cell phone.

好的，有問題的話，都可以打電話給我，貴公司有我的手機號碼。

談判停看聽 I've been in meetings like this. The other side was openly **hostile** and very **antagonistic**. But I **stood my ground**, didn't lose my temper, apologized for giving them bad news but not for anything I did. And I answered every question without hesitation or delay. I reviewed the meeting agenda and had everything ready for them. My preparation was better than what they were used to. I knew my business and I knew my product, and by the end of the meeting, they were eating out of my hand. They remained my clients for as long as I was in the business.

中譯 我曾經參加過這類型的會議，對方的敵意很明顯，但我堅持自己的立場，沒有發脾氣。給他們的回覆不夠好時，我會道歉，但只是因為答案不好，而不是因為我個人。在回答問題時，我不會遲疑或延誤。我會事先看過會議議程，準備他們可能需要的資料，我的準備總是比對方期望的還要詳細。我知道這一行產業，也熟悉我的產品。在會議結束時，他們簡直對我讚佩不已，後來我還在這一行時，他們也一直都是我的客戶。

Vocabulary　　重要字彙　　MP3-42

bang	大賺一筆
cram	填塞
believable	可信的
representative	代表
intimidation	威脅；不安
steamroller	強硬手段
indexed	編目好的
stapled	釘好的
commission	佣金
hostile	有敵意的
antagonistic	敵對的
stand one's ground	堅守立場
delay	延遲
eat out of one's hand	言聽計從

Chapter 18

Friendly Helpful Lawyers
友善助人的律師

For Your Information
背景介紹

MP3-61

This book has information about lawyers and their priorities. It covers how they look out for themselves and their clients, why they say there's no conflict of interest, and how no stone is left unturned for the client, regardless of cost. The **attorney** is tireless in checking every angle. This is basically because they are paid by the hour. The more time they spend on the case, the more they get paid.

中譯 這本書談到律師和他們處理事情的輕重緩急態度，也談到他們如何善於維護自身和客戶的利益，以及他們會不惜成本，強說事情沒有利益衝突，或堅稱客戶的情況會很順利的原因。在仔細調查事件層面時，律師從不感到疲倦，這是因為他們時數計費，他們花在案子上的時間越長，賺的錢越多。

The fact that an in-house attorney handles similar situations faster and cheaper than attorneys paid by the hour is one of those mysteries of life we mere **mortals** will never understand without the help of an attorney.

中譯 當企業雇有專屬的律師，律師處理案件的速度就會比較快，而收費也比外面按時計費的律師低。為什麼公司內部的律師處理案件的速度會比較快，恐怕不靠律師幫忙，我們這些平凡百姓也不會懂。

The only way to avoid **prolonged** legal sessions and get your lawyer to do things quickly is to hire one as an employee. Then, the mindset will immediately change to that of a normal employee. The only problem is American lawyers don't work cheaply, and many companies don't have enough work to keep a full time lawyer busy. So most of us are doomed to hiring a large law firm and paying through the nose.

中譯 要避免冗長的法律程序，讓律師處理事情的速度快一點，只有一個辦法──就是把他雇用為你的員工。一旦他成為你的員工，他的想法就會立刻改變，變得和其他同事一樣。唯一的麻煩是，美國律師的薪水都很高，多數公司沒有足夠的工作，可以讓一位全職律師保持忙碌。所以我們大部分的人沒有其他選擇，只好雇用大型法律事務所，多付很多的金錢。

Dialog　　　　　　　　　　　　　　MP3-43

There are ways to keep an attorney under control and things running smoothly. I think the best way to demonstrate this is through a dialog showing a negotiation session with an attorney. In the dialog, Tom is the head of sales and responsible for building the team. Pam is the attorney and they're discussing what Tom wants from Pam at the meetings.

有一些辦法可以掌握律師的工作，讓事情進展得順利一些。我認為只有從對話中，可以讓你清楚地了解到和律師談話的情況。在這個對話中，湯姆是銷售經理，負責帶領這個銷售團隊。潘是律師，他們正在討論，在會議中湯姆需要潘如何協助。

Tom：Hi, Pam. Thanks for coming.

嗨，潘，謝謝你過來一趟。

Pam：Hi, Tom. It's good to see you again.

嗨，湯姆，很高興又見到你了。

Tom：Have a seat and let's get right to it.

請坐，我們就直接談正事了。

Pam : Okay, shoot!

好，説吧！

Tom : I've never used you before on a negotiation and we need to set up the ground rules. Stop me if you have a problem.

我在談判時，從沒跟你合作過。我們現在要建立一些基本規則，如果你有問題的話，可以叫我停下來。

Pam : All right.

好的。

Tom : First of all, no **interruptions**, if you see a problem and it can't wait, whisper it to me, or hand me a note. Otherwise, wait until we're on break or after the session.

首先，不要打岔。如果你發現有問題，沒辦法等，你可以悄悄告訴我或傳紙條給我。要不然的話，請等到休息時或會議結束後，再告訴我。

Pam : I suppose, if that's the way you want it, but why?

可以，如果這是你的要求。但為什麼要這樣呢？

Tom : There shouldn't be anything complicated **airing** the negotiations, and I want to avoid **complications** if it's at all possible.

談判時，不可以有任何複雜情況出現，所以我想盡可能避免這種事發生。

Pam : Sure, I can live with that. Anything else?

當然，我可以做到。還有別的事嗎？

Tom : Not really, just that all your **comments** should come to me before anyone else. I get the final say on whether it gets into the meeting.

差不多了，只是你如果有任何意見，我一定要第一個知道；我有權決定要不要在會議上公開討論。

Pam : If you **squash** something I see as important, I'm going to inform your boss in writing.

如果你把我認為重要的事剔除，我會書面秉告你的老闆。

Tom : No problem, just be sure to cc me.

沒問題，但別忘了附送一份給我。

Vocabulary 重要字彙	MP3-43
mortal	平凡人
prolonged	長期的
doomed	註定的
law firm	律師事務所
pay through the nose	付了過高的價錢
interruption	打斷；打岔
airing	攪亂風聲
complication	複雜
comment	評論；意見
squash	壓碎
cc	附檔給……

Chapter 18

Part 2 商務談判
贏家關鍵 100 句

A

go across the street
到別處買東西

MP3-62

Idiom Definition

This is used if a customer or potential customer goes elsewhere to buy the same products or services you offer.

成語定義 當顧客或潛在顧客到別處購買的產品或服務和你所提供的相同時，就會用到這個慣用語。

Examples

例 I want you to make them so happy they won't even think about going across the street.

我希望你能讓他們覺得很滿意，這樣他們就會連到別家買東西的念頭都不會有。

例 We just never seemed to hit it off, so they went across the street.

我們不管怎麼好像就是談不攏，於是他們就到別處買東西。

Background

This goes back to neighborhood merchants much like things are in Taiwan today, and no one had an exclusive on anything. If a customer was dissatisfied he or she could walk across the street to a competitor.

背景資料 這句慣用語要回溯到鄰近商家密集，那種和今天台灣很像的情況，每家賣的東西都差不多。你賣的東西如果顧客不滿意，顧客就會過個馬路到對面的競爭對手那裡看看。

Alternatives 相關用語

◆ shop around	到處逛逛
◇ do some more shopping	多逛一下
◇ they might be back	可能回來買
◇ check out the competition	貨比三家

get (his) bearings
理出頭緒

`MP3-63`

Idiom Definition

This is the term used if someone is confused and disoriented about anything. It's what they do to get back on track. They pause long enough to figure out where they are, and what they should do.

成語定義 如果某人對某事感到困惑或迷惘時，就會用到這個慣用語。表示要做點什麼才能回到常軌。他們會停下來一段時間，想清楚現在所處的位置，接下來應該怎麼做等等。

Examples

例 No meetings on the first day, he'll use the time to get his bearings.

第一天不開會，他便利用時間好好理出個頭緒。

例 Things are happening so fast, I need a minute to get my bearings.

事情發生得太快，我需要一點時間理出頭緒。

Word Definition Used

"bearings" a person's orientation, the process of finding out where you are exactly in regards to your physical location, or the subject under discussion.

使用的字詞定義 「bearings」（方向）指的是一個人的方向，找出實際所在位置或討論主題目前進度的過程。

Originally used for physical location alone it is now frequently applied to political social and religious orientation.

背景資料 原來只用來指實際的地理位置，現在則經常用在政治、社會和宗教的方向上。

Business Use

This term describes the process of studying the details of a situation to determine what is the best way to handle it. It's also code, or a short version of what's between the quotation marks. "Give him the new data, let him rest up overnight so he has time to figure out what's what. Then we can discuss it tomorrow when he's rested."

商業用法 這種說法用來形容研究情況細節以決定最佳處理方式的過程。以下面這句引號裡的話為例：「把新資料給他好好想一個晚上，這樣他就有時間把來龍去脈弄清楚。等他想得差不多了，我們明天便可進行討論。」，這個慣用語便是描述這類情況的一種制式簡短說法。

Variations

The pronoun used is one of several possibilities. The parentheses indicate other pronouns could be substituted, and where they should go.

代替詞 這裡用的代名詞只是其中一種可能。括號的地方表示也可以用其他代名詞代替，依所要描述的對象而定。

Alternatives 相關用語

◇ figure out which end is up　　　想清楚後續情況

◇ find out what's what　　　　　把來龍去脈弄清楚

◇ see which way the wind is blowing
　看看風往哪裡吹（事情接下來如何發展）

put this deal to bed
告一段落

MP3-64

Idiom Definition

A statement meaning the speaker's intention is to settle or conclude the business at hand. Come to an agreement, shake on it and move on to something else.

成語定義 這個說法意指說話者企圖把手邊的事情給解決或結束掉。達成協議，把它擺一邊，然後把注意力轉到別的事上頭。

Word Definition Used

"to bed" is a term meaning finished.

使用的字詞定義 「to bed」這個詞是結束的意思。

Examples

例 Let's split the difference, and put this deal to bed.

我們把不同的地方分清楚，然後搞定它。

例 The talks looked endless, until Julie came and put this deal to bed.

談話看起來好像沒完沒了，直到茱莉來了才告一段落。

Background

This comes from newspapers where every step has a deadline. When the writing deadline is reached, the writers and editors go home to bed and they turn what they wrote over to the next printing department. The work goes to the printers; the presses are set up and the issue is run or printed.

這個説法來自報紙，因為發行報紙的每個步驟都有截止期限。當撰稿人截稿時間一到，撰稿人和編輯就會把稿子交給接下來的印刷部門然後回家睡覺。印刷的工作由印刷工負責把印刷機準備好，再把報紙印出來。

Business Use

Once a basic agreement is negotiated between the principals the same thing happens. The deal is turned over to staff people who work out the details.

商業用法 一旦決策者之間達成基本共識後，接下來也是一樣；會交由員工把決策的施行細節給處理好。

Alternatives 相關用語

◇ come to a meeting of the minds 達成共識

◆ hammer the last nail in place
把最後一根釘子釘上去（搞定收工）

B

bell ringer
就是這個；打開局面；扭轉乾坤

MP3--65

Idiom Definition

used to describe a very desirable or advantageous person, place or thing

成語定義 用來形容很有吸引力或好處很多的人事地物。

Examples

例 I really like that idea; I think it's a bell ringer.

我真的覺得這個點子不錯，靠它一定行。

例 We need a real bell ringer from research and development.

我們的研究發展需要有關鍵性的突破才行。

Background

This comes from carnivals and road shows that almost always have games to test one's skill or strength. One of the most popular is the hammer. Just about every show has one. The hammer is actually a wooden mallet. The contestant hits the raised end of a little seesaw as hard as possible. There's a metal slide resting on the other end, that shoots up the rod to ring the bell.

背景資料 這個詞是從嘉年華會或街頭表演那裡來的，當時有很多遊戲可以考驗參加者的技巧或力氣。其中最受歡迎的一項是鐵槌遊戲，差不多每個表演會場都有。說是鐵槌其實是木槌，參加競賽的人會用力敲打小蹺蹺板升高的那一頭，另一頭則有一個金屬滑板，會把一根棒子迅速升起，然後把鐘敲響。

It's used to identify a good person, place, or thing, but especially a good idea. It's also a code term for what's between the quotation marks. "This is an excellent idea, and in my opinion, exactly what we need."

商業用法　這個詞用來識別好的人事地物，但特別用來指想法。以下面這句引號裡的話為例：「這個主意真不錯，依我看來，它完全符合我們的需要。」這個詞便是描述這類情況的一種制式說法。

Variations

"That rings the bell."

"It rings my bell."

代替詞

這樣就對了。
我就是要這個。

Alternatives 相關用語

◇ good one	這個好
◇ that should do it	那個應該沒問題
◆ hit the mark	擊中目標；成功
◇ hits the spot	擊中要點
◇ wins the prize	得獎
◇ wins all the marbles	大贏家

big league

高階挑戰；競爭激烈的地方

MP3-66

Idiom Definition

This is said of any serious or important project worth a large amount of money to the participants.

成語定義 用來指任何對參加者而言值一大筆錢的嚴肅或重要方案。

Word Definition Used

"big league" is a term as well as an idiom meaning the above.

使用的字詞定義 「big league」是一個包含上述涵意的專門用詞，也是一個慣用語。

Examples

例 That kid stuff doesn't work here, you're in the big leagues now.

那些幼稚行徑在這裡可行不通，你現在面對的是高階挑戰。

例 This is the big leagues; we're playing for keeps here.

這裡競爭很激烈，我們要努力保持領先才行。

Background

Baseball is so popular it's organized on several levels. It Starts with Little League, for kids under twelve through school and church teams, company leagues, institutional teams, and several levels of professionals up to the major leagues.

The majors are the best, and often called the big leagues. The players are the best of the best, the cream of the crop. Each man's a professional, earning more than most Americans working full time.

These players treat the game like a business. They're playing for a living, not sportsmanship so only the strictest interpretations of the rules apply. Baseball here is a business where they play to win.

背景資料 棒球相當受歡迎,它分成好幾層不同的組織。一開始是少年棒球聯盟,主要是十二歲以下的孩子組成的學校球隊和教會球隊,然後是公司球隊、社團球隊,再往上是好幾層的職業球隊,最後是職業性運動聯盟。

這些職業球隊都是頂尖的球隊,通常也稱為大聯盟。這些球員都是棒球中的佼佼者,個個出類拔萃。每個人都很專業,也比大部分全職工作的美國人賺得還要多。

這些球員把球賽當事業來看,打球是為了維生而不只是喜歡這項運動而已,因此自我要求相當嚴格。棒球對他們而言,乃不斷爭取比賽勝利的一份事業。

Business Use

This is usually used as a warning that someone is now dealing with a sharper class of people, and should therefore be more careful. It is also used to congratulate someone on moving up in status.

商業用法 這個詞通常用來當做警告,表示某人正和一群精明的人打交道,因此需要更小心才行。它也用來恭賀某人高升。

Alternatives 相關用語

◇ the bigs	一級棒
◇ a big leaguer	超級戰將
◇ the shows	表現機會
◇ hard ball	堅毅
◇ playing hard ball	堅忍不拔
◇ this ain't the bush leagues	這可不是二流的(人、地方)
◇ major league	競爭激烈的地方
◇ major deal	過人一等
◇ big deal	了不起
◇ playing with the big boys	和重要的人打交道
◆ playing for keeps	努力保持領先
◇ big time	第一流的
◇ the majors	首屈一指的

B big ticket item
昂貴的東西；大生意；大買賣

MP3-67

Idiom Definition

This is used to describe any expensive item or service.

成語定義 用來形容任何昂貴的東西或服務。

Word Definition Used

"big" means expensive.

"ticket" refers to the price tag.

使用的字詞定義 「big」意指昂貴，「ticket」指的是標價。

Examples

例 That's a big ticket item, and it pays a good commission.

這是筆大生意，佣金很多。

例 I try to sell at least one big ticket item a month.

我設法每個月至少做成一筆大買賣。

Background

Big ticket is a slang term used to describe a price tag with an expensive price on it. To sales people, especially those working for commission the size of an item means little. The only thing that matters is the cost, because their commission is based on it.

背景資料 這個詞是一個俚語,用來形容標價上的價格很昂貴。對推銷員來說,尤其是那些靠佣金吃飯的人而言,東西的大小並不重要,唯一重要的是價格;因為他們的佣金全靠買賣價格多少而定。

Business Use

This is the term used to describe any expensive item by people in sales.

商業用法 這個詞用來形容任何推銷員推銷出去的昂貴產品。

Alternatives 相關用語

◇ the big stuff	大買賣
◇ high end	高級的
◇ major item	大生意

B
big time
有聲有色；高人一等；很有成就

Idiom Definition

This is used to describe anything done in a grand style. It's also used to describe anyone who has reached the highest levels in a company, or profession.

成語定義 用來形容任何漂亮完成的事，也用來形容某人在公司或該行業中爬到頂尖位置。

Word Definition Used

"big time" is a term as well as an idiom. When these exact words are used this way, they take on the unique meaning above.

使用的字詞定義 「big time」是一個專門用詞也是一個慣用語。每個字這樣連起來用時，表現的便是上述那種特別的意思。

Examples

例 He's a bright boy, he made the big time in just a few years.

他這不是蓋的，才不過幾年就幹得有聲有色。

例 We need to tell people we're big time and in it for the long haul.

長期而言，我們要讓別人覺得我們高人一等才行。

Background

This only recently became popular. Starting on

the streets it got to the boardroom with the seventies generation. The word 'time' uses the slang definition, meaning deal or event

背景資料 這個詞最近才流行起來。一開始是七年級生私下在用的，後來連辦公場合也在用。「time」這個字用的是俚語定義，意指交易或事件。

Business Use

This is mostly used in informal verbal exchanges. rarely in formal written reports, although that may happen in the future.

商業用法 這個詞大部分用在非正式的口頭交易上，很少用在正式的書面報告，或許將來也可能會用吧。

Alternatives 相關用語

◇ the bigs	一級棒
◇ a big leaguer	超級戰將
◇ the shows	表現機會
◇ hard ball	堅毅
◇ playing hard ball	堅忍不拔
◇ this ain't the bush leagues	這可不是二流的(人、地方)
◇ major league	競爭激烈的地方
◇ major deal	過人一等
◇ big deal	了不起
◇ playing with the big boys	和重要的人打交道
◇ playing for keeps	努力保持領先
◇ big league	高階挑戰
◇ the majors	首屈一指的

B

blind sided
被出賣（背叛）

MP3-69

Idiom Definition

This is used to describe an attack from an unexpected direction.

成語定義 用來形容被人從沒有料想到的地方攻擊。

Word Definition Used

"blind" is a slang term for an approach that is not watched.

使用的字詞定義 「blind」是個俚語，表示沒有注意到的方向。

Examples

例 She blind sided him, he never expected that question from her.

他被她出賣了，他從沒想過她會這麼做。

例 He was blind sided by a friend he thought he could trust.

他被一個他認為可以信任的朋友給出賣了。

Background

The word "blind" is a slang way of saying not watched. This is an old expression that always refers to something bad coming from a side, area or person. In war it refers to an attack from an area thought safe. In relationships it's a problem from an unlikely source. In

American football a tackle from a direction the runner wasn't watching or could not see, as from his direct rear.

背景資料 「blind」這個字是沒有注意到的俚語表達方式。這個說法由來以久，主要指一些人事地物的不好消息。在戰爭中，它指的是被以為安全的地方攻擊。在人際關係中，它指的是不可靠的問題關係。例如在美式足球裡，若要從跑者沒注意或看不到的地方加以擒抱，便是直接從他背後攻擊。

Business Use

The business meaning is much the same, and it gets a lot of use. It means an unexpected attack, or an expected attack from an unforeseen source, a betrayal.

商業用法 商業上的意義都差不多，也被人使用得很頻繁。它指的是意外襲擊，或是雖然可以預見攻擊，但對方卻在意料之外；也意指出賣。

Alternatives 相關用語

◇ climbed up my tail pipe	踩到我的痛處
◇ from my six (o'clock)	從背後襲擊
◇ climbed in my back door	從背後襲擊
◇ caught unawares	出其不意
◆ caught with his pants down	被逮個正著
◇ caught flat footed	缺陷入困境
◇ asleep at the switch	被欺騙

B (he) blinked
讓（某人）緊張了一下

Idiom Definition

To make an opponent pause to rethink things, or cause a small reaction when none was expected.

成語定義 讓對手停下來重新想一想，或是出其不意造成一些小反應。

Examples

例 We didn't win, but we made the big guy blink.

雖然我們沒有贏，但至少讓那個大個子緊張了一下。

例 They expected to walk away with the win, but we made them blink.

他們本預期可以輕鬆獲勝，但我們還是讓他們緊張了一下。

Background

This comes from American boxing. When a boxer is surprised by his opponents attack he often blinks as he takes a defensive stance to think about what just happened. It means the weaker man surprised his opponent, it doesn't mean the weaker man might win. It means the superior man will not have the easy victory he expected.

Now it's used to describe any successful action performed by the weaker side against a much bigger or stronger foe.

背景資料 這個用法來自美國拳擊。當拳擊手遭對方攻擊而嚇一跳時，往往會瞇著眼採取防禦姿勢，以便思索一下發生了什麼事。它的意思只是說較弱的一方讓對方嚇住，而不是說較弱的一方可能會贏；所以較強的一方不會像自己期待那樣贏得那麼輕鬆。

現在則來形容任何由較弱的一方對實力懸殊或強壯對手所完成的成功行動。

Business Use

This is used to describe an unexpected success against a superior foe.

商業用法 這用來形容對較強對手所採取的意外成功反擊。

Alternatives 相關用語

◇ made a good showing	表現很好
◇ put up a good fight	打了一場漂亮的仗
◆ caught (him) napping	使（某人）慌張失措
◇ did well for himself	表現得還可以
◇ made his presence known	讓人注意到自己
◇ scored a few points	得到一些認可

B

the bottom line
結果

Idiom Definition

When used in non-financial matters it refers to the end result. In financial matters it can only mean the total profit or loss for the project being discussed, or the entire business.

成語定義 用在非金融方面指的是最後結果。如果是金融方面，它指的便是所討論的專案，或是整個企業的盈虧。

Examples

例 He hurries people along by saying, get to the bottom line.

他用「替公司賺錢」的口號來催促別人。

....

例 The bottom line is we earned 2% more this month than last month.

整個盈虧情況是我們這個月比上個月多賺了 2%。

....

Background

This comes from the financial world, where the bottom line is the figure reached once all computations are complete, or the total profit or loss. This is mostly used to discuss finances.

However, its use is so popular in financial meetings, as well as the financial portions of other types of meetings, that it's been adopted by most people. It refers to the end result.

背景資料 這個用法來自金融界,指的是加總後的金額或是總盈虧。這大部分用在財務討論上。

然而,除了金融會議普遍使用這個詞以外,其他各類型會議有關金融那部分也經常用到,所以大部分人都已接受這種用法。它也指最後的結果。

Business Use

It's a short version or code term for what's between the quotation marks.

商業用法 以下面兩句引號裡的話為例,這個詞便是描述這類情況的一種制式簡短說法。

(Financial) "After all assets are added and expenses deducted the total profit or loss is shown on the last line of the report."

(和金融有關)「加總全部資產再扣除費用後,總盈虧會顯示在報表的最後一行。」

(Non-financial) "Once all factors are considered the final outcome is stated."

(和金融無關)「一旦考慮了所有的因素,最後結果便可加以確定。」

Alternatives 相關用語

◇ what it all comes down to is	總計
◆ in the final analysis	歸根究底
◇ in the end	最後
◇ to cut to the chase	只談重點

B (I'm) not buying (it)
我才不信

Idiom Definition

This is often used as an expression of disbelief and is another way of saying the speaker thinks something is a lie.

成語定義 這句話通常用來表現一種懷疑的態度，或是某人覺得某件事是謊言的另一種說法。

Word Definition Used

"buying it" is a term that takes on the unique definition above.

使用的字詞定義

「buying it」是一個表現上述獨特定義的專門用詞。

Examples

例 I know that's what you said but I'm not buying it.
我知道你有那樣說，但是我才不信。

例 We saw what happened and we aren't buying it.
我們有看到發生什麼事，但我們都不信。

Background

A person buys something only if they believe it will do what the salesman claims. If they don't believe the claims then they don't buy.

背景資料 會買某個東西是因為相信店員的介紹，如果不相信就不會買了。

Business Use

When used, this may have nothing to do with actually buying or not buying anything. In most cases it is simply a statement of disbelief, or a polite way to say some statement is a lie.

商業用法 使用這個慣用語和實際上有沒有買東西一點關係都沒有。大部分情況下，它只是一種懷疑的表達方式，或是一種認為某人說謊的婉轉說法。

Note 備註

Used without the negative it has the opposite meaning.
不用否定句便是相反之意。

Alternatives 相關用語

◇ yah, yah, yah.
是是是（表示不愉快的嘲笑聲音）

◇ am I supposed to believe that? 我應該相信嗎？

◇ you can't sell that to me
你不能把那賣給我（你不能要我相信）

◇ I don't believe you	我不相信
◇ bull shit	胡說
◆ that's a crock	胡說八道
◇ you're full of it	聽你在鬼扯

B

deal breaker
協議破壞分子

Idiom Definition

This is used to describe a person or situation that causes negotiations to break down, or sabotages a successful deal causing one or more parties to back out.

成語定義 用來形容某人或某種情況導致協商破裂，或破壞成功交易，造成有人退出。

Word Definition Used

"deal" is an agreement, or arraignment.

使用的字詞定義 「deal」指的是協議或約定。

Examples

例 He has a reputation, the rumor is, if he's involved he has been the deal breaker.

雖然他名聲不錯，不過有謠傳如果他有涉及此事，那協議破壞分子就是他。

例 The split is 50/50, anything less is a deal breaker.

講好二一添作五，更低就破壞規矩了。

Background

This comes from playing cards; it refers to the time after the cards are distributed, but before actual play begins. When not playing cards a deal is when all parties agree the preconditions are met and activity may begin. As in a card game, each player has a role to play. Unlike a card game, the roles don't have to be equal, only agreed to, and one or more players may be forced to participate.

Any person, place or thing that causes one or more players to stop acting in his or her role in the deal is called a deal breaker. A deal breaker could appear at any time, as the deal is being formed, negotiated or after it's agreed to.

背景資料 這個詞來自紙牌遊戲，和牌發好後，但還沒真正開始玩之前那段時間有關。如果不是在打牌，交易指的是各家都同意所有先決條件後再開始後續動作。和打牌一樣，每個玩家都有各自所要扮演的角色；和打牌不同的是，每個角色並不具對等性，僅是對條件的一種同意，也或許有人是被迫加入的。

任何導致另一方停止扮演在交易中所應扮演角色的人事地物，都叫做協議破壞分子。一旦交易成立、經過協商或達成共識，協議破壞分子隨時都可能出現。

Business Use

This idiom is a short version of what's between the quotation marks. "If this isn't changed I refuse to participate, regardless of any agreements reached during negotiations, and any possibility of a deal lost."

商業用法 以下面這句引號裡的話為例：「無論談判期間達成任何協議，或是有可能談判破裂，只要這一點不改變，我便拒絕參加。」，這個慣用語便是描述這類情況的一種簡短說法。

Alternatives 相關用語

◇ the kiss of death
死亡之吻（表面上看來無害，實際上具毀滅性的事物或行為）

◇ an end   結束

◇ it's all over, except for the crying
全毀了，只差沒哭出來

call back
修補

MP3-74

Idiom Definition

This is the term used to describe when a contractor is asked to return to a completed job to repair or redo something that failed or was found substandard.

成語定義 這個詞用來形容已完成的工作不合格或被發現未達標準時，要求將其退還給承包人，請他加以修復或重做。

Examples

例 The job had problems from the start, and it ended with three callbacks.

這個工作一開始時問題重重，最後完成時留下三個需要修補的地方。

例 I feel good about this job. I bet we won't have any callbacks.

我對這分工作很有好感。我肯定會把工作做好，不會東漏西漏。

Background

This is a vital term in construction. A call back when the client calls the contractor and asks him to return to fix one or more items found to be substandard. This is never something to look forward to, but they are an expected part of doing business.

背景資料 這個詞對營造業來講相當重要。當發現有不合標準的地方時，客戶會打電話給承包商要求重新修復。雖然沒有人喜歡這種事，但做生意時遇到這種情況是免不了的。

Business Use

Things get missed, mistakes are made and errors have to be corrected. A company is as good as the work they do, and how quickly they respond to call backs. This idiom is a short version of what's between the quotation marks. "After completion of the job, problems were discovered with your work. Some repairs are needed before the job can be considered done. Please refer to the attached list and schedule the work."

商業用法 事情沒做好或是做錯，必須設法彌補。員工必須把工作做好，沒做好時要盡快補起來，公司才會越來越好。以下面這句引號裡的話為例：「工作雖然已完成，但發現了一些問題。要設法把問題解決掉才算真的完成。請參考附件安排修補工作。」，這個慣用語便是描述這類情況的一種簡短說法。

called into play

調動；發揮

MP3-75

Idiom Definition

This is used when someone or something is pressed into service.

成語定義 當某人或某事被加以利用時，會使用這個慣用語。

Word Definition Used

"Play" means to use.

使用的字詞定義 「play」指的是使用。

Examples

例 The company was losing the account when Johnson was called into play.

公司調用強森後，就失去了該名客戶。

例 We were getting nowhere until the new device was called into play.

新設計未啟用前，我們卡在原地動彈不得。

Background

This comes from the sports world where it refers to when a player, sitting on the bench, is sent into the game.

背景資料 這個慣用語來自運動界，指的是原本坐冷板凳的球員被換上場時。

Business Use

This is often used to describe when someone or something not then in use is brought into the activity. For Examples, it's used when an employee is temporarily replaced to take a vacation, or for an extended illness. It also refers to when an overwhelmed employee is replaced by a better one. It can also refer to machinery, tools or ideas

商業用法 這通常用來形容用不到的某人或某事又重新加以利用。例如當員工休假或請長期病假時找人暫代,便會用到這個慣用語。也可以用來指受不了工作壓力的員工被較好的員工所取代。也可以用在機器、工具或想法方面。

Alternatives 相關用語

◇ pressed into service	利用
◆ put on line	冒險從事(某事)
◇ given a shot	給機會表現
◇ asked to step in	要求介入

C

(we) can't lose
一定沒有問題

MP3-76

Idiom Definition

This is said when something looks so good, it's inconceivable it could fail.

成語定義 事情看起來很順利，很難想像會搞砸時，便會用到這個慣用語。

Word Definition Used

"can't lose" is a term as well as an idiom. When these exact words are used this way, they take on the unique meaning above.

使用的字詞定義 「can't lose」是一個專門用詞也是一個慣用語，每個字這樣連起來用時，表現的便是上述那種特別的意思。

Examples

例 With all the preparation Jimmy did, you can't lose.

吉米已做了萬全的準備，不會有問題的。

例 You might think you can't lose now, but anything can happen.

或許你現在覺得一定沒有問題，不過世事無常，沒什麼一定的。

Background

This term is frequently used in games of skill and chance, but it has a different meaning than the one from the dictionary. Actually, there is no guarantee of success, just an extremely high possibility.

背景資料 這個詞經常用在需要技巧和機會的遊戲裡，不過它和字典上的意義不同。實際上並不保證成功，只不過成功機會極高。

Business Use

This is used everywhere the outcome is not sure including business, where it gets a lot of use.

It's often used as a deliberately over confident statement. It's very popular and used whenever attempts are made, and the outcome isn't guaranteed, but relatively certain.

商業用法 任何無法確定結果的場合都用得到這個慣用語，包括商業場合在內，而且還用得特別多。它往往用來刻意表示一種自信，任何雖不保證結果、但相當肯定的嚐試都用得到。

Alternatives 相關用語

◇ a sure thing	一定會成功的事
◇ a lead pipe cinch	很簡單的事
◇ a no brainier	很簡單的事
◇ as easy as falling off a log	易如反掌
◇ a piece of cake	很容易的事
◇ easy as pie	很容易的事
◇ duck soup	輕而易舉
◆ no sweat	輕而易舉
◇ as easy as one, two, three	輕而易舉
◇ child's play	輕而易舉

C caught flat footed
陷入困境;無計可施

MP3-77

Idiom Definition

To be attacked when you're unprepared, and suffer because of it.

成語定義 毫無準備時遭受攻擊並因此而受苦。

Word Definition Used

"flat footed" is a term referring to a physical stance.

使用的字詞定義 「flat footed」這個詞和身體姿勢有關。

Examples

例 I never expected that, they caught me completely flat footed.

我從來沒想到會被他們給逼到走投無路。

例 They won because their defense caught us completely flat footed.

因為他們的防禦讓我們無計可施,所以取得了勝利。

Background

This comes from the sports world. A prepared athlete stands on the balls of his feet, idiomatically referred to as on his toes, ready to respond quickly to anything. If you're standing flat-footed it means you have an additional step to take before you can respond.

背景資料　這個慣用語來自運動界。一個做好準備、全神貫注的運動員，準備快速回應任何事件；如果你採取一種果斷的站姿，表示你在做出反應之前，還可以採取額外的步驟。

Business Use

In business this means the subject was not ready to respond to a specific thing, or anything in general.

商業用法　在商業上意味著，尚未準備好對特定事情或任何一般事情做出回應。

Alternatives 相關用語

◇ caught unawares	出其不意
◇ caught with his pants down	被逮個正著

come up a little
多加一點

MP3-78

Idiom Definition

This means to increase the amount of an offer.

成語定義 意指增加提供的數量。

Word Definition Used

"come up" is a term as well as an idiom meaning the above.

"a little" is also a term but the definition for little may not mean something small.

使用的字詞定義 「come up」是一個表現上述含義的詞和慣用語。
「a little」也是一個詞，不過它的定義指的不是小東西。

Examples

例 If you come down half way, we can come up a little and meet you.

如果你多走一點路，我們就可以多過去一點去接你。

例 I can come up a little, but I can't afford to pay that big an increase.

我可以多付一點，但是多太多就沒辦法負擔了。

Business Use

This is a term mostly limited to negotiations, specifically it refers to money. The term a little may be a soft way of saying more money must be offered, and although we are calling it a little you may think it's a lot.

商業用法　這個詞大部分只用在協商的過程，特別和錢有關。「a little」是種婉轉說法，意思是要求提供更多的錢；雖然嘴巴講「一點點」，心裡想的可是很多。

Alternatives 相關用語

◇ juice up the bid	價格越喊越高
◇ let me see what I can do	我看看還可以怎麼做
◇ let me try again	讓我再試一次

C price concession
降價

Idiom Definition

This describes a price reduction for an item or service.

成語定義 用來形容東西或服務價格的調降。

Word Definition Used

"price concession" is a term as well as an idiom. When these exact words are used this way, they take on the unique meaning above.

使用的字詞定義 「price concession」是一個專門用詞也是一個慣用語。每個字這樣連起來用時，表現的便是上述那種特別的意思。

Examples

例 We did get a price reduction, but I'm not sure it's enough.

價格是降低了，但我不確定幅度夠不夠。

⋯⋯⋯⋯⋯⋯⋯⋯⋯⋯⋯⋯⋯⋯⋯⋯⋯⋯⋯⋯⋯⋯⋯⋯⋯⋯⋯⋯⋯

例 His idea of a big price reduction is what I call a good first step.

他那個大幅降價的想法，就是我所謂的好的起步。

⋯⋯⋯⋯⋯⋯⋯⋯⋯⋯⋯⋯⋯⋯⋯⋯⋯⋯⋯⋯⋯⋯⋯⋯⋯⋯⋯⋯⋯

Business Use

The standard definitions could apply, but it only refers to a lower price. The reduction could be a gesture of good faith granted prior to negotiations, or as a result of the talks, it doesn't matter. The amount and whether or not it's sufficient is also unimportant. Any reduction regardless of when and how granted, as well as the amount is a price concession.

商業用法 標準定義即可適用，但特別指較低的價格。降價是協議前雙方的一種信任，或是商量後的結果，都不重要；金額多少或夠不夠也不是重點。降價和價格協議的時間、方式和數量都沒有關係。

Alternatives 相關用語

◇ price abatement　　　　　　　減價

◇ price cut　　　　　　　　　　減價

the cream of the crop

最優秀的；出類拔萃；菁英

MP3-80

Idiom Definition

This is used to describe the best of what is available.

成語定義 用來形容出類拔萃的人。

Word Definition Used

"cream" means the best.

使用的字詞定義 「cream」的意思是最好的。

Examples

例 This is the cream of the crop, our ten best graduates this year.

今年最優秀的十個畢業生出爐了。

例 Of the applicants these five are the cream of the crop.

這五個人是所有申請人當中最出色的。

Background

Cream is milk fat that floats to the top of raw milk. That's the key ingredient and where the nourishment is. It's the best part of the milk, and anything called the cream is being called the best.

背景資料 「cream」是漂浮在生乳上面的乳脂，是生乳最重要的成分和營養所在，可以說是牛奶最棒的部分。任何被稱為「cream」的東西等於是「最好」的意思。

Business Use

It's a short version for the following. "Of all the candidates I considered, these are the best I could find"

商業用法　「在所有候選人當中，我認為這幾個人最為出色」的一種簡短說法。

Alternatives　相關用語

◇ it doesn't get any better	找不到更好的了
◇ the short list	候選名單
◇ the A list	A 級名單

permanent crimp
壓接;抑制;造成打擊

MP3-81

Idiom Definition

Crimping is a mechanical process where two parts are attached to each other by sharply bending them and thereby locking them together. It's also a metaphor, meaning to slow down or stop the free flow of something, as folding a water hose will stop the water flow.

成語定義 「crimp」是一種機械過程,經由猛烈地彎曲讓兩部分彼此接在一塊而加以固定。它也是一種比喻,意指減慢或阻止某事物的自由流動,好比把水管摺疊起來不讓水流出來一樣。

Examples

(Mechanical)
(和機械有關)

例 By permanently crimping the pieces together we cut costs.

把每個部分壓接在一起可以節省成本。

例 A permanent crimp is cheaper than using a screw.

壓接比用螺絲釘便宜。

(Metaphoric-creativity)
(比喻用法-創意)

例 If you put limits on me it will put a permanent crimp on my style.

如果你對我設限太多,我就無法發揮個人風格了。

例 Using this format will put a permanent crimp in my speed.

用這種形式會讓我的速度快不起來。

(Metaphoric-competition)

（比喻用法－競爭）

例 The larger administrative staff puts a permanent crimp on our bottom line.

行政人員過多，對整體盈虧造成影響。

例 Their lower price puts a permanent crimp in our profits.

他們的低價策略對我們的利潤造成競爭壓力。

Background

In manufacturing it's when two metal pieces are joined without fasteners by using a stamping process. Two pieces are placed side by side held together and bent locking them in place.

The metaphoric definitions come from the mechanical. A crimp or bend, is when something like a hose is sharply bent restricting the flow of material through it, bent sharply enough it could stop the flow completely.

It's used to describe a situation where the free flow of something, like goods in a supply line or creative ideas are hindered or stopped.

背景資料　在製造業中，這指的是兩個金屬部分經由壓製而連接在一起，並不用加上固定物。兩部分並排放一起彼此接合，再經由彎曲而卡在固定位置上。

比喻用法來自機械領域。捲曲或彎曲，便像水管猛烈弄彎一樣，限制水流出來；如果彎得夠兇，水就完全流不出來了。

這用來形容東西原本流通得很順利（如物品運輸線或創意），卻被加以阻礙或阻止。

Business Use

There are three separate uses, but they're all based on the mechanical crimping process, given above. Because all three uses could come up in a negotiation they're all shown.

The mechanical version is used in discussions on manufacture and assembly processes. The metaphoric uses come up in discussions of the flow of materials as with shipping and ideas in the creative process. To reduce confusion two Exampless of the three uses are given above.

商業用法 三種用法不同，不過都以上述機械壓接過程為基礎。這三種用法都可能在協商中出現，故全部加以說明之。

機械方面用在製造業和裝配過程的討論；比喻用法則用在貨物運輸或創意發揮的討論上。為了減少混淆，上面便列出三種不同用法的兩類（機械和比喻）例子。

Alternatives 相關用語

◇ get in the way	擋路
◇ put a damper on things	掃興
◇ slows the process	讓過程變慢
◇ it's a pain in the ass	痛苦之源
◇ take the wind out of our sails	不知如何是好
◇ slows things down	減速

cut to the chase
只談重點；直接了當地說

`MP3-82`

Idiom Definition

Skip over an unimportant part and go right to the heart of a matter, or skip to the closing.

成語定義 跳過不重要的部分直接進入正題，或者直接跳到結尾。

Word Definition Used

"cut to" is a term meaning delete everything between here and the important part.

使用的字詞定義 「cut to」這個詞意指將目前位置到重要部分之間的內容予以刪除。

Examples

例 Cut to the chase; just tell me the bottom line.

細節跳過，直接告訴我結果就好了。

例 We don't have a lot of time, please cut to the chase.

我們時間不多，請直接了當講重點。

Background

During the silent film era, Max Senate produced many of the most popular comedies. Most of which ended with a big chase scene, where the Keystone Cops chased the star. Sometimes the best part of the movie was the chase, in every case the chase was a crowd pleaser.

The term "cut to the chase" in the film industry means delete the film between here and the chase scene. So the term literally means go right to the last scene in the movie.

背景資料 在默片時代，Max Senate 公司出產很多風靡一時的喜劇，其結尾大部分都有一段拱石州（賓州）警察追捕明星的大型追逐場景。有時候電影最棒的部分就是那段追逐場景，大家都喜歡得不得了。

電影工業裡的「cut to the chase」這個詞指的便是將中間刪掉，直接跳到追逐場景。所以它字面上的意思就是直接跳到電影最後的場景。

Business Use

In business it means get to the point. It's a short version for what's in the quotation marks. "Skip this, if we have questions we can come back to it later. Get right to the bottom line."

商業用法 在商業上指的是直接了當講重點。以下面這句引號裡的話為例：「這個先跳過去，如果有問題待會再回來解決。先討論盈虧狀況（結果）。」這個慣用語便是描述這類情況的一種簡短說法。

Alternatives 相關用語

◆ give us the short version	大概介紹
◇ skip to the bottom line	直接跳到結果

it's a <u>deal</u>
就這樣設定；成交

MP3-83

Idiom Definition

This is used to state that the terms offered are accepted.

成語定義 用來陳述所提出的條件已被接受。

Word Definition Used

"deal" an arraignment agreed to by all sides

使用的字詞定義
「deal」指的是各方同意的協議或約定。

Examples

例 I think I can do that, it's a deal.

我覺得我辦得到,那就這樣設定了。

⋯⋯⋯⋯⋯⋯⋯⋯⋯⋯⋯⋯⋯⋯⋯⋯⋯⋯⋯⋯⋯⋯⋯⋯⋯⋯⋯⋯

例 It's a deal only if you agree to pay for shipping.

只要你同意運費由你付就成交。

⋯⋯⋯⋯⋯⋯⋯⋯⋯⋯⋯⋯⋯⋯⋯⋯⋯⋯⋯⋯⋯⋯⋯⋯⋯⋯⋯⋯

Background

This comes from card playing, when the cards are distributed, but before play begins. Everyone in the deal has a role to play; they don't necessarily have to be equal, only agreed to. For Examples, one member may do nothing more than fund the enterprise, another may lend his or her expertise, and a third could furnish a list of contacts and introductions.

Partners in the deal may not share equally in the profits. Anything is possible; to participate in the deal the partners need only agree to the terms.

背景資料 這個慣用語來自紙牌遊戲。牌發好後但還沒開始玩之前，每個玩家都有各自所要扮演的角色；他們並不具對等性，僅是對條件的一種同意。例如，有人可能只負責為企業提供資金，有人可能貢獻個人專業，也有人可能只是人脈很廣，便負責開拓客戶。

各方合夥人在利潤的分配上可能也不盡相同。只要大家同意即可合作，除此之外，其他什麼事都有可能發生。

Business Use

This is said when one member of a negotiation finds the terms acceptable. It means he or she agrees to honor them as long as the other sides honor their commitments.

商業用法 協商的其中一方覺得條件可以接受時便會用到這個慣用語。意思是說只要對方也遵守承諾，自己便同意雙方所協議的條件。

Special Considerations

This idiom is often said quickly and excitedly like an exclamation as the right hand is offered for a handshake. Sometimes the words are omitted and only the hand offered, but rarely. Almost always the words and handshake are simultaneous.

特別留意 用到這個慣用語的場合往往會像驚叫一樣，說得又快又興奮，同時右手也會伸出去和對方握手。有時候會省略言語直接握手，不過很少見。說話和握手差不多都是同時發生。

Alternatives 相關用語

◇ done	沒問題
◇ I agree	我同意
◇ I can live with that	我可以接受
◇ sounds good to me	聽起來不錯
◇ I think we have a bargain	就這樣說定了
◇ let's do it	那就開始吧

D deal with the devil
和魔鬼打交道

MP3-84

Idiom Definition

Used to express a willingness to deal with whoever the speaker needs to, to attain his or her goals, including a long time enemy, or someone the speaker personally dislikes.

成語定義 用來表示當事人為了達到目的，即使是長久以來的敵人，或是自己對他沒有好感的人，只要有必要，都願意和對方打交道。

Word Definition Used

"the devil" a metaphor meaning someone not liked

使用的字詞定義 「the devil」是一種比喻，意指不喜歡的人。

Examples

例 To stay in business I'm willing to deal with the devil himself.

為了讓公司經營下去，我願意和魔鬼打交道。

....

例 A deal with the devil can be very costly, you may lose your self-respect.

和魔鬼打交道的代價非常昂貴，你可能連自尊都會失去。

....

Background

In western culture the devil is the embodiment of evil, the opposite of everything good. A few hundred years ago it was believed the devil would tempt men to stray from god to worship him. To win people to his side he offers gifts and favors for the man or woman's soul. Those who enjoyed great and or sudden success could be accused of having made "a deal with the devil" by a jealous rival or envious neighbor.

At the time such accusations were taken very seriously and often resulted in a trial. If found guilty the defendant would be tortured until he or she confessed, then put to death. Leniency was a quick, painless death, few were ever acquitted. To be accused of dealing with the devil could be a death sentence.

The term "the devil" originally referred to Satan, now it's used to describe someone that is an enemy, or for who the speaker has no respect or trust.

背景資料 在西方文化中，魔鬼乃邪惡的化身，與一切良善相對立。幾百年前的人認為魔鬼會引誘人類誤入歧途，離開上帝而去崇拜魔鬼。為了騙取人類的心，他會用禮物和願望來和人類的靈魂進行交換。那些快速發跡、成就斐然的人，便可能被嫉妒他的競爭對手或羨慕他的鄰居控告「和魔鬼打交道」。

那時對於這類的指控乃非常嚴重的事情，當事人往往會被審判。如果罪名成立，被告會被嚴刑逼供直到認罪，然後處以死刑。獲判無罪的很少，能夠無痛苦地快速死去已經算是仁至義盡了。被控「和魔鬼打交道」差不多都是宣判死刑。

「the devil」這個詞原本指的是撒旦，現在則用來形容敵人，或是自己不尊敬、不信任的人。

This is a humorous way of saying. I will work with whoever I need to deal with. It's a short version of what's between the quotation marks. "I don't like him, and I don't trust him, but I have no choice. I'm willing to do just about anything to get this deal, including work with that man."

商業用法　這是一種幽默説法，用來表示自己願意和任何有需要的人打交道。以下面這句引號裡的話為例：「雖然我既不喜歡他也不信任他，但我沒有選擇餘地。只要能完成這項交易，我願意做任何事，包括和那個人合作在內。」這個慣用語便是描述這類情況的一種簡短説法。

Alternatives 相關用語

◇ do whatever is necessary	不擇手段
◆ leave no stone unturned	千方百計
◇ try and try again	一試再試
◇ hang in there	堅持下去
◇ go for broke	孤注一擲
◇ never say die	不要氣餒

done
沒問題

MP3-85

Idiom Definition

Usually said as an exclamation meaning the speaker agrees to the terms of the deal as presented.

成語定義 通常會用叫喊的方式說出，表示說話者同意協商所提出的條件。

Word Definition Used

"done" is a term as well as an idiom meaning the above.

使用的字詞定義 「done」是一個表現上述含義的詞和慣用語。

Examples

例 I listened to his proposal, said done, stood and offered my hand to a very surprised man.

我聽了他的建議，便說沒問題，並起身把手伸出去，把他給嚇了一大跳。

例 I thought negotiations were going badly, and then he smiled and said, "Done."

我原本以為協商過程很糟，結果他竟笑著說「沒問題」。

In verbal negotiations one side presents a set of terms for discussion. If the other side finds them agreeable and they say, "Done!" This meaning the terms as stated are acceptable and they agree. This is usually followed with a handshake.

背景資料 在口頭協商過程中，有一方提出一些條件來討論；如果對方覺得同意便會說「沒問題！」。意思就是這些提出來的條件可以被接受，而對方也同意了。通常講完後雙方接著會握手。

Business Use

The handshake could be the end of it. At this point a verbal deal exists, and sometimes that's enough. It depends on those involved.

It's not unusual for those who reached an agreement to do something to turn the matter over to their staff to iron out the details. Then sign a formal document written by lawyers.

Less formally, either party may write a memo to the other stating their understanding of the deal, asking for confirmation. The memo usually states that unless the writer hears otherwise he or she will assume the memo is correct. These memos have been upheld in court.

This is a short version of what's between the quotation marks. "I've listened to your terms and assume they're a proposal. I find them agreeable and will honor them. I assume we now have a deal."

商業用法 握手常表示協商完成，這時口頭交易便成立。有時這樣便已足夠，要看雙方的情況而定。

雙方達成共識後，接著將後續細節交給員工處理，並經由律師簽署正式文件，也是很常見的事。

比較沒那麼正式的情況是，雙方各寫了一張備忘錄給對方，上面寫著如果大家覺得沒問題便假設備忘錄所載無誤。這些備忘錄便具備法律效力。

以下面這句引號裡的話為例：「我已經聽了你提出的條件，並把它們當做提議來看。我覺得可以同意，沒有問題。那我們就這麼說定了。」這個慣用語便是描述這類情況的一種簡短說法。

Alternatives 相關用語

◇ you've got a deal	沒問題
◇ agreed	同意
◇ I agree	同意
◇ it's a deal	就這麼說定
◇ sounds good to me	聽起來不錯
◇ I accept	我接受
◇ let's do it	就這樣決定
◇ why not?	為什麼不？
◇ it doesn't get any better than that	這樣再好不過了
◇ let's boogie	我們開始吧
◇ These are just a few, the list is almost endless 類似的慣用語實在太多了，這裡只是其中一些例子	

draw the line
劃清界線

MP3-86

Idiom Definition

To draw a line is to make a boundary that cannot, or should not be crossed. It can be an actual line that may not be physically crossed. Or a metaphoric one used to define the limits of your behavior, and or those around you.

成語定義 劃清界線指的是劃分一條不能也不應跨越的分界線。它可以指實際上身體不能跨越的界線，或是一種比喻用法，用來規定行為之類的限制。

Examples

例 This is where I draw the line, let them seek services elsewhere.
這不是我負責的範圍，叫他們去找別人幫忙。

例 You have to draw the line somewhere, I admire him for that.
我就是欣賞他，你到別處去嗆聲吧。

Background

This describes an activity that's usually metaphoric but could be real. Drawing the line, is something boys do to determine their status. One boy draws a line in the dirt and dares another to cross it, threatening a fight if he does. Those who don't cross it accept the other's dominance. Crossing the line means you're willing to fight for leadership. The winner is the leader.

Status under the leader is determined in much the

same way. Young girls and women also establish status, but without fighting. The point is female executives in the U.S. are required to play the game just as the men do, and some of them do it very well. It's a right of passage everyone goes through and the basis for this idiom.

背景資料 這用來形容通常是比喻性質但也可以是真實的活動。劃清界線是男孩用來決定個人地位的方式。某個男孩在泥土上劃了一條線，並威脅別人敢過的話就單挑之類，用這種方式來刺激別人越線。那些不敢越線的人便等於接受對方比自己強。越線表示你要力爭領導地位－勝者為王。

領導以下的地位也大致依此決定。年輕女孩及女人一樣要建立地位，只不過不單挑。但是美國女性女管必須遵照男性的遊戲規則；有些做來得心應手。這個詞語表達的是通過的權利，每個人都經歷過。

Business Use

On the executive level competition is fierce and only thinly veiled behind a mask of team work. Executives are constantly vying with each other for dominance, on a daily basis. Drawing the line can describe a struggle for dominance, a warning defining of what's acceptable and what isn't, or the point at which no more concessions will be made.

商業用法 在經營管理層級，競爭可謂相當激烈；雖然外表標榜團隊合作，私底下的鬥爭卻幾乎毫無遮掩。經理主管經常彼此想壓過對方，競爭無一日休止。劃清界線可以用來形容優勢地位的鬥爭，一種限定什麼可以接受，什麼不可以接受的警告；或是讓別人明白最後讓步的底限在哪裡。

Alternatives 相關用語

◇ take a stance	採取一種立場
◇ take a stand	採取一種態度
◇ got his back up	讓他生氣
◇ got his dander up	讓他生氣
◇ call his bluff	叫他證明看看
◇ have a showdown	攤牌

D the impossible dream
不可能的夢想

Idiom Definition

A lofty goal impossible to reach, yet a dream you should never give up on.

成語定義 一個不可能達成的崇高目標，卻也是你永遠不該放棄的夢想。

Examples

例 I know it's an impossible dream but I want to try for it.

我知道這是不可能完成的夢想，但我仍要努力一試。

··

例 What was the impossible dream for our grandfathers is possible for us.

祖父那一輩人不可能的夢想，到我們這一代卻是有可能實現的。

··

Background

Understanding is easy if you know something about the Broadway Musical "Man of La Mancha." "The Impossible Dream" was a song from the play about a man who advises you should strive for the impossible, because you just might get it .

背景資料 如果你知道百老匯音樂劇「夢幻騎士」，這句話就不難理解了。「不可能的夢想」是劇裡的一首選曲，提到某個人要別人努力實現不可能的夢想，因為還是有可能實現的。

Business Use

This is a short version of what's between the quotation marks. "Others may have failed to pull this off, but I believe it's very possible, and I'm going to do my best."

商業用法 以下面這句引號裡的話為例：「別人可能都無法成功，但我雖然也認為不可能，仍要盡力而為。」，這個詞便是描述這類情況的一種簡短說法。

Alternatives 相關用語

◇ a goal	目標
◇ shoot for the stars	不可能的事

pipe dreams
白日夢；空想

MP3-88

Idiom Definition

This is used to describe any farfetched, impossible plan or scheme not grounded in reality.

成語定義 用來形容任何不腳踏實地的、既牽強又不可能的計畫或方案。

Examples

例 Call it a pipe dream, but I want to be the largest company in town.

儘管叫它白日夢沒關係，我就是想把公司弄成全鎮最大的。

⋯⋯⋯⋯⋯⋯⋯⋯⋯⋯⋯⋯⋯⋯⋯⋯⋯⋯⋯⋯

例 It's just a pipe dream, it will never happen.

那只是白日夢，永遠不可能成真。

⋯⋯⋯⋯⋯⋯⋯⋯⋯⋯⋯⋯⋯⋯⋯⋯⋯⋯⋯⋯

Background

This goes back to the nineteenth century when opium dens were legal. The opium was smoked with a long metal pipe, causing hallucinations referred to as pipe dreams. The dens are gone but the idiom remains. It refers to any fanciful desire so impossible the chances of it happening could correctly be termed a hallucination.

背景資料 這要回溯到十九世紀當時鴉片館還是合法的時代。抽鴉片用的是一支長金屬煙斗 (pipe)，由於抽了以後會產生一些幻想，所以就稱為「pipe dream」。它指的是任何可以稱之為幻想的任何不可能發生的古怪慾望。

Business Use

It's a short version of what's between the quotation marks. "It would be nice if it happened, but I doubt it."

商業用法 以下面這句引號裡的話為例：「這件事如果可以成真該有多好，不過我很懷疑。」這個慣用語便是描述這類情況的一種簡短說法。

Alternatives 相關用語

◇ the impossible dream	不可能的夢想
◇ a flight of fancy	異想天開
◇ fairy tales	神話故事

dumping
傾銷

MP3-89

Idiom Definition

This is a trade tactic where a company sells a large number of products cheaply to gain a bigger market share and reduce competitor's profits.

成語定義 這是一種貿易策略，指的是一家公司用較便宜的價格大量販售某種產品以爭取市占率，並削減競爭對手的利潤。

Word Definition Used

"dumping" is a term meaning the above.

使用的字詞定義 「dumping」是一個包含上述涵意的專門用詞。

Examples

例 They used a tax subsidy to finance it and started dumping VCR's

他利用關稅補貼籌措資金，開始傾銷 VCR。

例 They dumped DVD units in the U.S. and almost started a trade war.

他們在美國傾銷 DVD 零組件，差點引發貿易戰。

Background

The word dumping generally refers to discarding trash or unwanted items. Sometimes it's used to describe emptying a container of water to flood a specific area. In this case it's used to describe a sales tactic known as flooding the market.

背景資料　「dumping」這個字通常指的是丟棄垃圾或不要的東西，有時也會用來形容把水箱裡的水全部倒到某個特定地方。在本例中，它用來形容一種將產品在市場上拋售的行銷策略。

Business Use

This is a new international trade term used when a company with a special advantage, like tax credits or government subsidies floods the market with cheep products priced well below what competitors can match. It's often strongly protested by competitors and their governments in trade talks. It's been known to start trade wars.

商業用法　這是一個新的國際貿易專業術語。當一家擁有特別優勢的公司（如稅賦減免或政府補助），將廉價產品以遠低於競爭對手可以抗衡的價格大量充斥到市場時，「傾銷」就被引用。「傾銷」在貿易談判上經常遭到競爭對手及該國強烈的抗議。這就是所熟知的「開啟貿易戰爭」。

E

I'm all ears
全神貫注地聽；洗耳恭聽

MP3-90

Idiom Definition

This indicates the subject wants to hear what's about to be said.

成語定義 表示聽者想要把話的內容給聽清楚。

Word Definition Used

"all ears" is a term meaning the above.

使用的字詞定義 「all ears」是一個包含上述涵意的專門用詞。

Examples

例 If you know what happened, I'm all ears.

如果你知道發生什麼事，我已準備洗耳恭聽。

例 If you give her the chance she'll be all ears too.

如果你給她機會，她也會洗耳恭聽的。

Background

The speaker is obviously more than just a pair of ears, so this figure of speech is a lighthearted semi-humorous way to state the speaker wants to hear the news.

背景資料 說這句話的人顯然不只是兩隻耳朵（是一個人），所以這句話是一種輕鬆愉快的半幽默式比喻說法，表示說這句話的人想要把事情聽清楚。

Business Use

It's a short version of what's between the quotation marks. "Until you finish telling me everything you have on this subject, I am nothing but a pair of ears listing to every word."

商業用法 這句是下面這個引用句的簡短説法。「直到你完完全全告訴我此事的來龍去脈之前，我只不過是一對專心聽講的耳朵。」

Alternatives 相關用語

◇ I want to hear this	我想要知道
◇ I'm very interested	我很有興趣
◇ I want to take notes.	我要記下來
◇ I would pay money to hear this	花錢來聽都值得

enough is enough
我受夠了

MP3-91

Idiom Definition

This is used to express the speakers disgust with a specific behavior pattern or action. It means that whatever it is, it will no longer be tolerated.

成語定義 用來表示說話者對某種行為模式或舉動感到厭惡，意思是說不管那是什麼，都已無法再忍受下去。

Word Definition Used

"enough" the first one indicates some specific thing was already done

"is enough" indicates the previous repetitions may have been allowed, but it will not be allowed in the future.

使用的字詞定義 第一個「enough」表示已經做過的某特定事情。「is enough」表示先前做過的事或許有被允許，但未來將不再被允許。

Examples

例 I say enough is enough, let's get this over with.
我說我已經受夠了，一切到此為止。

例 Enough is enough you had your chance, now let someone else try.
已經給過你機會，我受夠了，現在讓別人來試試。

Background

Repeating enough is something usually forbidden by the rules of good English. It's allowed here to add emphasis to the statement. This use demonstrates the thing referred to is unpleasant, unwanted, undesired, or perhaps all three, and will no longer be tolerated.

背景資料 通常在好的英文中，規定是禁止重覆使用「enough」這個字的。不過這裡的用法是一種強調作用，表示所指的事情是討厭的、不想要的、不受歡迎的，或者也可能三種都有，而這件事再也無法被容忍。

Business Use

It's a short version or code term for what's between the quotation marks. "This will not be tolerated any more. It ends now."

商業用法 以下面引號裡的話為例，這個詞便是描述這類情況的一種制式簡短說法。「這件事再也不被容忍接受，到此為止。」

Alternatives 相關用語

◇ let's not go there	再這樣下去就不好玩了
◇ not again	不要再來一次
◇ no more	不要再發生
◇ we're done	到此為止
◇ I'm out of here	我走了
◇ been there, done that 狂歡過後（曾經蒼海難為水，除卻巫山不是雲）	
◇ hit the road	上路
◇ I'll pass	我跳過去
◇ you're done	你玩完了
◇ this is so not good	這樣實在不太好

factor in
將…列為重要因素；考慮進來

Idiom Definition

This means the speaker projected the effect an external matter will have on an operation, or that the operation will have on other related and unrelated things.

成語定義 意指說話者在闡述某個外在事件對事情本身的影響，或是事情對其他相關或無關事物的影響。

Examples

例 For this study, we factored in the worst case scenarios.

為了進行研究，我們把最糟糕的案例也列為重要因素。

例 We factored in every possibility we could think of.

我們把想得到的各種可能性都考慮進來。

Word Definition Used

"factor" means part or a fraction of a whole.

"in" is, to include

使用的字詞定義 「factor」意指整體的部分或片段。
「in」是包括的意思。

Background

Putting these words together roughly translates into include the parts. And that's pretty close to the definition shown above.

背景資料 把這些字放在一起大概可解釋為「把各部分包括進來」的意思，和上述定義相當接近。

Business Use

Use always refers to an estimated effect, and prepared studies use the word factor to refer to isolated areas in the report. It's almost always used in the singular, although to prepare an accurate study every area is addressed. Usually each factor is reported as a separate line item. I've only seen factors addressed one at a time, so the singular is used.

This idiom is a short version of what's between the quotation marks. "We understand this operation is made up of several parts. And a different hand guides each one operating from self-interest. After studying every factor, their likely interaction and outcome, we determined its most likely effect on the deal."

商業用法 這個詞的使用通常都意指一個大約的估計結果，一些預備研究可能用這個詞，來指出該報告中一些沒有考慮到的因素。儘管在準備準確的報告時，每一個因素都要提及，但當使用到這個詞時，幾乎清一色地使用單數。通常每個因素都會分開報告，我只看過每個因素分開討論，所以英文都用單數表示。

這個慣用語是較簡短的說法，原文是「我們了解這個操作過程有好幾個部分，每個部分都扮演了不同的角色，再研讀過每個部分及它們之間的互動與結果後，我們決定了這個交易最可能發生的結果。」

Alternatives 相關用語

◇ to allow for	考慮到
◇ make allowances for	考慮到
◇ that's what we think will happen	事情預估會如此

F

fairy tales
神話故事;天方夜譚;謊言

Idiom Definition

A story so wild and farfetched that it's disbelieved.

成語定義 故事過於荒唐和牽強,沒有人相信。

Word Definition Used

"fairy tales" is a term as well as an idiom meaning the above.

使用的字詞定義 "fairy tales" 是一個包含上述涵意的專門用詞,也是一個慣用語。

Examples

例 I think his story is a fairy tale, but I can't prove it.
我覺得他的故事根本是天方夜譚,不過我無法加以證明。

例 He's telling fairy tales to avoid the blame.
他不想被責怪,於是編了一套謊言。

Background

A fairy tale is a story told to children for entertainment, with a moral to help build a good value system. They're about a time long ago, filled with make believe creatures like dragons, dwarfs, giants and magicians. They are fun stories designed to entertain children, but are too incredible to be believed by adults.

背景資料 神話故事（或童話故事）是專門講給小孩子聽的，有寓教於樂的功能。故事背景通常是在很久以前，人物包含像是龍、侏儒、巨人和巫師等虛構角色。這些故事都很有趣，主要做為孩童娛樂之用，不過內容難以置信，不會有大人相信。

Business Use

A fairy tale is any reason or excuse too wild to be believed. It's a polite, slightly humorous way to call someone a liar. It's a short version for what's between the quotation marks. "He has an excuse, but it's so wild I don't believe it."

商業用法 童話故事一詞用來意指某人所提供的理由或藉口，讓人無法信服，這是一種比較禮貌、幽默的方式，指稱說話的對方在扯謊。這個詞原來始自「他有個藉口，但實在有夠離譜，我實在無法相信他的話。」

Alternatives 相關用語

◇ the impossible dream	不可能的夢想
◆ a flight of fancy	異想天開
◆ pipe dreams	白日夢

F (I'd) hate to see this deal fall apart
沒看到這件事成功，我會很遺憾

MP3-94

Idiom Definition

The speaker is indicating a strong desire to see a deal made.

成語定義 説話者表達一種希望達成共識的強烈慾望。

Word Definition Used

"fall apart" a metaphor for become undone

使用的字詞定義 「fall apart」是結果失敗的比喻。

Examples

例 After all the time you spent on this project, I'd hate to see this fall apart.

你花了那麼多時間在這個計畫上，沒看到這件事成功，我會很遺憾。

例 We put in a lot of hours on this, and we'd hate to see it fall apart.

我們花了那麼多時間在這上頭，沒能成功會很遺憾。

Background

When an agreement is reached people say the parties were "brought together." The opposite of bring together, is fall apart, which is the basis of this idiom..

背景資料 達成協議時，我們會說大家「關係友好」，相反情況則是「關係結束」，這句慣用語便是以此為基礎。

Business Use

Please note this indicates the speaker's strong desire to see negotiations succeed. American's, like the British, tend to under state things.

商業用法 請注意，這個表達法指出說話者有著強烈意願，希望看到談判成功，美國人也和英國人一樣，常常會這樣強調事情。

Alternatives 相關用語

◇ I want to see this puppy fly	很希望這件事成功
◇ I wish you the best of luck	衷心祝你好運
◇ break a leg	祝你好運
◇ go for broke	孤注一擲

figure of speech
比喻說法

MP3-95

Idiom Definition

A word or phrase used as an expression with a dictionary meaning that makes little or no sense at all. However, it also has a clearly defined meaning which is usually a language shortcut, taking the place of a long complex tedious description, much like an idiom.

成語定義 某個單字或片語若用字典上的定義來看可能意義不大或毫無意義,不過在語言功能上仍有其清楚定義,只是用簡短形式來表達複雜冗長的描述,和慣用語很像。

Word Definition Used

"figure" represents something larger and more complex.

"of speech" something used vocally

使用的字詞定義 「figure」代表較大較複雜的東西。
「of speech」是口頭表達的東西。

Examples

例 "A cross to bear," is a commonly used figure of speech.

「A cross to bear」(重責)是一種常用的比喻說法。

例 He confused everyone by using too many figures of speech.

他用了太多比喻說法,大家都被他搞混了。

Background

The word "term" is interchangeable with the longer and much older phrase "figure of speech," which was very popular but is now seldom used.

背景資料　「term」這個字可以和「figure of speech」這個較長又較老式的片語交替使用，過去很流行，不過現在已很少這樣用了。

Business Use

This phrase is now seldom used and only in a very fancy ornate way, by a speaker trying to impress.

Alternatives　相關用語

◇ manor of speaking	措辭	
◇ term	措辭	
◆ catch phrase	標語；警語	

flight of fancy
異想天開

Idiom Definition

A thought or desire so widely impractical it's unlikely to come true.

成語定義 過於不切實際而不太可能成真的想法或慾望。

Word Definition Used

"flight" to go somewhere

"fancy" something desired

使用的字詞定義 「flight」指的是去某個地方。
「fancy」是所渴望的東西。

Examples

例 It may be a flight of fancy, but I like to indulge myself from time to time.

或許是異想天開，但我有時喜歡讓自己高興一下。

例 It's a flight of fancy; no one can make it happen.

真是異想天開，沒有人可以讓它成真的。

Background

The word definitions used are old fashioned and now seldom seen in contemporary English. This was a very popular idiom from the nineteenth and early twentieth century.

背景資料 這裡所使用的字詞定義已經過時，現代英文中已很少看到。這個慣用語在十九世紀和二十世紀初相當流行。

Business Use

This is still used from time to time but rarely, and only by older people. The alternatives listed below are much more popular now.

商業用法 這個詞現今仍不時的被使用到，但機會不大，通常是老一輩的人比較會用到這個詞。下面所列出的其他表達法現今比較流行。

Alternatives 相關用語

◇ impossible dreams	不可能的夢想
◇ far fetched	牽強的
◇ day dreaming	白日夢
◇ wishful thinking	一廂情願的想法

Goosed

捏臀部；鼓勵；突然增加

MP3-97

Idiom Definition

This is used to describe when someone pinches a person on his or her rear end. It also describes when someone is spurred or inspired into motion, or to make a greater effort. It's used to describe a case whenever someone or something is caused to make a sudden increase in their activity level and or output.

成語定義 用來形容捏別人的臀部；或是激勵別人行動、更加努力之類。也可以形容行動範圍（人）或產量（物）的突然增加。

Word Definition Used

"goosed" is a brand new term meaning the above.

使用的字詞定義 「goosed」是一個包含上述涵意的全新用詞。

Examples

(a physical pinch)
（身體上的捏）

....

例 She got him fired because he goosed her.
她把他炒魷魚了，因為他捏了她的臀部。

....

例 Her husband can goose her, you can't.
只有她丈夫才可以捏她臀部，你不行。

....

(to inspire)
（激勵）

....

例 I went down to shipping and gave them a goose myself.
我去船運部門時，給了他們一番鼓勵。

例 After we talked he goosed up his offer.
我們談過以後，他便把報價提高。

Background

The goose is a large very aggressive domesticated fowl used by the Romans as watch animals. Their blunt beaks deliver a painful bite, usually to an intruder's rear end or crotch. The source for this term may be the goose's bite, the loud cry the victim usually makes, or it could be a combination of the two.

It's doubtful you'll find this definition in any but the most modern American dictionaries.

背景資料 鵝是一種又大又具侵略性的飼養家禽，羅馬人把它們用來當看門動物。被它們的鈍嘴咬到會很痛，通常會攻擊侵擾者的臀部或褲襠。這個專門用詞的來源可能是指被鵝咬到、被咬到的人通常會大叫的聲音，或是兩者兼具。

這個詞除了最新的美語字典外，你大概很難在別的字典裡找到它的定義。

Business Use

This has two common uses. It can describe a pinch, or when someone or thing is in some way motivated to do more or better.

When it describes a pinch, in some European cultures it means the pincher thinks the woman is attractive, and it's sometimes tolerated in non professional settings, but only if it's done by a very old man. Otherwise, it's looked upon as a sexual overture, and rarely, if ever allowed in the U.S. It's defiantly not allowed in a professional setting.

It's currently mostly used as a metaphor indicating that someone's attention was roused or they were spurred to a greater effort. It's a short version for what's between the quotation marks. "progress was slow, but a visit got them to speed up."

商業用法 這個詞有兩個較為常見的使用意義，它可用來描述某個吸引人的東西，會讓某個人想要把事情做的更好。

這個詞也可當作動詞，有「捏」的意思，在一些歐洲國家，這個用法表示做這個動作的人覺得某位女性很有魅力，通常當這個動作發生在非專業場合，而做的人又是年老男性時，多半人們都不太在意，願意容忍這樣的用法。否則，這樣的用法很容易被視為有著濃烈的性暗示，在美國幾乎完全不被允許。想當然的，在專業場合中，這個詞是絕對不能接受的。

現今，這個詞最常被當成譬喻法來用，意指某件事或某個人引起了他人的注意力，或可能讓他人對某事、某人更有興趣了。這個詞原來的版本是「儘管過程緩慢，但這樣做的結果還是讓事情加溫了。」

Alternatives 相關用語

◇ light a fire under his ass	刺激他行動，不要那麼懶
◇ held his feet to the fire	刺激他行動，不要那麼懶
◇ got him revved up	讓他躍躍欲試（很興奮）

(we've) got a deal
就這樣說定；成交

`MP3-98`

Idiom Definition

A statement, often used at the end of negotiations to indicate an agreement has been reached. It can also be used to remind the subject that a deal is in place that covers this situation.

成語定義 一句常用在協議結束時的陳述句，以表示雙方達成共識。它也可以用來提醒當事人先前的協議也適用目前的狀況。

Examples

例 We put our heads together and after a little work we got a deal.

我們坐下來談了一會便達成共識。

．．．

例 Great, if that's all you need then we've got a deal.

太好了，如果你要的就是這些，那我們就這樣說定了。

．．．

Business Use

It's popular with Americans, and often used as an exclamation.

商業用法 這個詞常被美國人使用，通常都會加上一點驚嘆的語氣。

◇ done	沒問題
◇ agreed	同意
◇ I agree	同意
◇ it's a deal	就這麼說定
◇ sounds good to me	聽起來不錯
◇ I accept	我接受
◇ let's do it	就這樣決定
◇ why not?	為什麼不？

◇ it doesn't get any better than that
這樣再好不過了

◇ let's boogie	我們開始吧

◇ These are just a few, the list is almost endless
類似的慣用語實在太多了，這裡只是其中一些例子

How does that grab you?
你有什麼感覺呢？

MP3-99

Idiom Definition

This is used to ask the subject how he or she feels about something.

成語定義 用來詢問當事人對某件事感覺如何。

Word Definition Used

"grab" means strike, or appear to you.

使用的字詞定義 「grab」意指感受或外在印象。

Examples

例 I'm getting the promotion, not you. How does that grab you baby?

要升官的是我不是你耶，你有什麼感覺呢，寶貝？

例 It looks like the dream's becoming a nightmare, how does that grab you?

那個夢想看來變成惡夢了，你有什麼感覺呢？

Background

This idiom is somewhat vulgar in its origin but most people don't know where it comes from, so feel free to use it. What's grabbed is a very sensitive part of the male anatomy.

這句慣用語的來源有點粗俗,不過大部分人都不曉得,所以就放心用吧。「被抓的部分」是指男性解剖學上相當敏感的部位。

Business Use

This is usually used to announce bad news, or when the speaker wants to gloat, and rub it in.

商業用法 這個用法通常被用在宣布壞消息,或在說話者想要慢慢地提及一件壞消息。

Alternatives 相關用語

◇ deal with it 　　　　　　　　面對現實吧

◇ put that in your pipe and smoke it
你好好琢磨琢磨吧

◇ here is something you'll have to come to grips with
有些事情要你解決一下

◆ I hate to tell you this 　　　我很討厭這樣跟你說

◇ I got some bad news for you 　我有壞消息要告訴你

◇ I hate to rain on your parade 　我不想掃興

◇ I don't like being a wet blanket, but ...
我不想掃興,但是…

grand
一千美元

MP3-100

Idiom Definition

This is a slang term for a thousand(s) dollars. Please note it doesn't matter if several thousands of dollars are involved the term grand is always singular.

成語定義 一千美元的俚語用詞。請注意不管是幾千塊，這個詞永遠都用單數。

Word Definition Used

"grand" very large

使用的字詞定義 「grand」是很大的意思。

Examples

例 I need a grand as a down payment.

我需要一千塊當頭期款。

. . . .

例 After five years a three hundred dollar investment earned me seven grand.

五年之後，原本三百塊的投資幫我賺了七千塊。

. . . .

Background

This is street slang from when a thousand dollars was a grand sum, and more money than the common man would be able to save.

背景資料 這個街頭俚語的來源是，當一千元是一筆大數目，一般人很少存到一千元以上時。

Business Use

A thousand dollars is no longer such a huge sum but it's meaning and use remain the same.

商業用法 一千元現在已經不再是筆大數字了，但其意思和用法仍和以前一樣。

Variations

Although this can be used alone it seldom is. The three dots indicate where the amount or number of thousands should be placed.

代替詞 雖然這個詞可以單獨使用，但很少如此。Grand 前面那三個點（… grand）表示可以放千元單位進去。

Alternatives 相關用語

◇ large	大
◇ K	千

come in handy
用得著；隨手可得

MP3-101

Idiom Definition

This is said of things which may be useful and or prove to be convenient.

成語定義　用來指可能用得到或是想用就有的東西。

Word Definition Used

"handy" something is placed where it can be easily reached

"come in" indicates an item has potential use.

使用的字詞定義　「handy」表示東西放在隨手拿得到的地方。「come in」表示某個東西可能用得到。

Examples

例 It's a useful thing to keep around, it'll come in handy.
這個東西留著還有用，總會用得著的。

例 I keep it because it comes in handy from time to time.
我把它留著是因為它有時會用得到。

Background

To be handy means a thing is close, and easily within

the grasp of the potential user's hand.

背景資料 「手邊」（handy）意指東西在附近，只要隨手一抓就很容易拿到。

Business Use

A thing or person that is readily available and may prove, or did prove to be useful. It's a short version for what's between the quotation marks. "Lets keep that close and remember where it is, I'm sure we will need it more than once.?

商業用法 當一件東西或一個人隨手可得時，可能會變有用的，原來的講法是「我們把那樣東西留在手邊，記住放置的位置，我確定會不只一次需要這樣東西。」

Alternatives 相關用語

◇ needful things	必需品
◇ all purpose	萬用的
◇ ready to hand	手頭備用的
◇ near to hand	隨手可得
◇ convenient	方便的

Hang tough
堅持到底

MP3-102

Idiom Definition

This is a direction to maintain a single position, and refuse to alter or change it in any way.

成語定義 一種保持同一立場的傾向，無論如何都拒絕改變。

Word Definition Used

"hang" to remain or last

"tough" unmoving

使用的字詞定義
「hang」意指維持或持續。
「tough」意指不動。

Examples

例 Just hang tough, if you get past this first interview you should be ok.

一定要堅持到底，只要通過第一次面試就沒問題了。

. . . .

例 I need you to hang tough, back me up and we'll be ok.

我需要你力挺我到底，我們就沒問題了。

. . . .

Background

This is a fairly new addition to the language that

appeared in the late 60's. It comes from the term hang around, meaning to loiter in a social group.

背景資料 這是 60 年代晚期才出現的一句相當新的慣用語。它來自「hang around」這個慣用語（意指在社交活動中消磨時間）。

Business Use

It's also a short version of what's between the quotation marks. "You need to hold your ground no matter what happens. Just hang in there and never say die.?

商業用法 這個用法是「不管發生什麼事，你需要堅定自己的立場，只要堅持下去，不要輕言放棄」的簡短版本。

Alternatives 相關用語

◇	maintain your position	堅守立場
◇	stick to your guns	堅持不讓步
◇	hang in there	堅持下去
◆	stand tall	昂然挺立
◇	take a stand	堅持己見
◇	don't flinch	不要退縮

in a heartbeat
立刻

MP3-103

Idiom Definition

This is said when a decision was or will be made very quickly and was or will be used at the next opportunity.

成語定義 當需要很快做決定，下次出現機會便用得到時的慣用語。

Word Definition Used

"heartbeat" the amount of time it takes for the human heart to beat once

使用的字詞定義 「heartbeat」是指人類心臟撲通跳動一次所需要的時間。

Examples

例 I'll do that for you in a heartbeat.
我會立刻幫你處理。

例 I'll do it in a heartbeat, if I ever get the chance.
只要我有機會，就會立刻去做。

Background

The normal heart rate for an adult is between 70 and 90 beats per minute, or more than one per second. So the speaker is saying he or she will not have to think for very long before acting.

背景資料 成年人一般的心跳次數介於每分鐘 70 到 90 下之間，或是每秒一下以上。所以說這句話時表示當事人在行動之前並沒有想太久。

Business Use

This is usually connected with the decision making process. Technically it means the speaker will need the time it takes for his heart to beat once to reach a decision when the opportunity comes. In actuality it means the decision is already made.

It's a short version for what's between the quotation marks. "Allthough I'm saying I'll make a decision when the time comes, the truth is I already made the decision and I'm only waiting for the opportunity to use it."

商業用法 這個用法通常和做決定有關。就技術層面來看，這個用法意指說話者需要一些時間，在適當的機會時，讓自己的心跳再次確定某個決定是否正確。在實際情況中，這個用法意指決定已經做好了。
這個用法較長的版本是「雖然我說會在適當的時機做出決定，但事實上我已經做出決定，我只是在等待適當的機會，採取行動而已。」

Alternatives 相關用語

◆	in a New York second	傾刻間
◇	without giving it a second thought	想都不想

with no place to hide
無處可躲；無所遁形

MP3-104

Idiom Definition

This indicates there is and or will be no opportunity to hide errors or guilt, and no opportunity to shift blame.

成語定義 表示沒有機會隱藏錯誤或過失，也沒有機會逃避責難。

Examples

例 His signature on the memo left him no place to hide,
備忘錄上的簽名讓他無所遁形。

例 You've got no place to hide; I suggest you face the music.
你已無處可躲，勸你勇敢地面對困難吧。

Background

When someone discovers they did something they feel ashamed about they look for a place to hide their deed or themselves. This idiom says that things are set up in such a way there won't be any way or place to hide.

背景資料 當某人發現自己做了一些覺得丟臉的事情，會設法掩蓋自己的行為或是找個地方躲起來。這個慣用語用來指事情已沒有任何辦法或地方可以加以隱藏。

Used to describe someone who did something that didn't turn out well. It says the guilty party can't hide, but really means the evidence can't be hidden, nor is there a possibility to shift or share the blame to or with another.

商業用法 這個詞被用來描述某個人做了一件事，結果不是很好。這個用法描述做錯事的一方沒有躲藏之處，但真正的意思是無法掩飾證據，也沒有把過錯推到他人身上或和他人共擔責任的可能性。

Alternatives 相關用語

◇ caught red handed	當場逮個正著
◇ caught with egg on his face	當眾出糗
◇ the buck stops here	責無旁貸

high power
值錢的；很能幹的

MP3-105

Idiom Definition

This is used to describe any person, place or thing worth a lot of money or usually used to make a large amount of money. It is often used to describe a very competent businessman or woman.

成語定義 用來形容任何很值錢，或可以用來賺一大筆錢的人事地物。也經常用來形容一個很能幹的生意人。

Word Definition Used

"power" money

使用的字詞定義 「power」意指金錢

Examples

例 She's a real heavy hitter, very high power.
她是個真正的大人物，能力相當強。

例 That was my first high power negotiation.
這是我第一次參與涉及重大金額的協商。

Background

Using the definitions in a standard dictionary this idiom means something carrying or using a large amount of electricity. If you substitute the word "power" with "money" you get a business term, you'll know which applies by the context.

The term came into being because big money means power, and people able to deal with big money situations are considered high power.

背景資料 如果用標準字典的定義，這個慣用語意指某事物帶有或使用大量電力。如果你把「電力」用「錢」這個字來代替，就會變成商場用語，也可以從上下文知道其正確涵意。

之所以有這個慣用語是因為有錢代表力量，而有能力處理涉及重大金額情況的人會被認為很能幹。

Business Use

This is used to identify certain people places and things as being very good at what they do and able to deal with large valuable assets and concepts.

商業用法 這個詞意指有些人、地方或事情，擅長扮演自己的角色，能夠處理很有價值的財產或觀念。

Alternatives 相關用語

◇ big league	高階挑戰
◇ major league	競爭激烈的地方
◇ heavy hitter	大人物
◇ hot stuff	了不起的人（事物）
◇ one of the big ones	出類拔萃
◇ a big fish	要角
◇ top drawer	最高級的
◇ top notch	第一流的

price hike

漲價

MP3-106

Idiom Definition

This is used to indicate an increase in the price.

成語定義　用來表示價格的上漲。

Word Definition Used

"hike" raise or increase

使用的字詞定義　「hike」意指上升或增加。

Examples

例 When they raised their prices the whole industry had a 3% price hike.

他們漲價後，整個業界也跟著把價格調漲了 3%。

例 We don't enjoy these price hikes, but our costs go up every year.

雖然我們不喜歡漲價，但是成本每年都在增加。

Background

A hike is usually a long walk, but here it means an increase.

背景資料　「hike」通常指遠足，不過這裡的意思是指增加。

This is the term preferred by most business people to discuss an increase in prices to meet rising costs.

商業用法 這個專用詞大多被商業人士使用，目的在討論增漲價格，以符合漸增的成本。

Alternatives 相關用語

◇ A rate increase	費用提高
◇ inflation adjustment	通貨膨脹調整

hit it off
處得來；相處融洽

`MP3-107`

Idiom Definition

This is used to describe when people meet and get along or work well with each other.

成語定義 用來形容大家認識後相處融洽，或是彼此合作愉快。

Word Definition Used

"hit it off" is a term as well as an idiom. When these exact words are used this way, they take on the unique meaning above.

使用的字詞定義 「hit it off」是一個專門用詞也是一個慣用語。每個字這樣連起來用時，表現的便是上述那種特別的意思。

Examples

例 We hit it off right from the start.
我們打從一開始就處得很好。

例 It's important to hit it off with your coworkers.
和同事處得來很重要。

Background

A hit is a success. In baseball the idea behind the game it for the batter to hit the ball away from the control of the team on defense and run as far as possible before they regain control of the ball.

Following that rational, any successful project is a hit, a hit book, movie, song, play and the list goes on.

背景資料 「安打」(hit) 是成功的意思。在棒球賽裡的概念便是,打擊者把球打出去讓球脫離防禦對手的控制,然後能跑幾壘就跑幾壘,直到對手重新控制球為止。

順著這樣的思路,任何成功的方案便是一個「hit」,成功而叫座的書、電影、歌曲、表演等等,什麼都可以套用。

Business Use

The term "hit it off", is an old one, and it still gets a lot of use. When it's said that two people hit it off it means they became good friends right from the very start, almost best friends.

商業用法 這個短語有著相當的歷史,但至今仍廣為使用。當有人說某兩個人一拍即合時,意思是這兩個人一開始就成為好友,幾乎是至交。

Alternatives 相關用語

◆ get along	和睦相處
◇ as thick as thieves	親密無間
◇ best buddies	好搭擋
◇ pals	好夥伴
◇ close friends	好朋友

H

hold (your) own
不輸給別人；獨當一面

MP3-108

Idiom Definition

This is used to describe a person or group that is able to defend themselves, or protect their own interests.

成語定義 用來形容一個人或一個團體能夠自我防衛，或保護自身利益。

Word Definition Used

"hold" remain in control

"own" a position or stance on something

使用的字詞定義

「hold」是保持控制之意。

「own」是對某事的立場態度。

Examples

例 She has a pretty strong personality; she can hold her own in any meeting.

她個性很強，任何會議場合都表現得不輸別人。

....

例 Executives have to hold their own against people in their own company.

業務主管在公司裡不能輸給其他人。

....

The word "own" could refer to an actual physical thing or location.

背景資料 「own」這個字可以用來指實際上摸得到的東西或位置。

Business Use

In the business world it seldom means anything physical, more often it refers to a person or company's ability to defend itself from the competition in the open market place. It's a short version for what's between the quotation marks. "You're a big boy (girl) now and you'll have to protect what's yours, by yourself. No one will do it for you".

商業用法 在商業界，這個詞很少意指身體上的防衛，通常只的是一個人或公司在公開市場中，捍衛自己的能力。較完整的用法是「你現在長大了，有能力保護自己的東西，因為沒有別人會保護你。」

Alternatives 相關用語

◇ watch your back　　　　　　　小心你的背後

◇ taking care of business.　　　　做該做的事

do (your) homework
準備工作

MP3-109

Idiom Definition

Prepare for a meeting or event

成語定義 為會議或討論做好準備

Word Definition Used

"homework" is a term meaning the preparation work for an event, like a meeting.

使用的字詞定義 「homework」這個詞意指該做的準備工作，例如會議前的準備。

Examples

例 We get a lot done because you do your homework.

你準備工作做得很好，省了我們很多麻煩。

例 She did her homework and did quite well.

她準備工作做得相當充分。

Background

The standard definition refers to a child reviewing materials for discussion in the next class. This is a good corollary for the business world. The preparation could be done at home, but more likely at the office.

標準定義原指小孩為了下堂課要討論的東西而溫習功課。對商業界而言,準備工作做好必然會有好結果。準備工作可以在家裡做,但更可能是在辦公室裡進行。

Business Use

In business it means to prepare for an event prior to the event and be completely ready before the event starts.

商業用法 在商業界,這個用法的意思是在某件事發生之前,做好萬全的準備。

Alternatives 相關用語

◇ study up	鑽研
◇ burn the midnight oil	日以繼夜地工作

get hot
生氣

MP3-110

Idiom Definition

This is used to describe an event where tempers flair and people become angry.

成語定義 用來形容人們情緒激動而生氣的場合或事件。

Word Definition Used

"hot" angry

使用的字詞定義
「hot」指的是生氣。

Examples

例 There's no need to get hot about it, we can work something out.

沒有必要對這件事生氣，我們可以搞定的。

例 Things were getting hot so we called a lunch break.

氣氛開始越來越不對頭，於是我們決定休息一下。

Background

When a person loses his or her temper their body temperature does rise.

背景資料 人發脾氣時體溫會上升。

Any reference to an increased body temperature in a business context means the subject has become stimulated or excited and most likely angry.

商業用法 在商業用法上，體溫增加指的是説話者被刺激到，最常見的用法是描述他人生氣了。

Alternatives 相關用語

◇ hot under the collar	勃然大怒
◇ things got heated	火爆場面
◇ a heated exchange	火爆場面
◇ tempers flared	情緒激動
◇ a three alarm argument	嚴重爭議

in house
內部

MP3-111

Idiom Definition

This is used to describe when work is done by a company's permanent staff, and not a contractor, or someone specifically hired for a specific situation.

成語定義 用來形容公司的工作由公司固定員工,而非由契約員工或因應特別情況而特別雇用的人來完成。

Word Definition Used

"in house" is a term as well as an idiom. When these exact words are used this way, they take on the unique meaning above.

使用的字詞定義 「in house」是一個專門用詞也是一個慣用語。每個字這樣連起來用時,表現的便是上述那種特別的意思。

Examples

例 We do the landscaping in house, it's cheaper and we have more control.

我們內部自己完成環境美化設計,一來比較便宜,二來我們可以更好控管。

例 We did the painting in house at half the cost of a contractor.

內部員工自己油漆比外包給別人要省下一半成本。

The words "in house" means the work was done by employees already in the house, or on the payroll.

背景資料 「in house」這兩個字意思是工作由公司內員工或現職員工所完成。

It indicates the work was all performed by employees on staff, or in the house. A contractor was not hired for this job alone.

Alternatives 相關用語

◇ with the talent on hand   身邊的高手

◇ using our own staff   用內部員工

in a run
一次;一輪;一期

MP3-112

Idiom Definition

This is used to describe a case where several repetitions of a single task are performed without a single planned interruption.

成語定義 用來形容一種情況:單一工作之不斷重覆的部分執行時,不受刻意的中途干擾。

Word Definition Used

"run" a series or actions or units

"in a run" is a term as well as an idiom. When these exact words are used this way, they take on the unique meaning above.

使用的字詞定義 「run」是一個系列、活動或單位。
「in a run」是一個專門用詞也是一個慣用語。每個字這樣連起來用時,表現的便是上述那種特別的意思。

Examples

例 We plan to set up once and make all the units in a run.

我們打算只弄一次,就要把所有的組件做出來。

例 We can make twenty-five units in a single run.

我們一次可以完成 25 個單位。

A walk is a series of steps which may or may not have a purpose. A run always has a specific goal.

背景資料 走路由連續的步伐所形成，可能有目的或者沒有。跑步卻往往有特定目標。

Business Use

In this idiom a run refers to a series of actions. For Examples, a printer sets up his press to print one thousand images before he stops to print a different image, and so on. Each image, regardless of the actual number printed is considered a "run."

Likewise, the number of burgers a cook can fry at one time, or the total units produced by an assembly line in one unbroken streak are also referred to as a run.

商業用法 在這個用法中，「a run」意指一連串的行動。舉例來說，一個印刷商要印製一千份的圖片，在動工之前，他先把油印機架設好。不管份數為何，每一份都要跑一圈。運用到類似的情況下，一個廚師一次可以準備的漢堡數量、一條生產線一次可以製造的全部數量，都可稱為「動工一次」。

Alternatives 相關用語

◇ per setup	每次的安排
◇ before you retool	重新更換以前
◇ nonstop	不休息地；直達車

industry wide
整個業界的

MP3-113

Idiom Definition

This is used to describe any action, concept or anything else that is the established norm, or normal for everyone in a particular industry.

成語定義 用來形容任何本身為確立基準，或為特定行業業內人士所遵循的行動、概念等等。

Word Definition Used

"ride" throughout, from one end to the other, completely

"industry wide" is a term as well as an idiom. When these exact words are used this way, they take on the unique meaning above.

使用的字詞定義 「wide」意為遍及、從此端到彼端、完全。

「industry wide」是一個詞，也是一個慣用語，當這些字一起使用時，有上述的意思。

Examples

例 It's an industry wide requirement imposed on us all by state law.

這項業界需求乃州法律強制規定的。

例 The pricing is industry wide; it's regulated by a state agency.

這是政府部門制定的業界共同價格。

Background

The word "wide" can refer to every member of a group.

背景資料　「wide」這個字可以指團體內的每個成員。

Business Us

This is used to describe something as a condition concept or problem everyone in the same line of work has to deal with. It's also a short version of what's between the quotation marks. "Every business in this field has to deal with this problem."

商業用法　這個詞用來描述在某一個行業中，大家都要處理的情況、觀念或問題。描述這個詞的較長版本是「這個產業中的每家公司都要處理這個問題。」

Alternatives 相關用語

◇ across the boards	全面的
◇ no exceptions	沒有例外

(we) jumped on it
把握良機；抓住機會

MP3-114

Idiom Definition

This is used when the speaker is reporting his group took imitate advantage of an opportunity.

成語定義 要團隊成員立即掌握機會時，便會用到這句慣用語。

Word Definition Used

"jumped" pounced as a hunting animal

使用的字詞定義
「jumped」是指像狩獵動物一樣一把捉住獵物。

Examples

例 When an opportunity arose, we jumped on it.
一旦機會來臨，我們便要善加把握。

....

例 When they called to tell us there was a vacancy we jumped on it.
他們打電話來告訴我們有空缺時，我們立刻把握良機。

....

Background

Again this is a fairly recent addition to the language that started in the 1970's. The term "jumped on" came from "pounce" the way a cat attacks it's pray.

這句慣用語相當新，也是 1970 年代以後才有的用語。「jumped on」這個詞來自「pounce」，是指貓攻擊獵物的方式。

Business Use

This term describes any situation where an unexpected opportunity opens up and someone there moves, usually on his or her own authority, to take advantage of it.

商業用法 在任何一個情況中，當一個意想不到的機會突然來臨或某個人突然有所行動時，通常其上司會善加利用這個情況，這時候就會用到這個表達法。

Alternatives 相關用語

◇ take advantage of	利用
◇ strike while the iron is hot	打鐵趁熱
◇ make hay while the sun shines	良機勿失
◇ take the money and run 拿了錢就跑（嚐到甜頭就閃人）	

keep up (my) end
遵守承諾

MP3-115

Idiom Definition

This means the speaker will honor his or her obligations.

成語定義 意指說話者會履行義務。

Word Definition Used

"keep up" is a term meaning to continue or maintain.

"end" side of a deal

使用的字詞定義

「keep up」這個詞意指繼續或維持。

「end」是交易的其中一邊。

Examples

例 I made you a promise, and I'll keep up my end of the deal.

我答應過你，自然會遵守承諾。

例 Tell them I'll keep up my end, if they do the same.

告訴他們只要他們守信用，我也一樣會遵守承諾。

This refers to two or more workers carrying a load together. They make an agreement to cooperate, then each picks up an end and holds it until it's where it's supposed to be.

背景資料 和兩個或兩個以上的工人一起扛著重物有關。他們協議大家合作，一人抬一邊，合力抬到目的地。

Business Use

This means to keep your agreements for as long as promised. It's a short version for what's between the quotation marks. "Tell them we made an agreement and we'll stay true to our word."

商業用法 這個詞的意思是盡可能地信守你的承諾，原來較長的用法是「告訴他們，這是我們的協議，我們會信守承諾。」

Alternatives 相關用語

◇ I'll keep my word	遵守諾言
◇ honor my commitments	遵守諾言

locked in
不能更動；無法改變

MP3-116

Idiom Definition

This is used to describe a situation where an agreement is in place, or more precisely, a portion of an agreement is set for a specific period, and not subject to change.

成語定義　用來形容已達成協議的情況，或者更精確地說，協議中有限定特定期限內，某些部分是不能更動的。

Word Definition Used

"locked in" is a term as well as an idiom. When these exact words are used this way, they take on the unique meaning above.

使用的字詞定義
「locked in」是一個專門用詞也是一個慣用語。每個字這樣連起來用時，表現的便是上述那種特別的意思。

Examples

例 The price is locked in for five years, then we renegotiate.

價格五年內都不能更動，到期後我們再重新協議。

例 We were locked in for a year, and we have three more months to go.

我們綁約期限是一年，目前還有三個月可以利用。

Background

"locked in" means can't change, and it's a recent addition to the language from the military. Radar, closed circuit TV and other electronic devices sometimes guide modern long-range weapons. In most cases the target image is acquired, then the aiming system is locked onto the image. The guidance system takes control adjusting the flight path until the projectile impacts and detonates.

The meaning is the image or goal is locked in the system, "locked in" also means held in a room or cell. Both sources fit, but use started after the military technology developed smart weapons.

背景資料　「locked in」意指無法改變，是源自軍中用語的新詞。雷達、閉路電視和其他電子儀器有時會用來導引現代長程武器。大部分情況是：先鎖定目標影像，接著瞄準系統鎖住該影像，再來由導彈系統控制飛行路線的調整，直到導彈撞擊目標後爆炸為止。
這個詞的意義便是影像或目標由系統所鎖定，另外也有關在房間或牢房裡的意思。兩個來源都可以解釋，不過一開始是由於軍中科技發展出更先進的武器才開始使用的。

Business Use

This describes the conditions of an agreement not subject to change at this time. It's a short version of what's between the quotation marks. "We have an agreement, in place that sets the price for now. You can count on that, and any planning you do should reflect it."

商業用法 這個詞描述在現在的情況下，協議不容許任何改變。原來較長的版本是「我們之間有個協議，所以現在的價格是鎖定的，你可以信任我們，你們所做的任何計畫，也應該反映這個情況。」

Alternatives 相關用語

◇ that's carved in stone	無法改變
◇ it's set in concrete	無法改變
◇ you can take that to the bank	保證兌現
◇ we have a contract	我們有協議
◇ it's an iron clad contract	合約有嚴格規定

in for the long haul

長長久久；堅持到最後

`MP3-117`

Idiom Definition

This is used to express a commitment to something for a long time, usually until the very end.

成語定義 用來表示長久承諾某事，通常是直到最後一刻。

Word Definition Used

"in it" is a term meaning committed.

"haul" duration

"long haul" is a term meaning from beginning to end.

使用的字詞定義

「in it」這個詞意指承諾。

「haul」表示持續。

「long haul」這個詞意指從開始到結束。

Examples

例 I'm in for the long haul; I intend to make this a career.

我打算以此為業，打的是長期戰。

例 We need someone in for the long haul, someone who'll be here for years.

我們需要的是可以待很久的人，最好是可以待上個幾年。

Background

The terms "in it" and "long haul" when put together mean "committed to something for a long time."

背景資料 「in it」和「long haul」放在一起時便意指「長久承諾某事」。

Business Use

This is used to describe the speaker's intention to do something from beginning to end. He/she wants to see the project completed.

商業用法 這個詞被用來描述說話者打算要把一件事從頭到尾做完，希望看到這個計畫完成。

Alternatives 相關用語

◇ committed	堅持下去
◇ dedicated	專注
◇ willing to see it through	願意奉陪到底

break things loose
打破僵局

MP3-118

Idiom Definition

This is used to describe ending a situation where nothing is happening, where a stalemate is in place. The intention being to create or restart activity in a stalled project

成語定義 用來形容結束風平浪靜、陷入僵局的狀態。表示一種想要讓停滯的計畫重新開展的企圖。

Word Definition Used

"reak" to unclog

"loose" to restore action

使用的字詞定義
「break」是使暢通的意思。
「loose」是恢復活動的意思。

Examples

例 Bill was able to break things loose with his jokes.

比爾只要一講笑話，僵局就會打破。

....

例 Jill tried to break things loose but they wouldn't budge.

吉爾設法打破僵局，但徒勞無功。

....

Background

The words "beak loose" is a term meaning, start activity, "things" are unspecified items. Put together the meaning is fix whatever is wrong and get things moving.

背景資料 「break loose」這個詞意指展開活動;「things」則是不特定對象。兩個放在一起意指修復有錯誤的地方,然後繼續前進。

Business Use

The business meaning is the deadlock is unacceptable, we have to get things moving again.

商業用法 這個詞的商業用法意指說話者無法接受某個僵局,所以得要做一些事來打破現狀。

Alternatives 相關用語

◇ jump start things	重新展開
◇ end the deadlock	打破僵局
◇ get things moving again	繼續進行

lousy
討厭的

Idiom Definition

This is used to describe anything bad, uncomfortable or unpleasant.

成語定義 用來形容任何不好、不舒服或不愉快的事情。

Examples

例 That was a lousy thing to do.

做那件事很討厭。

例 It's a good deal for us and a lousy one for them.

這個協議對我們來說很棒,對他們來說可就爛透了。

Background

This idiom comes from the military, specifically the trenches of World War I. From the viewpoint of the common soldier, living conditions were worse then, than in any other conflict of the modern era. Lice infestation was inescapable.

The American soldiers, called doughboys brought the term, meaning infested with lice, back with them. Since then Americans expanded the definition, and it's been a part of the language ever since.

背景資料 這個慣用語來自軍中,尤其是第一次世界大戰的戰壕。從一般士兵的觀點來看,當時的生活條件比任何現代戰爭都來得差,因為虱子橫行,無處可逃。

所謂步兵的美國大兵便把這個用詞帶回來，意指被虱子騷擾。從那時
起，美國人便把這個詞的定義加以擴大，成為英文裡的一部分。

Business Use

This is used to describe anything felt to be of poor quality, or unpleasant.

商業用法 這個詞用來描述某個人覺得某件東西的品質很差，讓人無
法接受。

Special Considerations

Please note that pronunciation differs from the spelling. Speakers should pronounce it "lou-zee." That's "lou" as in loud and "zee".

特別留意 請注意發音和拼字不同。說法是 "lou-zee"。 就是 loud 唸
成 "lou"，再來是 "zee" .

Alternatives 相關用語

◇ Substandard	不合標準的
◇ sub par	低於標準
◇ inferior quality	次等品質
◇ below grade	次級的
◇ deficient	有缺陷的
◇ unacceptable	不令人滿意的
◇ shoddy	劣等的
◇ trash	垃圾

M

make believe
假裝

MP3-120

Idiom Definition

This is usually thought of as a children's saying, used to express something that is not real, but only pretended to be real for a game.

成語定義 通常被認為是小孩子的説法，用來表示遊戲中的某件事雖然不是真的，卻假裝是真的。

Word Definition Used

"make believe" is a term as well as an idiom. When these exact words are used this way, they take on the unique meaning above.

使用的字詞定義 「make believe」是一個專門用詞也是一個慣用語。每個字這樣連起來用時，表現的便是上述那種特別的意思。

Examples

例 Now it's only make believe, but someday, if we work hard we can do it.

雖然我們現在只是假裝它是真的，但只要我們努力工作，總有一天可以夢想成真。

例 This is not make believe, I'm very serious about this.

我對這件事可是很認真，一點都沒有做假。

Background

This is one of the most well used terms in the English language. These are the magic words used to lead children into play. "Let's play make believe" is the phrase used to start English-speaking children's play all around the world. The literal meaning of the words "make & believe" is "create & assume to be true" or "create an alternative set of rules for the game we're about to play."

As a native speaker I'm no stranger to the land of make believe. I've been there many times as a child, and again I've brought children there as well. And those magic excursions were always pleasant adventurers.

背景資料 這是英文裡最普遍的用詞之一。就是這些神奇的字眼帶領孩子們進入遊戲世界的。「來玩家家酒」對全世界講英文的小孩來説，是一句用來開始玩耍的片語。「make&believe」這些字詞的字面意義是「創造＆假定是真的」或「替我們要玩的遊戲創造一組可以選擇的規則」。

就一個以英文為母語的人而言，我對這個世界並不陌生，從小便接觸過許多次，現在也會帶孩子到那個世界探險。那些神奇之旅永遠都是令人愉快的冒險。

Business Use

I've also been brought there by unrealistic young executives and the wishful thoughts of bosses. So yes, this term does have a place in the business world. It's sometimes used to introduce a scenario that's possible if not exactly correct at the time as a first step to create a plan for that set of circumstances, if they come up.

商業用法 我曾經碰過不實際的年輕商業主管，也聽過一些老闆們的不實際想法。所以這個詞在今日的商業界仍被使用。有時，這個詞被用來介紹一種情況，該情況在當時也許僅有可能，但不是完全正確。如果有某一些情況發生了，就可以利用原來的情況來做計畫。

Alternatives 相關用語

◇ Never, Never Land	忘憂谷
◇ The Emerald City	翡翠之城
◇ pretending	假裝
◇ just in case	以防萬一
◇ a what if	假設情況
◇ in a perfect world	在完美世界中
◇ let's just say	我們不妨說
◇ for the fun of it	為了好玩
◇ it could happen	有可能發生

get (the talks) moving
突破僵局；打開局面

`MP3-121`

Idiom Definition

This is a direction to someone to make progress with negotiations.

成語定義 某人讓協商進行下去的方向。

Word Definition Used

"moving" progress, nearing completion

使用的字詞定義

「moving」意指前進（進步）而接近圓滿。

Examples

例 I say reduce the price 2% to get the talks moving again.

我說把價格降 2%，才打破了僵局。

例 I'll do whatever I have to do to get the talks moving.

只要能打破僵局，做任何事我都願意。

Background

The word "moving" mean progress. The speaker is telling the subject the negotiations are stalled and he or she has to make progress.

「moving」這個字意指前進，說這句慣用語的人在告訴當事人協商已陷入僵局，必須打破才行。

Business Use

This idiom means a negotiation is stalled and something has to be done.

商業用法 這個慣用語意指協商因某種原因停滯，需要採取行動讓會談繼續才行。

Alternatives 相關用語

◇ jump start things	重新展開
◇ end the deadlock	打破僵局
◇ break things loose	打破僵局

none the less
仍然

MP3-122

Idiom Definition

This is used when the speaker wants to acknowledge a statement or condition but discounts it as unimportant because it has little or no effect on the matter at hand.

成語定義 說話者想要承認某句話或某個情況的重要，但由於對手邊的事情很少或沒什麼影響，便漠視其重要性。

Word Definition Used

"none" not any

"the less" diminishment, to reduce or make smaller

"nonetheless" is a term as well as an idiom. When these exact words are used this way, they take on the unique meaning above. Please note this idiom can be spelled as three separate words or single words, both are correct.

使用的字詞定義 「none」表示一個都沒有。「the less」是減少、降低或變小的意思。

「nonetheless」是一個專門用詞也是一個慣用語。每個字這樣連起來用時，表現的便是上述那種特別的意思。請注意這個慣用語可以拼成三個不同的單字也可以連在一起，兩個都是正確用法。

Examples

例 I know Jones has been here longer, but nonetheless the job is yours.

雖然我知道瓊斯比較資深，但這個工作還是會交給你。

例 He did get off to a bad start, but nonetheless he did very well.

他一開始的確沒有弄好，不過仍然表現得很棒。

Background

This is actually a formal word included here for those that hear it spoken, assume it's three words and want to find out what it means. Originally, it was three words, but use and rapid pronunciation sort of rolled the three words into one. This is one idiom that has been around long enough to make it into the dictionary.

背景資料 假設這個慣用語包含三個字而聽者又想知道其意義為何，那這個慣用語對聽者而言其實是一個正式的單字。起初雖然是三個字，但由於講得太快而黏在一起，三個於是變成了一個。因為這個慣用語用得夠久，故字典也將其收錄在內。

Business Use

This is used to acknowledge the existence of something and state that it has no effect on the matter at hand. It's a short version of what's between the quotation marks. "I'm not saying it's of no importance, only that it has no effect here."

商業用法 這個詞用來指出某件事的存在，但說明它對手邊發生的這件事沒有任何影響。原來較長的表達版本是「我不是說這件事不重要，只是想說明它在這個情況下沒有任何影響力。」

Alternatives 相關用語

◇ be that as it may	雖然如此
◇ of no consequence	無足輕重
◇ dismiss it	不管它
◇ it matters not	無關緊要

established norm
已制定的標準

MP3-123

Idiom Definition

This is used to describe the standard adopted as the normal state or condition of something. For Examples it's normal rate of production

成語定義 用來形容某事之一般情況所採用的標準。例如標準產出率。

Word Definition Used

"established" proven

"norm" the short way to say normal

"established norm" is a term as well as an idiom. When these exact words are used this way, they take on the unique meaning above.

使用的字詞定義

「established」意指被證明的。

「norm」是正常（normal）的簡短寫法。

「established norm」是一個專門用詞也是一個慣用語。每個字這樣連起來用時，表現的便是上述那種特別的意思。

Examples

例 They operate at right around the established norm for the job.

他們依工作上已制定的標準來進行。

例 We maintain an average rate just above the established norm.

我們保持在已制定標準的平均水平之上。

Background

Non-native speakers may not recognize "norm" as a short form of the word "normal." This is a very popular term used with everything technical.

背景資料 不是以英文為母語的人可能不知道「norm」可以當做「normal」的簡寫。任何需要專業技術的領域都經常用到這個詞。

Business Use

This is a good way to state the usual rate at which something operates.

商業用法 這是描述在一般狀況之下，進行某件事的常規，是個不錯的表達法。

Alternatives 相關用語

◇ standard operating procedure	標準作業程序
◇ S.O.P.	標準作業程序
◇ running at norm	正常進行
◇ up to speed	瞭若指掌；經驗豐富

N not too bad, even if I do say so myself
還不錯嘛，要是我自己來也差不多一樣好吧

MP3-124

Idiom Definition

This is used when the speaker wants to take credit for something he or she did well.

成語定義 用來形容說話者想要對自己若也同樣表現不錯時加以讚揚一番。

Word Definition Used

"not too bad" is a term meaning good, or done well.

"even if" is a term meaning despite the fact, or even though.

使用的字詞定義

「not too bad」這個詞意指好，或是表現不錯。
「even if」這個詞意指雖然、儘管。

Examples

例 The design is not too bad, even if I do say so myself.

這個設計還不算太壞，就連我自己都這麼認為。

例 The final result was not too bad, even if I do say so myself.

這個最後結果不算太糟，就連我自己都這麼認為。

Often used in a semi humorous way. The term "not too bad," is an understated way of saying something was well done in the opinion of the speaker. The second term, "even if" is a second term meaning despite the fact, indicating some may disallow the statement because of the following statement.

"I do say so myself" is of course, an immodest statement because the speaker is talking about himself, and therefore boasting.

背景資料 這個表達法常用來表達詼諧效果。其中的「還不算太壞」其實意指相反，表示說話者覺得事情做的真的很不錯。其中的「就連…」是「即使」的另一種說法，表示前半句話可能會因為後面要講的話，而無法成立。
「我自己都這麼認為」當然是不怎麼謙虛的表達法，因為說話者講的是自己，所以有一些自誇意味。

Business Use

This is often used whenever the speaker comments on something he or she did add that it was done well. It's almost as if using this idiom will pardon the speaker for being immodest.

商業用法 這個表達是用來表達說話者對自己所做之事的評語，還外加了覺得自己做的很好的意思。用這個表達法，就好似說話者想要藉此說明自己其實沒有那麼自誇。

Special Considerations

The first part of the term, "not too bad" is usually said flatly, as a statement of fact not open to debate. The second part of the term, "even if I do say so myself" is usually added quickly with a smile because the speaker is being immodest.

特別留意

這個表達法的第一部分講到「還不算太壞」時，說話者的語氣會很平，彷彿不希望有人質疑他的意見，但第二部分的「就連我自己都這麼認為」通常會很快加上，說此話時，臉上還會帶著一絲笑意，因為說話的人並不謙虛。

Alternatives 相關用語

◇ that's my work	那是我的傑作
◇ patting myself on the back	好好獎勵自己一番

numbers people
和數字為伍的人

Idiom Definition

This is used to describe anyone connected with the financial part of business. For Examples, CPAs, accountants, bookkeepers, or anyone that works with numbers having to do with money.

成語定義 這個詞通常用來描述任何和商業的財務有關的人。例如，認證會計師、會計、管帳的人或任何和金錢數字為伍的人。

Word Definition Used

"numbers people" is a term as well as an idiom. When these exact words are used this way, they take on the unique meaning above.

使用的字詞定義
「numbers people」是一個詞，也是一個成語。當這些詞在某種場合被用到時，有上述獨特的意思。

Examples

例 Let me give this to my numbers people, and I'll get back to you.

讓我把這個交給公司中搞數字的人，之後再回覆你。

例 My numbers people disagree with your numbers people's projections.

我們公司管數字的人不同意你們公司代表所預測的數字。

Background

Numbers is used because these workers work with numbers. "People" is used in this case because either gender may apply. It could just as easily be a numbers guy or a numbers gal.

背景資料 這裡用到「數字」這個詞是因為這些人的工作與數字有關。這裡用「人」這個字是因為沒有性別之分。當然如果想標上性別，也是可以的〈就可以用 numbers guy 或 numbers gal 的用法〉。

Business Use

This is the slang term mostly for workers that keep books and perform financial projections, or anyone that works with financial numbers.

商業用法 這是一個俚語，通常用來描述管帳目和預測財務數字的人，其他和財務數字為伍的人也可以用這個詞描述。

Alternatives 相關用語

◇ number crunchers	斤斤計較的人
◇ bean counters	錙銖必較的人

a very attractive offer

很誘人的提議

MP3-126

Idiom Definition

This is used to describe a very good sales offer. It would be a high price if said by the seller or spoken from the seller's viewpoint, and low if said by the other side. The point is what it is exactly depends on the speaker.

商業用法 這個表達法用來描述一個很好的銷售提議。如果説話的人是個銷售員，或從他們的説話立場來看，這表示價格很高。但如果是從買家的立場來看的話，就表示價格很低。這句話的意思要看説話的人而定。

Word Definition Used

"attractive" desirable

使用的字詞定義

「誘人的」：吸引人的

Examples

例 They made us a very attractive offer, and we jumped on it.

他們提供我們一個非常誘人的提議，所以我們立刻就接受了。

例 It's a very attractive offer that I don't think I can beat.

那是個非常誘人的提議，我想我的提議無法更好。

Background

The word "attractive" is usually used in connection with a sexy, beautiful woman, by inference it means the proposal is sexy and beautiful.

背景資料 「attractive」這個詞常用於形容性感、美麗的女人,指的是這個提議非常誘人、讓人非常動心。

Business Use

This is used to express the speakers opinion that an offer is better than just good or acceptable, but highly desirable.

商業用法 這個詞常用來表示說話者覺得這個提議不只是好、可以接受而已,而是令人非常動心。

Alternatives 相關用語

◇ a good deal	很好的交易
◇ a keeper	一個誘餌

this isn't an official offer
這不是正式報價

MP3-127

Idiom Definition

This is used when an offer isn't made, or put on the table, but a feeler, to learn where the other side's position may be, the offer is suggested.

成語定義 這個表達法用於試探性質,它告訴對方這並非正式議價,只是為了試探對方的立場,它的確暗示了報價。

Word Definition Used

"Official offer" is a term meaning a bid to buy or sell something. If accepted the transaction will take place.

背景資料 「official offer」這個詞表示了要購買或賣出一項東西時的提議價格,如果對方接受了這個提議,便可以做成交易。

Examples

例 This is not an offer, but if you like it we may offer something like...

這不是一個報價,但如果你喜歡這個價格,我們也許可以提供類似的…

例 This is an unofficial offer, just to test the waters.

這不是正式報價,只是要試試看對方的反應。

Background

The negative words before "official offer" are code meaning this isn't a bid, and if accepted, no transaction will occur.

背景資料 置於「official offer」一詞之前的負面語氣,旨在告知對方這不是報價，即使對方願意接受，也不見得可以做成交易。

Business Use

This is usually used when talks are stalled, and one side wants to find out what the other side really wants. If you're approached with this phrase, you should take it very seriously, and relay it at once to the boss.

This is a code phrase meaning what's between the quotation marks. "It looks like the talks are stuck and we want to make a deal, so let's say enough is enough, of this crap. We want to get things moving, but we don't want to appear weak, overly anxious or needful. So we're making this unofficial offer. If you are interested, let us know."

商業用法 這個表達法通常用於雙方議價停滯時，如果其中一方想要知道對方意欲為何時，就會用這樣的話語。如果對方用這種詞語和你交談，你應該嚴肅看待這個反應，立即向老闆反應這個事實。

這個表達法也是一個暗號，引號間的字詞「正式報價」隱含了一些意義，對方想要告訴你，「我們的談話似乎已經陷入僵局，但我們還是想和你們做生意，所以就不多說廢話了，我們想要事情趕快有結果，但是又不想要讓你覺得我們削弱了自己的立場，好像迫不及待要和你做生意一樣。因此我們希望聲明這個提議是非正式的，如果你對此也有意的話，讓我們知道你的想法。」

Alternatives 相關用語

◇ under the table	檯面下的 …
◇ through back channels	走後門的
◇ this is off the record	以下談話不列入紀錄
◇ I didn't say this, but, …	這不是我的意見，但…
◇ you didn't hear this from me	你別說這話是我說的
◇ this is not an official offer	這不是正式報價
◇ this is an unofficial offer	這是非正式報價
◇ this offer isn't official	這報價不具任何效力

operating losses
營運損失

MP3-128

Idiom Definition

This is used to describe financial loses from the cost of operating a business.

成語定義 這表達法用於描述公司因營運不佳，而遭受到的損失。

Word Definition Used

"operating losses" is a term as well as an idiom. When these exact words are used this way, they take on the unique meaning above.

使用的字詞定義

「operating losses」是一個詞，也是一個慣用語。當這兩個字一起使用時，便會有上面提到的獨特意義。

Examples

例 He reduced the operating losses, and showed a profit in two months.

他減少公司的營運損失，在兩個月中就看到公司賺了錢。

....

例 The operating losses disappeared when the old floor manager was fired.

當前任工廠經理被炒魷魚後，營運損失就不再發生了。

....

Business Use

This describes losses from normal operations such as wages, utilities, taxes and office supplies, the cost of staying in business. It's different from manufacturing costs, the cost of making a product, and may be due to a large office staff, workers who don't make the product but process orders and deal with the government.

商業用法 這個表達法描述公司在正常營運下的損失，像是薪資、設備、稅務及辦公室文具用品，這些都是公司的必然營運成本。不同於製造成本，製造成本是製造產品的成本，營運成本的產生也許是因為公司有很多員工，這些員工不負責製造產品，他們的工作是處理訂單、和政府機關打交道。

Alternatives 相關用語

◇ the cost of doing business　　　做生意的成本

◇ the cost of keeping the doors open
讓公司經營下去的成本

on the other hand
另一方面來說

MP3-129

Idiom Definition

This is used to introduce a different interpretation of a situation or event.

成語定義 這個詞用於介紹對某一情況或事件的不同詮釋或解釋。

Word Definition Used

"on the other hand" is a term as well as an idiom. When these exact words are used this way, they take on the unique meaning above.

使用的字詞定義
「on the other hand」是一個詞，也是一個慣用語。當這些字一起使用時，便會有上面提到的獨特意義。

Examples

例 True, it is half empty, but, on the other hand, we could call it half full.

沒錯，這瓶子一半是空的，但另一方面來說，我們也可以把它稱為半滿。

例 But, on the other hand, this could be the opportunity we've waited for.

但另一方面來說，這可能是我們等待已久的機會。

Background

The idiom refers to the difference between things made for the left and right hands, like tools and clothing. A molded pistol grip is an asset when held by the hand it was made for, and a liability when held in the other hand.

背景資料 這個慣用語指的是事情的兩種看法，像是工具或服飾，左手和右手會有不同的操作手法。一支鑄模手槍如果落到了會用槍的人手裡，它會是一項資產，但若入了不會用槍的人手裡，可能會成為帶來危險的工具。

Business Use

This is a verbal device used to introduce an alternative set of circumstances, or a different set of rules.

商業用法 這個表達是一個語言上的轉折詞，主要被用來介紹一些情況的另種詮釋，或另外一套規則。

Alternatives 相關用語

◇ but then again...	相對的 ...
◇ or you can take the other side	另一個角度來看

pretty much
差不多就是…

Idiom Definition

This technically means "almost," but not quite the thing wanted. However, it is also used as an understatement, meaning the thing referred to is exactly what's needed.

成語定義 這個表達法意味著「幾乎」，但意思稍有差距。但它也可以用來「淡化」語氣，表示所提及的東西正是說話者需要的東西。

Word Definition Used

"pretty much" is a term meaning "not quite"

使用的字詞定義

「pretty much」這個詞表示「並不全然是…」

Examples

例 Well, what happened is pretty much what I wanted, so I'm happy.

這樣說吧，發生的情況差不多就是我想要的，所以我很滿意。

....

例 Things went pretty much like we figured, so we were ready.

事情的發展和我們所預期的差不多，所以我們有做好準備。

....

Background

The definition of the word "pretty," when used in front of an adjective or adverb, becomes "quite or rather."

背景資料　當被用在形容詞或副詞之前時，pretty 這個字的意思和「相當、差不多」一樣。

Business Use

This in an understated way to say that the thing referred to seems to be what is needed.

商業用法　這是一種淡化語氣的講法，表達所談到的事情似乎和預期的差不多。

Alternatives 相關用語

◇ close enough	差不多一樣
◇ almost there	幾乎一樣
◇ just a bit short	差強人意
◇ pretty well	還不錯啦

asking price
起價

MP3-131

Idiom Definition

This is the price the seller asks for his product or service prior to the start of negotiations.

成語定義 這指的是賣方在議價過程開始之前，對某一產品或服務所出的價格。

Word Definition Used

"Asking price" is a term as well as an idiom meaning the above.

使用的字詞定義 「asking price」這個詞，也是個慣用語，有著上面所解釋的意思。

Examples

例 I bought the car for 15% below the asking price.

我用低於起價百分之十五的價格，買到這部車。

例 He said the asking price was firm, but when I turned, he dropped it 10%.

他說這個起價很死，但當我表示不能接受，要離開時，他降價百分之十。

Background

Whenever an item or service is offered, the seller has to post a price, referred to as the asking price. The original price is not necessarily the selling price; in fact. it rarely is. The actual price could be higher but usually is lower.

This is common with big-ticket highly negotiable items, like homes and cars. The asking price tends to be high because the seller expects to be negotiated down. It's part of the sales strategy. Americans take pride in working out a good deal, so the asking price is inflated, allowing the seller to slash the price, but still make a profit.

背景資料 每當某種服務或商品在報價時，賣方必須先貼出一個價格，這就是所謂的起價。一件物品或服務的原始價格並不一定是起價，應該說，通常原始價格都不是起價。實際價格可能會高一些，但通常都低於起價。

這種情況通常發生於價錢較高、議價空間較大的商品，像是房子及車子。它們的起價通常都很高，因為賣方知道這個價格會被買方殺價。這些都是銷售策略中的一部分。美國人都很自豪他們達成好交易的能力，所以通常起價都會偏高，這讓賣方即使碰到殺價，都還能小賺一筆。

Business Use

The asking price may actually be paid by a few, but it's usually only the starting point for serious negotiations.

商業用法 實際上，有些人可能會以起價達成交易，但起價通常是嚴肅談判的起點。

Alternatives 相關用語

◇ sticker price	標籤價格
◇ advertised price	廣告價格
◇ posted price	公告價格

consumer price

消費者價格

MP3-132

Idiom Definition

This is the price paid by a customer in a retail store.

成語定義 這是消費者在零售店中所支付的價格。

Word Definition Used

"consumer price" is a term as well as an idiom, meaning the above.

使用的字詞定義

「consumer price」這個詞，也是個慣用語，有著上面所解釋的意思。

Examples

例 Sales increased dramatically when the consumer price was lowered.

當消費者價格降低時，銷售量會大大提升。

....

例 The consumer price is always high on the first line of a new product.

新產品剛剛推出時，總是有很高的消費者價格。（表示消費者願意花高價購買）

....

Background

This business term is formed with the basic dictionary definitions and a few shortcuts. If we restore the deleted language, the meaning is clear. The price the manufacture expects the consumer to pay in most retail stores under normal circumstances.

背景資料 這個商業術語是由基本字典定義和些許意思縮短所形成。如果我們把減掉的字都加回去的話，意思會很清楚。這個詞的意思就是：在正常情況下，製造商希望消費者在大多數零售店所需支付的價格。

Business Use

In conferences on marketing strategies, the consumer price is important. Either in terms of the competition prices, or if the product is unique, people in the meeting try to guess the most the general public would to pay for it.

商業用法 在制定行銷策略的會議中，消費者價格一詞非常重要。不管是考量到競爭價格或產品本身非常獨特，與會者會嘗試猜想大多數的消費者，會願意為這種產品支付多少價格。

Alternatives 相關用語

◇ retail cost	零售價格
◇ the cost to the end user	最終使用者成本
◇ cost to the general public	一般大眾成本

pull the fat out of the fire
解救危機

MP3-133

Idiom Definition

To save something from being lost and/or ruined.

成語定義 拯救某物，使其免於遺失或毀壞。

Examples

例 Our new IT man really pulled the fat out of the fire for us.

新資訊科技人員真的為我們公司解決了許多問題。

例 She's sharp; she's pulled the fat out of the fire more than once.

她非常精明能幹，不只一次為大家解救危機。

Background

The common definitions apply but it makes no sense to modern business people. This goes back to when man cooked over an open fire. Animal fat is very flavorful and used in cooking to baste meat and add flavor to vegetables.

Sometimes a piece of fat is placed on a lean portion of meat to keep it moist while it cooks. If the fat falls into the fire, it burns and its flavor is lost. So, pulling the fat quickly out of the fire before it burns is saving the meal.

背景資料 這個表達法可以用一般的定義來加以解釋，但那樣的解釋對於現在的商業人士來說，沒有什麼道理。這個表達法要追溯歷史，當時的人們在野外生火煮食。動物的油脂可以為食物增添許多口感，常常用在肉類的烹調中，或者用來為蔬菜增添味道。

有時候，一片肥肉會被放置在一片瘦肉上，用以在烹調的過程中保持瘦肉的滋潤度。如果肥肉掉到火裡面，就會被燒乾，那麼它的味道就會消失，所以很快地把肥肉撿起來，避免它被燒乾，就拯救一餐飯，免於口感全失。

Business Use

Few know where this idiom comes from, but it still gets a lot of use in rural and southern America. It means that, for a while, things were looking bad, but some action or string of events has turned things around.

商業用法 幾乎沒有人知道這個慣用語的由來，但這個表達法仍常常被引用，尤其是在鄉村及美國南方。這表示有一陣子，事情看起來很糟糕，但有人採取一些行動或發生了一些事情，而使事情的狀況好轉。

Alternatives 相關用語

◇ a shoestring catch	些微之差，差點保不住
◇ we saved it	我們保住了它
◇ we pulled it off	我們做到了耶！

pull the plug

停止（某事）

Idiom Definition

This means to suddenly stop, call a halt to or end something.

成語定義 這個表達法的意思是突然喊停、暫停或結束一件事。

Word Definition Used

"pull the plug" is a term as well as an idiom meaning the above.

使用的字詞定義

「pull the plug」這個詞，也是個慣用語，有著上面所解釋的意思。

Examples

例 It was losing money so I pulled the plug.
那是虧錢生意，所以我就把它停了。

例 We have six months to show a profit, or the boss pulls the plug.
我們有六個月的時間來使這個計畫賺錢，否則老闆會喊停。

Background

The words "pull the plug" refer to pulling an electric plug out of a socket, thereby suddenly stopping the flow of electricity to an appliance, turning it off. This is a substitution; the energy is money and authorization from above, which feed the operation.

背景資料 這個表達語是從電子儀器的使用而來的，指的是把電子儀器的插頭拔掉，這樣一來，電子儀器的電源就會停止，也就是把儀器關掉的意思。這種表達是一項替代用法，意指公司的精力來源是上頭所撥下來的金錢和授權。

Business Use

When a venture proves unprofitable and is unlikely ever to show a return, someone has to decide to end it. When they do, this is the term they usually use.

商業用法 當公司不賺錢、而且顯示不太可能轉虧為盈時，就得有人決定要喊停。當這樣的事情發生時，人們就會用到這個表達語言。

Alternatives 相關用語

◇ reallocate the funds	資金重新分配
◇ cut funding	經費刪減
◇ kill it	把它宰了
◇ cut the juice	斷絕資源
◇ cut the cord	剪斷資源
◇ stop the bleeding	停止供應
◇ cut your losses	停止損失
◇ dump it	丟掉吧
◇ cut it loose	放掉吧

punch list
問題清單

Idiom Definition

This is a list of defects or problems discovered with a recently completed construction job.

成語定義 這個詞是指一個表格，列出某件最近完成建築工作的缺失或問題。

Word Definition Used

"punch" to hit or do quickly

"punch list" is a term as well as an idiom, meaning the above.

使用的字詞定義

" punch" 這個字是打，或快速做某事的意思。
「punch list」這個詞，也是個慣用語，有著上面所解釋的意思。

Examples

例 I'll have this punch list faxed to your office by tomorrow.

我明天會叫人把問題清單傳真到你辦公室去。

....

例 You don't get a cent until the punch list is complete.

除非把問題清單中的事都解決了，否則你一毛錢也拿不到。

....

Background

This is a term unique to construction. It's a list of defects that must be fixed before the contractor is paid, so he's highly motivated to get it done. He gives each item a quick knockout punch, or repair, and moves on to the next.

背景資料 這個詞專門用在營造業方面。此表格列出一些建築商在請款之前，必須修理的事項，因為是請款之前，建築商才會比較積極。建築商會很快地修理每個項目，逐一完成表格列出的項目。

Business Use

This idiom is indispensable in construction, yet it's so specialized, it's not in the dictionary.

商業用法 這個慣用語在營造業中非常重要，但因為過於專業，所以沒有列在字典中。

Alternatives 相關用語

◇ call back list　　　　　　　抱怨代辦事項

P

put one over
對…惡作劇

MP3-136

Idiom Definition

This is used when the speaker wants to tell someone he or she was able to fool or trick someone.

成語定義　這個詞的使用場合是當說話者想要告訴某個人，他成功地愚弄了別人。

Word Definition Used

"put one over" is a term as well as an idiom. When these exact words are used this way, they take on the unique meaning above.

使用的字詞定義　「put one over」這個詞也是一個慣用語。當這幾個字一起使用時，便會有上面提到的獨特意義。

Examples

例 Are you trying to put one over on the old man?
　你是不是要對那個老人惡作劇？

....

例 I tried to put one over on him but he caught me.
　我試著要對他惡作劇，但被他逮到了。

....

Background

In the past, when farmers brought crops and livestock to market, they had to find a buyer and show their goods were of good quality. If the buyer didn't like what he saw, he'd close negotiations by dropping the bar, or closing his gate to the goods he didn't want.

If the farmer could sneak one more over the bar before the final tally was done, he'd get paid for one the buyer rejected. This is a very old idiom but it still gets a lot of service even if few people know where it comes from.

背景資料 在過去，當農夫們把農作物和牲口帶到市集時，他們必須找買家，然後讓他們看到所要買的東西品質很好。如果買家不喜歡自己看到的東西，他可能會把關牲口的門把關上，藉以表示他不想再議價了。

如果農夫能夠在最後交易計數時，成功地把幾隻牲口偷運過門把，那麼儘管買家拒買某隻牲口，農夫還是可能拿得到錢。這個用語非常古老，很少有人知道它的由來，但至今還是廣為使用。

Business Use

It's now widely used and still actually means to successfully fool someone although it seldom has anything to do with farmers selling their product.

商業用法 儘管這個詞和農夫販賣牲口已經沒有什麼關係，這個用法現在仍廣為使用，用來指「成功地愚弄某人」。

Alternatives 相關用語

◇ sneak in when nobody's looking 趁沒人注意時偷溜進去

◇ slip one past him　　　　　　繞過他偷偷過去

◇ running a scam　　　　　　　佈置騙局

Q every quarter
每一季

Idiom Definition

This means to do something once each three months, or approximately every 90 days.

成語定義 這個表達法的意思是説，做某事的週期是每三個月或大約每九十天。

Word Definition Used

"Every quarter" is a term as well as an idiom. When these exact words are used this way, they take on the unique meaning above.

使用的字詞定義 「every quarter」這個詞也是一個慣用語。當這幾個字一起使用時，便會有上面提到的獨特意義。

Examples

例 We have a minor in-house audit every quarter to check our status.

我們每季會有一次內部稽查，查看公司的情況。

例 Business taxes are paid every quarter in the U.S.

在美國，商業稅每季付一次。

Background

Accountants divide the year into four roughly equal periods. Each period is about 25% or 1/4 of a year also referred to as a quarter-year.

背景資料 會計師把一年大約分為四個時期，每個時期是一年的四分之一，又稱為四分之一年。

Business Use

Every quarter is a fiscal term referring to three months, or approximately 25% of the year. This is usually computed from the first day of each quarter to the last day of the third month.

The quarters usually start in January, April, July and October, but, a quarter could be any three consecutive months, and start on any day of the month, so long as it's consistent.

商業用法 「每季」是一個會計名詞，指的是每三個月，或大約是一年的四分之一。計算方法是從每一季的第一天到三個月的最後一天。
每季通常開始於一月、四月、七月及十月，但一季可以是任何三個連月，也可以從任何一天開始計算，只要算法一樣就可以。

Alternatives 相關用語

◇ every ninety days	每九十天
◇ four times a year	一年四次

Q no quarter is asked for and none will be given
不可能也沒有機會求饒

MP3-138

Idiom Definition

In war, this is the idiom usually used to describe a fight where no forgiveness or mercy will be asked for or given, a fight to the death. In business, it's a contest that will not stop until one side has won.

成語定義 在戰爭中，這個詞通常用來描述一場打鬥，其特色是不可能有機會要求會對敵人手下留情，這是一場生死之鬥。在商業上，這個詞意指一場比賽，不到其中一方獲得勝利，不會有人罷手。

Word Definition Used

"quarter" mercy or forgiveness

使用的字詞定義 "quarter" 寬恕或饒命

Examples

例 It's us against them; no quarter is asked for and none will be given.

這是我們對他們的爭戰，不可能也沒有機會求饒，一定要分出勝負。

例 No quarter is asked for and none given; we don't slow down or stop until the other guy is beaten and out of the running.

不可能、也不會求饒，除非敵手倒地不起或退出比賽，否則我們絕不鬆手或停止。

Background

Here, the word "quarter" uses a very old definition that we seldom see any more, meaning mercy or forgiveness.

背景資料 在這裡，quarter 這個字所用的定義是現在很少見的，指的是寬恕或饒命。

Business Use

This idiom, when used in business, means every trick that could gain an advantage over the other side will be used. Playing fair does not matter; only winning does. It's a short version for what's between the quotation marks. "This is important; we need to win this one. So the gloves are off on this project. We play to win.?

商業用法 當用在商場上時，這個詞的意思是敵對雙方會不擇手段來贏過對方。公平競賽不再是重點，最後誰贏是唯一重點。這個用語已經被簡化，原來的說法是「這個比賽很重要，我們必須要贏，所以把禮貌、文明都擺到一邊去，這場遊戲的目的就是要贏。」

Alternatives 相關用語

◇ play to win	要玩就要贏
◇ the gloves are off	文明暫且丟到一邊
◇ take no prisoners	不俘虜任何敵人、全部殺光
◇ play for keeps	守住要塞，不讓對方得手
◇ go for the gold	目的是得金牌

R swimming in red ink
在紅色墨水裡載浮載沉

MP3-139

Idiom Definition

This is used to describe when a project or company is rapidly losing a great deal of money.

成語定義 這個詞用來描述一個計畫、一家公司正快速地損失金錢。

Word Definition Used

"red ink" is a term as well as an idiom, meaning the company or project is losing money.

使用的字詞定義

「red ink」這個詞也是一個慣用語，指一個計畫或一家公司正在虧錢。

Examples

例 After a year of swimming in red ink, we made it into the black.

在紅色墨水中載浮載沉一年之後，我們終於轉虧為盈了。

例 We were swimming in red ink, so we did some serious cost cutting.

我們以前曾在紅色墨水中載浮載沉，所以做了很多成本縮減。

Background

Accountants used to post losses with red ink to prevent them from being misread as profit, so using red ink means you're losing money.

背景資料 以前，會計師們會用紅色墨水來指出虧損，以防大家把虧損誤讀為利潤，所以用紅墨水這個表達法被引申為虧錢。

Business Use

To say you're swimming in red ink indicates the losses are so bad that the accountant needs enough red ink for a man to swim in to record them all. This is often used in a semi humorous way, but it is nonetheless dead serious.

商業用法 當你說自己在紅色墨水中載浮載沉，你的意思是說你損失慘重，你的會計師所用的紅色墨水都多到可以讓人在其中游泳了。這個詞是一種常用的詼諧詞語，但情況其實是很嚴重的。

Alternatives 相關用語

◇ floundering in red ink	在紅色墨水中掙扎
◇ floundering	掙扎中
◇ going down for the third time	第三次倒下了
◇ all at sea	沉沒於大海之中
◇ sinking	沉溺
◇ sinking fast	快速沉溺
◇ drowning in red ink	被紅色墨水淹沒
◇ awash in a sea of red ink	被紅色墨水覆蓋

R   retainage
暫扣款

Idiom Definition

This is used to describe that portion of a construction payment kept by the client until the contractor has completed all punch lists to the satisfaction of the client.

成語定義 這個詞指的是建築商在完成客戶所指定的「問題清單」及其滿意度之前，所被扣住的款項。

Word Definition Used

"Retainage" is a term as well as an idiom meaning the above.

使用的字詞定義 「retainage」這個詞也是慣用語，有上面所述之意。

Examples

例 I'll pay the retainage as soon as you complete this punch list.

只要你一完成問題清單上的項目，我就會把暫扣款付清。

例 No contractor will accept more than 15 % retainage.

沒有任何一家承包商會接受高於百分之十五的暫扣款。

This word is unique to construction, and isn't in the dictionary. When the contractor is paid off, the client usually retains 10%, until the punch lists and callbacks are done.

This is to assure the contractor has a reason to take care of any problems quickly. Because this money is retained by the client, it is referred to as retainage. It may be a politically correct term, but use goes back to before the term "politically correct" became popular.

背景資料 這個詞只適用於營造業，並不在字典中。當顧客付錢給承包商時，通常會扣下百分之十的款項，直到所有問題清單上的工作項目完成為止，才將此款項付清。

這樣做是為了要確保承包商會把所有問題盡快解決。由於這個款項會被顧客暫扣，所以被稱為「暫扣款」。這也許是一個買賣公平的正確用字，但其歷史比所謂的「買賣公平」觀念要來的更早。

Business Use

In most contracts, the largest payment is made upon substantial completion, or when the contractor says all the construction work is done. There usually is some clean up work and equipment removal to do, but the building part is over. The contractor is then paid off except for the retainage.

商業用法 在大多數的合約中，最大的款項是在工程絕大部分都完成之後付清，或當承包商說他們已經完成工作時付清。此時，儘管通常工程部分已經完成，仍有一些善後或機器調動的工作尚未結束，因此承包商所得到的款項是扣除了暫扣款後的數目。

Alternatives 相關用語

◇ surety bond	受到保證的束縛
◇ performance bond	受到表現的束縛

get the ball rolling
開始進行某事

`MP3-141`

Idiom Definition

This is used to describe when the speaker wants to start things moving, or create activity in an area that should not be quiet.

成語定義 這個表達法用來描述當說話者希望某事開始進行,或想要在過於安靜的情況下,帶動一些氣氛。

Word Definition Used

"all" is substituted for the matter under discussion.
"rolling" moving

使用的字詞定義

"ball" 代替目前正在討論的事。
"rolling" 滾動

Examples

例 She was hired to get the ball rolling again.

雇用她是為了重新帶動這件事。

例 If we don't get the ball rolling, we'll be out of work.

如果我們再不開始這件事,可能會失業的。

Background

Obviously, if you are discussing work, there is no ball involved, so there is also nothing to physically roll. The word "all" refers to whatever the topic at hand is. It could be a business, project, idea, activity, game or anything else. And the word "rolling" is also a substitute for whatever action should be going on.

It comes from the playground or sports field where games often use balls which are kept in constant motion for the duration of the game. The term implies that motion is needed. On the playground or sports field, it's fun; in business, it is productive work.

背景資料 很明顯的，如果你在談論正事，當然不會用到「球」這個字，所以也不可能真正去滾動什麼東西。「球」這個字在這裡指的是人們所討論的事，可能是一筆生意、一個計畫、一個想法、一個活動、一個遊戲或其他等。「滾動」也是一個替代詞，意指應該進行的事。

這個詞來自遊樂場或運動場，在這兩個場所中，遊戲的進行常常會用到球，當遊戲進行時，球應該一直保持滾動的狀態。這個用法暗示聽話的人應該要採取某種行動。在遊樂場或運動場，這個表達語很好玩，但在商業用語中，這個詞指的是要有生產力。

Business Use

This term means the people involved aren't doing enough and any activity would be better than no activity.

商業用法 這個詞指的是某活動中的人們沒有在做事，在這種情況下，採取任何行動都比沒有行動要好。

Alternatives 相關用語

◇ light a fire under them	在他們屁股上點把火吧
◇ hold their feet to the fire	把他們的腳綁在火邊
◇ get things moving	開始動作了吧

R on the ropes
岌岌可危

Idiom Definition

This is used to describe when someone or something is in the process of losing, and about to be knocked out.

成語定義 這個表達語描述某人或某事可能面對失敗或一敗塗地的結果。

Word Definition Used

"on the ropes" is a term as well as an idiom. When these exact words are used this way, they take on the unique meaning above.

使用的字詞定義

「on the ropes」這個詞,也是個慣用語,當 on the ropes 這幾個字一起使用時,有著上述之意。

Examples

例 We're on the ropes now; we need this sale to stay in business.

我們現在岌岌可危了,需要這筆生意才撐得下去。

例 He was on the ropes, and then he got this account and saved his job.

他當時岌岌可危,後來得到這個大客戶,才保住了工作。

Background

This term describes a boxer doing poorly. Leaning on the ropes hampers mobility and is only done when a boxer is tired and/or injured. A key to winning a boxing match is to stay in the center of the ring so you can move, avoid attacks and launch your own. If a boxer is using the ropes for support, he's also reducing his ability to avoid blows.

背景資料 這個詞描述拳擊手的表現節節敗退。當拳擊手退守到拳擊台旁邊的繩索上時，他的移動空間就會受到限制，所以這種情形只有在拳擊手疲倦或受傷時，才會發生。在拳擊賽中獲勝的關鍵是讓自己留在拳擊台的中央，這樣才可以自由移動，躲避敵人的攻擊或計畫自己的出擊。如果一個拳擊手需要繩索來支撐自己的話，那他躲避敵手攻擊的空間也會縮小。

Business Use

This is used to indicate a business or individual in serious trouble.

商業用法 這個表達語用來指出某個公司或個人正面臨很大的麻煩。

Alternatives 相關用語

◇ last gasp	最後的喘息機會
◇ circling the drain	持續消耗
◇ going down for the third time	第三次敗北了
◇ running out of air	上氣不接下氣
◇ in trouble	麻煩大了

R run this (tactic) on
把這個（策略）用在⋯

MP3-143

Idiom Definition

This is used when the speaker is suggesting someone try something on someone, to attempt to run a ploy as part of an attack or a scheme to gain something.

成語定義 這個表達語用在當說話者要建議他人做某種嘗試，或嘗試某種方法，來攻擊或得到其他東西。

Word Definition Used

"run" to play something like a trick or scheme

"tactic" whatever the strategy may be

使用的字詞定義

"run" 對他人開玩笑或用計謀

"tactic" 策略、計謀

Examples

例 Why don't you run this on Jean? I still owe her one for last week.

你為什麼不在吉兒身上試試看這個呢？她上星期還欠我一次呢。

例 You can try to run this delaying tactic on Joe, but I doubt it'll work.

你可以在喬身上試試看這個拖延戰術，但我想不會成功。

Background

The correct definition for the word "run" is to use a strategy.

背景資料 「run」這個字在這裡的正確定義是使用某種策略。

Business Use

Using this idiom indicates the entire operation, from beginning to end, is all planned to achieve a specific effect.

商業用法 用這個慣用語是指整件事，從開始到結束，都計畫著要達成某種效果。

Alternatives 相關用語

◇ give it a shot	試試看吧
◇ nothing ventured, nothing gained	不試試看又怎麼知道呢？
◇ see if it works	試試看有沒有用
◇ the old college try	試試看老把戲

running the numbers
統計數字

MP3-144

Idiom Definition

This is used to describe when someone is doing the computations needed to find the information.

成語定義 這個詞描述某個人為了要找資料,而去做一些計算動作。

Word Definition Used

"running" taking basic information, then organizing and analyzing it until you get as complete a picture as possible from it

"running the numbers" is a term as well as an idiom. When these exact words are used this way, they take on the unique meaning above.

使用的字詞定義

"running" 拿到基本資料,加以組織、分析,盡可能得到完整的了解為止。

「running the numbers」這個詞,也是個慣用語,當這幾個字一起使用時,有上述的意思。

Examples

例 I finished running the numbers, and we're in great shape.

我把數字統計好了,目前狀況極佳。

例 He spent all night running the numbers, trying to make it work.

他花了整個晚上計算數字,試著把數字算對。

Background

The success or failure for any business venture is measured by its profitability. It's the computing that is done by taking the raw data and running it through an adding machine to get the needed information.

背景資料　任何一家公司的成功或失敗都取決於公司獲利。當公司把所有初步數字精算之後,才能得出有關獲利的資料。

Business Use

It applies to two actions, preparing a profit and loss statement, or a profitability study for a proposed project. To determine a business's status, its profit and loss history must be reviewed.

Likewise, the viability of a possible business venture is studied by projecting its assumed expenses and income in a mock profit and loss statement based on available data and market studies. Doing either is called running the numbers.

商業用法　這個用語可以用在兩個方面:準備損益表或研究一個提案的獲利率。要定義公司的狀況,就必須審視公司的損益歷史。

同時,一個商業計畫的可行性必須加以預測,利用可得的資料及市場研究,加上開支及收入,來預測可能的損益。這兩種作法都稱為統計數字。

Alternatives 相關用語

◇ do the math	你自己算算
◇ run the numbers	統計數字
◇ give it to the bean counters	把這個交給統計員或櫃員

S

save a step
省個步驟

Idiom Definition

This is used to describe when a process is analyzed in the hope it's possible to reduce the steps needed to produce a product.

成語定義 這個用語描述人們分析一個過程，其目的在於找出是否可能減少製造產品的步驟。

Word Definition Used

"save" eliminate

"step" operation

使用的字詞定義
"save" 減少
"step" 營運；操作

Examples

例 That will save a step and really help the bottom line.

那樣做能省個步驟，對底線有所幫助。

例 If we can save a step, maybe we can avoid a price hike.

如果我們可以省個步驟的話，也許可以避免價格上升。

Background

To eliminate a manufacturing step without losing quality is very desirable. To do so with a minor loss of quality but still make a product that falls within specifications is almost as good. It means an increased profit or lower consumer price.

背景資料 若公司可以在不損及品質的情況下,減少製造步驟,這是很好的事。或某種作法只引起些微品質損失,但所製造的產品仍在規格之內,也還是不錯的作法。這代表公司可以增加獲利或減低消費者價格。

Business Use

An eliminated step saves time and money by reducing costs. This applies to steps eliminated in the idea, planning or testing phases. That means an increased profit or lower consumer price.

商業用法 減少步驟是透過減低成本來省時、省錢。這適用於減少某個構思、計畫或測試階段的步驟。這也意味著獲利增加或消費者價格減低。

Alternatives 相關用語

◇ save a step or two	減少一兩個步驟
◇ cut out a step	跳過一個步驟
◇ trim down operations	把操作過程縮減

S

have a seat
請坐

MP3-146

Idiom Definition

This is used when the speaker gives someone an invitation to sit down.

成語定義 這個詞是說話者邀請對方坐下時的用語。

Examples

例 Please come in and have a seat.

請進,請坐。

例 You're welcome to have a seat and take a rest.

你可以坐下來、休息一下。

Background

This is included here because some words are omitted, and treated as understood, which may cause foreign students some confusion. Used as an invitation, this should start with please, but it doesn't . As a command, it could be used as is.

背景資料 儘管這句話中有些字省略了,但大家都了解它的意思,所以有時對外國學生可能造成困擾,因此把這個詞囊括在這裡。當這句話用來當作邀請時,這句話應該要加上 please〈請〉,但通常都省略了。如果當成命令,它的用法如上。

Business Use

This is the most common phrase used to order or invite someone to sit down. Tone, facial expression and context are the only way to tell how it's being used.

商業用法 在邀請或命令他人坐下時,這是最常用的表達法,要知道使用者的用意,必須從語調、面部表情及使用場合來判斷。

Alternatives 相關用語

◇ take a load off	休息一下吧
◇ grab a seat	找張椅子坐
◇ sit down	坐下
◇ make yourself comfortable	讓自己自在點

S

dead serious
非常嚴肅、認真

MP3-147

Idiom Definition

This is used to describe someone as being as intent and on purpose as possible, allowing no room for play.

成語定義 這個用語用來描述某個人對正在做的事，盡可能的專注，沒有玩樂的空間。

Word Definition Used

"dead" completely, nothing is open to interpretation, nor is there a possibility of error

使用的字詞定義
"dead" 指的是「完全」，沒有商量的餘地，也不可能出錯。

Examples

例 I'm not playing this time. I'm dead serious on this stuff.

我這次不是開玩笑的，我對這事非常認真。

例 This is dead serious; we need to get this done on time.

這件事非常嚴肅，我們需要準時完成這件事。

Background

A look at the definition used for the word dead should answer any questions.

背景資料 只要看到這個表達法中的 dead 這個字，這個表達法就不說自明了。

Business Use

This is used when the speaker wants to make it clear that all concern should concentrate on their job. It's a short version for what's between the quotation marks. "The time for games is past. We have to focus on the job and get it done right".

商業用法 當說話者想表明他們想把所有注意力放在工作上時，會用這個說法。這個用法的原文是「玩樂的時刻已經過去，我們必須把注意力放在工作上，把工作做好。」

Alternatives: 相關用語

◇ must win	非贏不可
◇ no holds barred	不能空手而回
◇ do or die	不做就死吧
◇ take no prisoners	沒有任何餘地

set up fees
修改費用

MP3-148

Idiom Definition

This is used to describe the cost of modifying a production line to produce a product.

成語定義 這個用法用來描述修正產品生產線所需花費的成本。

Word Definition Used

"set up" is all by itself a term meaning to make ready.

"set up fees" is a term as well as an idiom. When these exact words are used this way, they take on the unique meaning above.

使用的字詞定義

"set up" 這個字本身的意思是「準備」。

「set up fees」 這個詞，也是個慣用語。當這些字一起使用時，有上述之意。

Examples

例 If you double the order, I'll reduce the set up fees.

如果你把訂單數字乘二，我會把修改費用降低。

例 If I don't charge set up fees, I have to increase the unit price.

如果我不收取修改費用，就必須加高單價。

Background

Few machines are dedicated to producing only one item and nothing else. Whenever a new product is to be made, the machinery and production line have to be changed in some way, and that costs money. It's time spent not producing an income-generating product, which has to be paid for.

In some cases the customer is charged, in others the manufacturer pays. This refers to the cost of preparing the work area to produce a new product.

背景資料 很少機器只用來製造單一產品。因此每當要生產新產品時，機器設備和生產線就必須做某個程度的變動，這樣的過程需要花錢。廠商所花的時間並不是用來生產會賺錢的產品，而是做一些改變，這樣的花費還是要有人負擔。

有些時候，這筆錢要由顧客負擔，有時則由廠商負擔。這種費用是花在準備生產新產品的工作上。

Business Use

This idiom is indispensable in preparing proposals and invoices.

商業用法 這個詞在準備提案或報價時，是不可或缺的詞語。

S

Let's shake on it.
就這麼握手說定了。

MP3-149

Idiom Definition

This is used when an agreement is reached.

成語定義 這個表達法用在協議達成的時候。

Examples

例 That's a deal I can live with; let's shake on it.

這是個我可以接受的交易，就這麼握手說定了。

例 I think we can both make money with this deal; let's shake on it.

我想我們雙方都可以在這場交易中獲利，就這麼握手說定了。

Background

It's customary to shake hands when an agreement is successfully reached, and the word "shake" is a short cut meaning, "shake hands." Negotiations are always ended with a handshake.

背景資料 當成功做成一筆交易時，人們通常都會握手，在這個表達法中的 shake 指的是「握手」。當談判結束時，人們通常會握手。

Business Use

If a major player stops the talks with an exclamation,

357

"let's shake on it." It means he's agreed to the other's terms and there's a deal in place. If it's used as a question one party is asking if the other agrees to the terms as stated.

商業用法 如果交易中的主角在用這個表達法時，採取高亢的語氣，這表示他同意另一方的條件，交易已經達成。

Alternatives 相關用語

◇ Do we have a deal?　　　　我們達成交易了嗎？

◇ I think we have a deal.
我想我們剛剛達成交易了。

◇ Then it's agreed.　　　　那麼就這樣說定了。

◇ I think we're done.　　　　我想我們就這麼說定了。

◇ It was good doing business with you.
很高興能和你做生意。

(our) market share
（我們）的市佔率

MP3-150

Idiom Definition

This is used to describe the portion of sales in an area handled by one company, or that company's share of the market.

成語定義 這個表達法用來描述一家公司在一個地區所處理的銷售率，也就是該公司的市佔率。

Examples

例 With seven major players in the American market, we have a 22% market share, so we have more than our fair share.

美國市場中有七個主要廠商，我們有百分之二十二的市佔率，所以我們的比率比應有的要高。

例 I think if we have a sale twice a year we can increase our market share.

我想如果我們希望一年辦兩次特賣，那麼就可以增加我們的市佔率。

Background

Simply stated, market share is the fast and easy way to say the company's piece of the pie.

背景資料 簡單來說，市佔率是描述公司角色比重的一種簡單、快速的說法。

Business Use

This idiom is very important in finding out a product, or company's impact in the area it operates in. The number of units sold tells a lot, but it could be deceptive. Market share is an excellent way to get right to the core of the issue.

For Examples, if you have a 35% market share in a two-company competition, you aren't doing well but 35% in an eight-company race is very good.

商業用法　這個慣用語非常重要，因為它可以讓人們瞭解，某個產品或公司在其市場中的影響力。銷售數字顯示了許多訊息，但也可能造成假象。市佔率是直接點出議題的好方法。

舉例來說，如果在一場只有兩家競爭者的競賽中，你有 35% 的市佔率，這成績不是很好。但同樣的數字拿到了一個有八家競爭者的市場中，就是很不錯的表現了。

Alternatives 相關用語

◇ Our share of the pie	我們擁有的比率
◇ our end	我們這一方
◇ our cut	我們的比率

S sharpen (my) pencil
削尖（我的）鉛筆

MP3-151

Idiom Definition

This is used when the speaker wants to review a bid with the intention of lowering the price to make it more competitive.

成語定義 當説話者用到這個表達語時，他是想要再度審視一個投標，想要看看是否可以降低價格，讓投標更具競爭性。

Word Definition Used

"sharpen" to trim off the excess, make smaller and more exact

"sharpen my pencil" is a term as well as an idiom. When these exact words are used this way, they take on the unique meaning above.

使用的字詞定義

"sharpen" 把多餘的東西去除掉，讓東西變得更小、更準確。

「sharpen my pencil」是一個詞，也是一個慣用語。當這些字一起使用時，便會有上面提到的獨特意義。

Examples

例 Let me go home and sharpen my pencil; I'm sure I can do better.

讓我回家好好削尖我的鉛筆，我確信我可以做得更好。

例 I think if I sharpen my pencil, I can beat that price.

我想如果我可以削尖我的鉛筆，我可以提供更好的價格。

Background

This idiom is also a term, formed with a substantiation reasoned like this. You sharpen a pencil by shaving wood off the tip, and you make your bid more competitive by shaving the cost. Therefore, the more you sharpen your pencil, the sharper you make your bid.

背景資料 這個慣用語也是一個詞，其背後的含意是這樣的。當你削鉛筆時，你是把鉛筆的木頭部分削掉，你也可以藉由降低成本，來使你的投標更具競爭力。因此，鉛筆削得越尖，你的投標就會越好。

Business Use

This idiom is used quite a bit, always with the definition shown above.

商業用法 這個慣用語經常被使用，通常意思都如上所述。

Alternatives 相關用語

◇ Trim this down	把這個減少一點
◇ juice up my bid	把投標弄得更好一點
◇ work the numbers	好好計算一下數字
◇ play with the numbers	好好算一下數字
◇ let me see what I can do	我看看能做些什麼
◇ let me try it again	讓我再試試看
◇ sweeten the bid	把投標弄得誘人一點

S

shave the price
降低價格

MP3-152

Idiom Definition

This is used by the speaker to describe when he or she wants to reduce the price on an item being marketed.

成語定義 當講者話者想要降低他所想要販賣的商品時，會用這個表達法。

Word Definition Used

"shave" to make a little smaller

使用的字詞定義

"shave" 指的是把東西弄小一點。

Examples

例 We can shave the price a little to make this deal work.
我們可以把價格降低一點，來促成這個交易。

例 We shaved the price as much as we could, and made up the difference.
我們已經盡可能地降低價格，把價差拉近。

Background

This is a substitution idiom, the word "shave" indicates a reduced price, but only slightly smaller, not drastically cut. Sometimes, the word is used satirically to indicate the opposite. The speakers tone, body language and facial expression make the meaning clear.

背景資料 這是一個替代性說法，文中的 shave 這個字指的是降低價格，但通常降幅不大。用這個表達語時，通常都有點諷刺意味，意指相反的東西。說話者的語氣、肢體語言和面部表情，會讓這個表達法的意思更為清楚。

Business Use

This is used to indicate the price is made smaller, but more of an adjustment than a heavy cut.

商業用法 用這個表達法來指出價格已經降低，但調降的原因比較偏向「調整」意味，而不是大幅砍價。

Alternatives 相關用語

| ◇ at a reduced price | 降低價格 |
| ◇ made more competitive | 讓價格變得更有競爭性 |

shop around
到處比價看看

Idiom Definition

This is used to describe the action of going to different places or shops to compare the prices and services of several sources before buying.

成語定義　用這個表達語來描述在做出購買決定前，到處比較價格或服務品質。

Word Definition Used

"shop around" is a term as well as an idiom meaning the above.

使用的字詞定義

「shop around」是一個詞，也是一個慣用語，有著上述的意思。

Examples 例句

例 I'm shopping around for another source. Would you like to submit a bid?

我正在到處比價，找尋另一個供應商，你想要報個價嗎？

例 It's a good price, but I do have to shop around a bit.

這價格不錯，但我必須再到處比價看看。

Background

The term "shopping around" is an old one from the common sector meaning, comparison-shopping.

背景資料　「到處比價」是個適用於一般產業的古老表達語，意思就是價格的比較。

Business Use

In business circles, it's sometimes used like a joke, but the speaker is usually very serious.

商業用法　商業領域中，有時用法較為戲謔，但說話者通常都很嚴肅。

Alternatives 相關用語

◇ look around	到處看看
◇ see what else is out there	看看市場中有什麼東西
◇ test the waters	感覺一下市場價格
◇ solicit competitive bids	向場商索取價格

shopping list

購物單

MP3-154

Idiom Definition

This is used to describe a list of goods and/or services needed.

成語定義 這個詞用來描述説話者所需要的產品或服務清單。

Word Definition Used

"shopping list" is a term as well as an idiom, meaning the above.

使用的字詞定義

「shopping list」是一個詞,也是一個慣用語,有著上述的意思。

Examples

例 I have a whole shopping list of talents the new man needs to have.

對於新人要有的才能,我可有一整個清單呢。

例 The boss gave me a whole shopping list of items I have to research.

老闆給我一整張清單,列出了我要搜尋的項目。

Background

The idiom is an old term from the common sector

specifically meaning a number of items, services and or abilities needed.

背景資料 這個慣用語適用於一般產業，歷史頗為悠久，意思是好幾項需要的產品、服務或能力。

Business Use

In business circles, this is usually said with a smile, but don't let that fool you. The speaker is usually quite serious. A shopping list is an actual list of desired things, but they may or may not be available in a store.

For Examples, if the company needs a new director of training, the executives may compile a list of personality traits the replacement should have, and refer to it as a shopping list.

商業用法 在商業界中，說這句話時，通常會面帶微笑，但別被這個表情給騙了。說話者還是很嚴肅的。一張「購物清單」實際列有說話者所想要的東西，但在店裡面有可能找不到。

舉例來說，如果公司需要一個新的訓練主管，公司高層可能會收集一張人格特性清單，其中列有候選人需要的特色，並將這種清單稱為「購物清單」。

Alternatives 相關用語

◇ wish list	希望購買的物品清單
◇ criteria	購物標準
◇ bill of particulars	特別要購買的物品
◇ Christmas list	聖誕節禮物清單
◇ things we need from Santa	希望聖誕老公公送的東西
◇ The list is endless, so I'll stop here. 這一類型的詞語很多，在此就不多列了。	

stand your ground
堅守立場

Idiom Definition

This is used by the speaker to encourage someone to maintain his or her position despite verbal attacks specifically mounted to get them to change their mind.

成語定義 說話者用這個表達語來鼓勵他人，不管受到他人怎麼樣的言語攻擊，都要堅持自己的立場，不要改變自己的想法。

Word Definition Used

"stand" to remain where you are physically and or intellectually

"ground" one's position physically and or intellectually

"stand your ground" is a term as well as an idiom. When these exact words are used this way, they take on the unique meaning above.

使用的字詞定義

"stand" 意指你要保持處自己身體或理智的立場

"ground" 是一個人身體或理智所處之地

「stand your ground」是一個詞，也是一個慣用語。當這些字一起使用時，便會有上面提到的獨特意義。

Examples

例 He doesn't like you, but if you stand your ground, he'll respect you.

他不喜歡你，但如果你堅持自己的立場，他會尊敬你的。

例 No matter what happens, stand your ground and

you'll be fine.
不管發生什麼事，只要堅持立場，你就會安然無事。

Background

This is a substantiation idiom; "stand your ground" is a term that comes from the military. When soldiers fought in ranks, they had to hold the ground they stood on regardless of what happened, and it's still used today with the same meaning. However, the use and meaning have expanded to nonmilitary situations.

背景資料 這是一個實體化的慣用語，「堅守立場」這個表達法來自軍隊用語，當不同軍階的軍人進行爭鬥時，不論發生什麼事，他們都必須堅守崗位。這個詞沿用至今日，仍有相同的意思，但其用法及意義都已衍伸到其他非軍事的場合上。

Business Use

The term meaning to hold your position in a fight means exactly the same thing in a business deal, or an argument. It means the subject should stay with his or her original desire or belief that they shouldn't change.

商業用法 這個詞的意思是要對方在爭鬥中，保持自己的立場，在商業界或爭論中，這個用語有一樣的意思，希望聽話的人能夠堅守自己原來的想法，不要有所改變。

Alternatives 相關用語

◇ maintain his position	堅持自己的立場
◇ stick by his guns	緊握槍枝，不要放棄
◇ hang in there	撐下去
◇ stand tall	昂首站著
◇ take a stand	表態
◇ hang tough	表現出強勢的樣子

stop the presses
把手邊的工作停下來

MP3-156

Idiom Definition

This is used to indicate recent news is very important and must be shared as soon as possible. It's also used in a semi humorous way to temporarily halt an ongoing process to make changes required by the recent news.

成語定義　這個表達語意指最近的新聞非常重要，必須儘快讓大家都知道。其用法也可以很詼諧，目的是要讓一個進行中的活動停下來，以便進行這個消息所帶來的改變。

Word Definition Used

"the presses" whatever you're doing, the task at hand

"stop the presses" is a term as well as an idiom. When these exact words are used this way, they take on the unique meaning above.

使用的字詞定義
"the presses" 指的是你手邊正在做的事
「stop the presses」是一個詞，也是一個慣用語。當這些字一起使用時，便會有上面提到的獨特意義。

Examples

例 Stop the presses. I never thought they'd go for that
停下你手邊的工作，我從未想過他們會做的那麼過分。

例 Stop the presses; we have to adjust the contract.

停下你手邊的工作，我們必須要調整合約內容。

Background

Using the definitions in a standard dictionary will get you the literal meaning, presses being printing presses. It's a dramatic metaphor based on a period of American history. In the late nineteenth century, competition between newspapers was fierce. Reporters didn't share information and papers fought to print the most current news.

When a paper is put to bed, that's the end of the writing process. To change anything meant what was printed would be thrown away and redone. However, some news was thought to be so important the printing process was halted and a new story put on the front page.

背景資料 如果你去查字典的話，你會查到 press 這個字的意思是「印刷機」，這個表達法是一個隱喻，源自美國歷史的一個時期，在十九世紀晚期，報社之間的競爭非常激烈，記者們不會互相分享訊息，報社之間競相印刷最新的新聞。
當一家報社下班時，通常撰寫新聞的過程也結束了。如果要做任何改變的話，已經印好的東西要全部報廢、丟棄。但有些新聞非常重要，重要到印刷過程可以暫停下來，而把一個新的報導硬是加入成為頭版新聞。

Business Use

This idiom is used when something extremely important comes up, causing people to change their priorities. It means the impact of a new development is staggering in its nature. The second and the most common use is to ridicule someone's news, or at least make light of it.

當有一件非常重要的事情發生,而導致人們需要改變做事的先後順序時,就會使用到這個慣用語。它是指發生的事情本身可能很驚人,其次也是最常的使用情況是取笑有關他人的消息,抑或是把發生在他人身上的事情看得不甚重要。

Special Considerations

If it is used to ridicule, or make light of someone's news, it's usually said with mock surprise meaning the speaker already knows, or feels it really isn't that important.

特別留意

如果這個用語被用來嘲笑他人、或看輕某人身上所發生的事,通常說話的語氣會透露出嘲諷的驚訝味,目的在顯示說話者早已知道或覺得發生的情形並不重要。

Alternatives 相關用語

◇ say what	說啊
◇ hold the phone	佔著電話線
◇ wait a minute	等一下
◇ run that by me again	再跟我說一次
◇ are you sure?	你確定嗎?
◇ I never saw that coming 我一點都沒意料到這事會發生	
◇ well, I'll be...	讓我再 ... 看看

S stop (them) dead in (their) tracks
把（某人）堵的死死的

MP3-157

Idiom Definition

This is used when the speaker wants to describe bringing someone or something to a complete and sudden halt.

成語定義 當說話者用這個表達語時，主要在描述要把一個人或一件事給完全停下來。

Word Definition Used

"dead" unmoving

"stop them dead in their tracks" is a term as well as an idiom. When these exact words are used this way, they take on the unique meaning above.

使用的字詞定義

"dead" 不會動了

「stop them dead in their tracks」是一個詞，也是一個慣用語。當這些字一起使用時，便會有上面提到的獨特意義。

Examples

例 When I told them the results it stopped them dead in their tracks.

當我告訴他們結果時，他們被堵的死死的。

例 The light stopped them dead in their tracks.

那道光線把他們給堵死了。

This term goes back to hunting. Game tastes better if it's shot in a relaxed unexcited state, without fear produced adrenalin pumped through its body. So making a kill with one shot while the animal was unaware it was being stalked is very desirable. The key here is the target was unaware anything was wrong, and that is the concept to keep in mind in the metaphoric uses of this idiom.

背景資料 這個詞源自於狩獵。當獵物被射殺時,如果牠們處於放鬆的情況,身體裡面沒有因恐懼而產生的腎上腺素,會比較美味。因此當獵物不注意時,一槍把牠們射死,這種做法比較好。這裡的關鍵是要標的物不注意到事情不對勁,這也是這個慣用語的主要觀念。

Business Use

This is usually used to indicate the opposition was caught completely by surprise, and unable to mount any counter measure, much less a successful one.

商業用法 這個用法通常適用於把對方堵個正著,讓對方無法採取任何應變措施,就算採取措施,也不會成功。

Alternatives 相關用語

◇ stopped cold	趁其不備
◇ caught napping	趁其不備
◇ asleep at the switch	攻其不備
◇ caught unawares	趁其不備

S a string of
一連串的

MP3-158

Idiom Definition

This is used to describe a situation where several similar items happen in consecutive order, or a chain of items similar, but do not necessarily come from the same source.

成語定義 這個詞用來描述好幾件相似的事情,一件接著一件發生,但它們不見得有相同的來源。

Word Definition Used

"string" a series

使用的字詞定義
"string" 一系列

Examples

例 Recently she's had a lucky string of wins, one after another.

最近她有一連串的好運氣。

例 To earn a raise, you have to have a string of wins behind you.

要想加薪,你必須要有一連串的好運氣。

One standard dictionary definition for the word "string" is a piece of twine. Twine is commonly used to tie things together as with a series of articles. If a string ties actual things together, the meaning can be expanded to include events, etc.

背景資料 字典對 string 的標準定義之一是麻繩。麻繩常用來把東西綁在一起。如果一條繩索可以把實物綁在一起,那麼這個意思就可以進一步擴展用到事情上面。

Business Use

This is used to describe any series of items or events that happen by chance, design or a combination of both.

商業用法 這個表達語描述任何一系列的東西或事件,其發生原因可能是巧合、可能是安排好的,也可能兩者兼具。

Alternatives 相關用語

◇ a chain of	一連串的
◇ a series	一系列的
◇ one after another	一個接著一個

S substantial completion
大體上均已完成

Idiom Definition

This is the term used to describe when a construction project reaches the point when the major work is complete and only cleanup, inspection and minor repairs remain.

成語定義 這個表達語用來描述興建計畫,當到了快要結束的時刻,只剩下一些結尾工作、檢查或一些極其微小的修理。

Word Definition Used

"substantial completion" is a legal term in the construction industry. When these exact words are used this way, they take on the unique meaning above.

使用的字詞定義
「substantial completion」是一個用在建築界的專業術語。當這些字一起使用時,便會有上面提到的獨特意義。

Examples

例 I can't give you another dime until you reach substantial completion.

除非大致上你已完成這項工作,我不會再給你任何一毛錢。

例 We'll reach substantial completion on Thursday, can

we meet then?

我們在星期四時會大致完成這個計畫，要不要碰個面？

....

Business Use

This is an indispensable construction term with special significance and plays an important part in construction negotiations and contracts. It describes an important stage in construction that sets things, determined during negotiations, into motion.

商業用法 這是一個非常重要的建築專業字彙，有著獨特的重要性，並在建築協商和合約協調過程中，扮演重要的角色。這個用語在於描述建築計畫中的一個重要階段，在這各階段中會把很多協議達成的內容付諸行動。

S

(it) sucks
爛透了

MP3-160

Idiom Definition

This is used to describe the thing referred to as very bad. It's often used as an expression of disgust.

成語定義 這個表達語用來描述事情的狀況很糟，通常使用這個詞時，會有很厭煩的表情。

Word Definition Used

"sucks" very bad

使用的字詞定義
"sucks" 很糟糕

Examples

例 The price is right, but the quality sucks.

這個價格沒錯，但品質糟糕透了。

例 I know it sucks, but that's the way it is.

我知道情況很爛，但實際情形就是這樣。

Background

This is a term with a unique meaning and an obscure origin. It's not listed in every dictionary because its use is considered crude by most, and vulgar with sexual overtones which many women find offensive.

這個表達語有著特殊意義及一個很模糊的由來，並不是在每本字典中都有註明，因為大多數人認為它的用法很粗陋，可能有很嚴重的性暗示，冒犯到很多女性。

Business Use

This is used to describe a person, place or thing as being very bad, or of poor quality.

商業用法 這個用語可以描述人、地方或事物，形容他們很糟糕、品質很差。

Alternatives 相關用語

◇ it blows	將 ... 搞砸
◇ it's a piece of crap	全是狗屁

S sweeten the offer
將報價「弄得更好」

MP3-161

Idiom Definition

This is used to describe an improved bid, made better because it was increased.

成語定義 這個表達語描述經過改進的報價。

Word Definition Used

"sweeten" make more attractive

"sweeten the offer" is a term as well as an idiom. When these exact words are used this way, they take on the unique meaning above.

使用的字詞定義

"sweeten" 讓…變得更為吸引人

「sweeten the offer」是一個詞,也是一個慣用語。當這些字一起使用時,便會有上面提到的獨特意義。

Examples

例 Then let me sweeten the offer.

這樣的話,讓我把價格報的更好一點。

例 I reran the numbers and found a way to sweeten our offer.

我又把數字看過一遍,找到了報出更好價格的方法。

This term works because it's a substitution. Most people like sweets and are attracted to them. Therefore, to sweeten something means to make it more attractive, to do something that will improve it to those it's offered to.

背景資料 這個詞是一個替代語。大多人喜歡吃甜食，會受到甜食的吸引。所以英文中用了 sweeten 這個字來表示把某件事變得更好，讓它更吸引人，這個動詞有「改進」的意思，讓一件事變得更吸引人。

Business Use

Usually sweetening the offer means adjusting the price but it could also be done by offering better terms.

商業用法 通常這個用語的意思是調整價格，但也可能單純意指「提出更好的條件」。

Alternatives 相關用語

◇ Trim this down	把這個東西再修剪一下
◇ juice up my bid	把我的報價加點料
◇ work the numbers	把數字再改一下
◇ play with the numbers	把數字再改一下
◇ let me see what I can do	讓我想想還能再做點什麼
◇ let me try it again	讓我再試試看
◇ sharpen my pencil	把鉛筆再削尖一點
◇ come up a little	再做一些調整

on the table
攤開來說

MP3-162

Idiom Definition

This is used to describe the terms and or conditions discussed in a negotiation.

成語定義　這個表達語用來描述談判中所提到的條件或但書。

Word Definition Used

"on the table" is a term as well as an idiom. When these exact words are used this way, they take on the unique meaning above.

使用的字詞定義

「on the table」是一個詞，也是一個慣用語。當這些字一起使用時，便會有上面提到的獨特意義。

Examples

例 It's on the table, so we can talk about it.

都攤開來說了，這樣我們就可以討論看看了。

例 We can discuss anything on the table.

我們可以談論任何攤在桌面上的議題。

Background

Understanding this one is easy if you know something about playing the American card game, poker. Each player bets according to how good he thinks his hand is. In stud poker cards are dealt one at a time with a round of betting between each card. Players must match the bet made to remain in the hand or fold his cards and quit, forfeiting any bets made.

If a player can't match the bet, he has to quit, unless the "Table Stakes" rule is called prior to play. It means no player is required to bet more money than is on the table in front of him. If the largest bet is far more than he has, he can bet everything and if he wins, he only wins the bets equal to or less than his. If he loses, he can go get more money to continue playing or quit. The original amount of cash brought to the game and all money won must stay on the table for as long as a player stays in the game.

The term "on the table" refers to "table stakes," everything on your list of demands. The items you are negotiating for are all tradable, but once you start a negotiation, you're not allowed to introduce more items.

背景資料 如果你知道如何和美國人玩撲克牌的話，就很容易理解這個用語。每個玩家都依照自己手上的牌來下注。玩撲克牌時，每一盤都會重新發牌，大家會下注。玩家們必須跟得上彼此所下的注，否則就必須蓋牌、不跟，放棄已下好的注。

如果任何一個玩家不能跟上他人所下的注時，除非在遊戲開始之前，參賽者有定下「桌上注」的條件，這個詞的意思是任何一個玩家所下的注，不得超過他面前所有的錢，如果別人所喊的注比他手上的錢大時，該玩家可以把全部的注押下去，如果他贏的話，他所贏的錢只能是他原來有的錢或更少而已。如果他輸的話，他有兩條路，一是去想辦法弄到更多的錢，二是停手不玩。每個玩家一開始帶到牌桌的錢，只要這個玩家不停手，那錢就會一直留在桌面上。

「on the table」這個用法指的是「桌上注」，也是玩家們需要的所有東西，玩家想要談判的任何一件東西都必須有交換的價值，一但談判開始，玩家們就不能再提及新的談判籌碼。

Business Use

The term refers to every item on your list of demands. The items you are negotiating for are all tradable, but once you start a negotiation, you're not allowed to introduce more items.

商業用法　這個用語涉及玩家們需要的所有東西。玩家想要談判的任何一件東西都須有交換價值，一但談判開始，他們就不能再提及新的談判籌碼。

Alternatives: 相關用語

◇ in play	考慮周詳
◇ open to discussion	還有商量的餘地

take stock
善加評估

MP3-163

Idiom Definition

This is used to describe when someone stops to reevaluate his or her position and or condition, to take inventory.

成語定義 當某人停下來重新評估自己的立場或情況時，便可用這個表達法來描述此「審慎評估」的做法。

Word Definition Used

"stock" one's own needs, wants, hopes, desires, condition, and so forth

"take stock" is a term as well as an idiom. When these exact words are used this way, they take on the unique meaning above.

使用的字詞定義

"stock" 某個人的需求、意欲、希望、慾望、情況等等。

「take stock」是一個詞，也是一個慣用語。當這些字一起使用時，便會有上面提到的獨特意義。

Examples

例 You need to take stock and decide if you want to continue.

你需要善加評估，再決定你想不想要繼續下去。

例 I need time to take stock before I can answer you.

我需要時間來善加評估，才能答覆你。

....

Background

"Taking stock" means to take inventory in very old-fashioned English. Today, it assumes the definition shown above. The stock is now his or her needs, wants, hopes, desires, condition, and so forth.

背景資料 在老式的英文中，這個詞指的是「清點庫存」。今日，這個詞有了上述提及的意思。在這裡，stock 這個字指的是說話者的需求、意欲、希望、慾望、情況等等。

Business Use

In short, this means to evaluate one's position because he/she has to decide whether to continue or choose a different course of action.

The original definition was to take inventory as in a store, but now this term is limited to one's personal feelings and condition.

商業用法 簡單來說，這個詞的意思是評估一個人的立場，因為他必須決定是否要繼續或選擇不同的做法。
這個詞的原始定義是要為一家店進行「庫存」，但在這裡，這個詞的用法只限於某個人的自我感覺與情況。

Alternatives 相關用語

◇ rethink things   重新考量一些事情

◇ realign one's priorities   重新調整事情的先後順序

talk turkey
討論重點

Idiom Definition

This is used to describe when only the heart of a matter is discussed. When only serious talks are welcome, no delaying tactics or side issues are welcomed. The speaker is saying he or she intends to settle the matter here and now.

成語定義 當討論只涉及某件事的中心議題時,會用到這個表達法。當討論者只想討論重要的事情時,不希望任何一方使用拖延戰術或涉及次要議題。用這個詞的說話者想要表達的是他想要把該件事項立刻解決。

Word Definition Used

"turkey" open and frank

"talk turkey" is a term as well as an idiom. When these exact words are used this way, they take on the unique meaning above.

使用的字詞定義

"turkey" 指的是公開的、坦誠的

「talk turkey」是一個詞,也是一個慣用語。當這些字一起使用時,便會有上面提到的獨特意義。

Examples

例 Let's talk turkey and settle this argument.

讓我們討論重點吧,把這個爭議給解決掉。

例 Are you ready to talk turkey, or are you going to play around some more?

你準備好要討論重點了嗎？或是你還想再玩玩？

Background

The American Wild Turkey is a very shy, crafty, resourceful game bird known for its ability to evade the most resourceful hunter. Its call is loud and unmistakable; it can't be mistaken for anything else.

背景資料 美國野生火雞是一種很害羞、很狡猾、很機智的野生禽類，以其躲避聰明獵人的能力著稱。火雞的叫聲很大聲，一般人不可能會誤認，把牠認成其他動物。

Business Use

"To talk turkey" is to be open, frank completely honest and above board, like the turkey.

商業用法 「to talk turkey」是指雙方要完全地開誠佈公、誠實，就像火雞一樣。

Alternatives 相關用語

◇ frank and open discussion	坦誠、公開的討論
◇ being completely candid	完全坦誠
◇ getting to the real issues	討論真正的重點
◇ cut to the chase	把不重要的事略過

(my) hands are tied
（我的）雙手被綁了

MP3-165

Idiom Definition

This term is used to indicate that the person referred to is unable to respond differently than he/she already has regardless of any mitigating circumstances.

成語定義 當說話者使用這個詞時，他的意思是無法做出任何其他的回應，不管情況有任何改變。

Word Definition Used

"tied" can't be used

"my hands are tied" is a term as well as an idiom. When these exact words are used this way, they take on the unique meaning above.

使用的字詞定義

"tied" 不能用了

「my hands are tied」是一個詞，也是一個慣用語。當這些字一起使用時，便會有上面提到的獨特意義。

Examples

例 I wish I could help, but my hands are tied.

我也想幫忙啊，但我的雙手都被綁住了。

例 It won't do any good to talk to the operator, their hands are tied.

跟經營者談什麼都沒用的，他們是無能為力的。

Background

No one's hands are actually tied; that's a figure of speech. The speaker's hands are tied by the rules, not rope. The logic is a person usually uses his or her hands to do things, but if his/her hands are tied, he/she can't do anything, even if he/she wanted to.

背景資料 當使用這個表達法時,沒有任何人的手被綁住,這只是一種譬喻而已。説話者的手是被規則所束縛住了,而不是真正被繩子給綁住了。這種用法的邏輯是通常一個人都用他的雙手來做事,如果他的雙手被綁住了,就算想做什麼事,也是無能為力。

Business Use

This is handy if referring to lower level workers who listen to complaints, then respond as directed by policy. They've no authority. It's also used when a customer requests something unreasonable or beyond the users authority to grant.

It's a code phrase meaning what's shown between the quotation marks. "I've heard your complaint; it's just like the others I hear all day, every day. There was nothing I could do for them, and there's nothing I can do for you because I have no authority."

"My job is to listen to people like you, and take the heat for my superiors who actually have the authority to help you but won't . They're under strict orders not to budge on this point. If you ask to talk to one of them, you can, but I doubt you'll get anything more than what I just gave you."

商業用法 當層級不高的人員聽到一些抱怨時，這個表達語彎好用的，因為這些人沒有什麼權力，所以這是個很制式化的回應方式。當顧客對員工提出不合理或非能力所及的要求時，員工們可以用這樣的方式回答。

這是固定用語，意思是說話者的「雙手被縛」，說話者想表達的是「我聽到了你的抱怨，這些抱怨我每天都在聽，可是我什麼事也不能做，對你和他們都是一樣，因為我沒有任何權力去做改變。」

「我的工作是聆聽像你這一類型的人，看看你們有什麼意見，做我老闆的擋箭牌，他們有能力幫你，可是不想幫。他們接到的指令是不可以在這個議題上，做任何讓步。如果你想和他們談談，當然可以，但我想你從他們那裡得到的，絕對不會比從我這裡得到的更多。」

Alternatives 相關用語

◇ I have no authority	我沒什麼權力
◇ there's nothing I can do	我無能為力
◇ I wish I could help, but...	我很想幫忙，但 …
◇ as deaf as a traffic court judge 我就和交通庭的法官一樣充耳不聞	
◇ impotent	無力
◇ window dressing	我只是個裝飾品而已

at the time
當時

MP3-166

Idiom Definition

This is used to describe circumstances at a point in time that is now past, when the event referred to took place.

成語定義 這個片語用於描述一件已經發生的事情，事發當時的狀況。

Word Definition Used

"at the time" is a term as well as an idiom. When these exact words are used this way, they take on the unique meaning above.

使用的字詞定義

「at the time」是一個詞，也是一個慣用語。當這些字一起使用時，便會有上面提到的獨特意義。

Examples

例 I was willing to do that, at the time.

在當時，我是很樂意那樣做的。

例 I was way ahead at the time, so I helped him a little.

當時，我遠遠超前，所以就幫了他一下。

This term is used to describe someone's feelings and emotions as well as the events leading up to a cretin point in time when something the speaker said or did needs to be clarified.

商業用法 這個表達語用來描述某個人的感覺、情緒和一些事件，說話者想澄清為何他會做出一些事或說出一些話。

Alternatives 相關用語

◇ circumstances being what they were
當時的情況是

◇ according to the lay of the land
根據當時的情形

◇ events seemed to indicate
情況似乎指向…

◇ it seemed like a good idea at the time
在當時，那樣做似乎是個不錯的處理方式

◇ it's just the way things were
這是當時的情況

tried and true
試過之後，果然如此

MP3-167

Idiom Definition

This is used to describe any person or thing that's been tested and found reliable.

成語定義 用這個表達法來描述某個人或某件事受到考驗之後，發現很不錯。

Word Definition Used

"tried and true" is a term as well as an idiom. When these exact words are used this way, they take on the unique meaning above.

使用的字詞定義

「tried and true」是一個詞，也是一個慣用語。當這些字一起使用時，便會有上面提到的獨特意義。

Examples

例 Let's get one that's tried and true. I know the green one works, take it.

讓我們找一個已經通過考驗的，我知道綠色那個很有用，就選它吧。

例 That one is tried and true. I used it yesterday.

那個有人試過了，很有用，我昨天才用過呢。

This idiom is so popular because it has flow.

這個慣用語很受歡迎，因為在英文中，tried 和 true 有相同的韻頭。

Business Use

This is used to refer to any person, place or thing used before for the same purpose and found reliable.

商業用法 這個表達語指的是任何一個人、地方或事情，在之前被實驗過，結果讓人很滿意。

Alternatives 相關用語

◇ it works	有用呢
◇ old reliable	很可靠
◇ it's dependable	它直得信賴
◇ trustworthy	直得信賴

played (her) trump card
亮出（她的）王牌

MP3-168

Idiom Definition

This is used to describe when someone uses whatever power, authority or favors they have to get their way. Often they use it a lot more than necessary, just to be sure they succeed. This is used when one succeeds even though he/she was expected to fail.

成語定義 當某個人使用權力、權威或請人幫忙，來達到目的時，就可以用這個表達法。通常人們常常這樣做，因為想要確定自己能得到自己想要的東西。這個表達語通常使用於當人們認為某個人會失敗，但他卻成功的時候。

Word Definition Used

"trump" an automatic win

"play her trump card" is a term as well as an idiom. When these exact words, except the pronoun may be replaced with another pronoun or noun, are used this way, they take on the unique meaning above.

使用的字詞定義

"trump" 自然而然的勝利

「play her trump card」是一個詞，也是一個慣用語。當這些字一起使用時，便會有上面提到的獨特意義，但其中的所有格可以替換掉。

Examples

例 She got her way, but she had to play her trump card to get it.

她得到她想要的了，但代價是必須亮出她的王牌。

例 It looked like we'd win, until Jean played her trump card.

那時看起來我們會贏，但吉妮亮出她的王牌後，情況就改觀了。

In cards, one of the four suits is designated as trumps. Any trump card beats all non trump cards to win the trick.

背景資料 在玩牌時，J、Q、K、A 都可以被指定是王牌，任何一張王牌都勝過非王牌的牌。

Business Use

When this idiom is used in other than card playing situations, it means the subject did something completely unexpected or the expected unexpectedly well, and was able to outperform the competition.

A real life trump card could be almost anything. If it is not a task well done as above, then asking that a favor owed be repaid, a relationship with the person making the decision, anything that could influence the decision.

商業用法 當這個表達語被用於非撲克牌遊戲時，意思是被談論的主角做了大家意想不到的事，因而贏得比賽。

現實生活中，王牌可能意指任何事情。如果情況不佳，可以叫他人償還以前欠下的人情，在這種情形下，有人必須做出決定，任何可以影響他人決定的事，都可以稱為王牌。

Alternatives 相關用語

◇ call in a favor	找人幫助
◇ use up a marker	找人幫忙
◇ collect on an old debt	向某人討舊債
◇ win against the odds	讓人跌破眼鏡的勝利
◇ beat the odds	居然成功了
◇ pull it off	成功了

get in under the wire
及時趕上

`MP3-169`

Idiom Definition

This is used to describe when someone completes something either just before the deadline, or just after and it was accepted anyway.

成語定義 這個表達語描述某個人恰恰好在期限截止之前，完成一件工作，或僅錯過期限一些些，對方仍願意接受的情況。

Word Definition Used

"under the wire" is all by itself a term, meaning to beat the deadline.

使用的字詞定義

"under the wire" 本身就是一個詞，指的是「趕上期限」。

Examples

例 Regardless of the expense, we have to get it in under the wire.

不管要花費多少，我們必須在期限之內得到那樣東西。

例 He's hoping to get it in under the wire.

他希望能在期限之內，得到那樣東西。

This is a metaphor that often refers to a qualifying round. To get to the next level, you must do something prior to the deadline. When the time expires, a wired gate is lowered, baring the way to further entries.

背景資料 這是一個隱喻，常用來描述合格標準。要晉升到下一個階段，你必須要在期限來臨之前，採取行動。當期限到時，電纜門會降下來，阻擋任何人的進入。

Business Use

To get in under the wire is to be, do or have something just in time.

商業用法 要趕上期限，就必須及時去做一些事。

Alternatives 相關用語

◇ An eleventh hour entry	第十一個小時進入
◇ a last minute try	最後一分鐘的嘗試

unit cost
單元成本

MP3-170

Idiom Definition

This is used to describe the cost of a single item in a run after all expenses and savings are taken into account, including volume discounts, if any.

成語定義 用這個表達語來描述一項物品的成本，此成本的計算已將所有花費及可以節省的費用納入考量，包含任何可能的大幅折扣。

Word Definition Used

"unit cost" is a term as well as an idiom. When these exact words are used this way, they take on the unique meaning above.

使用的字詞定義

「unit cost」是一個詞，也是一個慣用語。當這些字一起使用時，便會有上面提到的獨特意義。

Examples

例 We need the unit cost as a basis to set the unit price.

我們需要單位成本來當作設定單位價格的基礎。

例 If our unit cost is lower, why does our product cost more?

如果我們的單位成本已經降低了，為什麼產品更貴了呢？

This idiom uses the standard definitions. The idiom is also a term; that's why it's here.

背景資料 這個慣用語有著標準定義,它也是一個詞,因此收錄在這裡。

Business Use

This is an extremely important term in sales negotiations, where this figure is vital in setting the unit price.

商業用法 這個用語在銷售談判中非常重要,因為在談判中,這個數字對於決定單位售價扮演了很重要的角色。

U up (the) offer
提高價格

`MP3-171`

Idiom Definition

This is used to describe when a proposed price is increased in order to get the shipment.

成語定義 這個表達語用來描述為了要確保訂得到貨,把報價提高的做法。

Word Definition Used

"up our offer" is a term as well as an idiom. When these exact words, except the article the may be replaced with a pronoun or noun, are used this way, they take on the unique meaning above.

使用的字詞定義

「up our offer」是一個詞,也是一個慣用語。當這些字一起使用時,便會有上面提到的獨特意義,但定冠詞可以換成其他的所有格。

Examples

例 If we want this contract, we're going to have to up our offer.

如果我們想得到這份合約,就必須提高價格。

例 The Chaney Corporation is hungry, they will up their offer.

如果錢尼公司很想要得到這些貨的話,他們就會提高價格。

This idiom uses the standard definitions. The idiom is also a term; that's why it's here.

背景資料 這個慣用語有著標準定義，它也是一個詞，因此收錄在這裡。

Business Use

This is a very important idiom and term you'll run across often, so it's listed here.

商業用法 這是個你常常會用到的重要表達語或慣用語，因此收錄在這裡。

Alternatives 相關用語

◇ juice up my bid	把報價報得更好
◇ work the numbers	把數字再修正一下
◇ play with the numbers	在調整一下數字
◇ let me see what I can do	我看看還能做些什麼
◇ let me try again	讓我再試試看
◇ sharpen my pencil	削尖我的鉛筆
◇ boost the bid	把價格提高
◇ goose the bid	提高價格
◇ juice the bid	把報價報得更好

up to speed
趕上進度

MP3-172

Idiom Definition

This is used to describe when someone is current on all information relevant to something, or when someone should be informed of all recent developments, so they can operate in an informed way. This term means to know as much about something as everyone else involved.

成語定義　這個表達語描述某個人對某事的相關資料應該瞭如指掌，或某人應該知道最新發展，這樣才能做出正確的決定、採取正確的行動。這個詞意指必須盡可能了解牽扯的人或事物。

Word Definition Used

"up to speed" is a term as well as an idiom. When these exact words are used this way, they take on the unique meaning above.

使用的字詞定義

「up to speed」是一個詞，也是一個慣用語。當這些字一起使用時，便會有上面提到的獨特意義。

Examples

例 Before I can say anything I have to be brought up to speed.

在我表達任何意見之前，必須要先趕上進度。

例 He's up to speed and ready to go.

他已經趕上進度，隨時可以開始。

Background

This has nothing to do with rate of travel and has everything to do with amount known about something. If two cars are moving at the same speed, they can easily exchange things. Likewise, if two people agree on the basic facts, then they are said to be up to speed with each other. Then their conversation can center on what to do.

背景資料 這個表達法和旅行的速度沒有任何關係，而和某件事情的任何已知情況有關。如果兩部車子以同樣的速度前進，對他們來說，要交換東西是很容易的事。同樣的，如果兩個人對一些基本資料都有共識，就可以說他們兩人趕上了彼此的進度。這樣一來，他們的對談就可以專注在要進行的事情上。

Business Use

Think of it this way, two people have comparable knowledge on a subject, so they can discuss it without one having to explain details to the other. They can be said to be working at the same speed.

If a third person with less knowledge joins them, the process will be slowed while things are explained to the third. Once he/she is informed, he or she is up to speed and the discussion will move on rapidly.

商業用法 這樣想吧，兩個人對一個主題有相當程度的知識，所以他們不需要任何解釋，就可以開始討論正事，我們可以說他們的工作進度相同。

如果第三者加入他們，可是他的背景知識不夠，整體的做事速度就會慢下來，因為他們要向第三者解釋一些事情。一但第三者了解進度，他就可以趕上來，那麼他們的討論就可以進行的更為快速。

Alternatives 相關用語

◇ up to date	最新進度
◇ current	現況
◇ up to the minute	最新進度
◇ fully briefed	完全知曉現況
◇ ready for anything	完全做好準備
◇ loaded for bear	做好萬全準備

wait (him) out
等著（他人）採取行動

MP3-173

Idiom Definition

This is used to describe when a decision is made to defer action until the other side moves.

成語定義 這個表達語用來描述當某人決定阻止某事的進展，直到另一方採取行動為止。

Word Definition Used

"out" out last or out wait

"Wait him out" is a term as well as an idiom. When these exact words, except the pronoun may be replaced with another pronoun or noun, are used this way, they take on the unique meaning above.

使用的字詞定義

"out" 比…更久
「wait him out」是一個詞，也是一個慣用語。當這些字一起使用時，便會有上面提到的獨特意義，但其中的所有格可替換成其他的所有格或名詞。

Examples

例 I say we should wait him out and see what he does.

我建議應該要等到他採取行動，看看他會怎麼做。

例 We decided to wait him out, let him make the mistakes, then do it right.

我們決定等著看他要怎麼做，讓他去犯錯，然後他就會做出正確的事。

....

Background

The word "out" of course means the speaker intendeds to do a better job of waiting than the subject. This is a fairly recent addition to the language.

背景資料 這個表達語中用了 out 這個字，因為說話者打算要比另一方等的更久，這是一個嶄新的表達法。

Business Use

This is a common tactic in the business world. It's a short version for what's between the quotation marks. "Let's not act first, but let the other side have that privilege so we can go the other way, and criticize whatever they do."

商業用法 這種做法在商業界中很常見。它是個簡短版本，原文是：「讓我們先別採取行動，把這個榮幸讓給對手，這樣就換到我們來批評他們的做法了。」

Alternatives 相關用語

◇ bide our time	慢慢等吧
◇ let's watch and wait	讓我們走著瞧吧
◇ let him take the risks	讓對方去冒險

W there's more than one way to skin a cat
要達到目標，方法不只一種

MP3-174

Idiom Definition

This is used to describe a situation where there are many ways to do something. If one won't work, then just try a different way.

成語定義 這個表達法用來描述做一件事的方法有很多種。如果一種方法行不通，就試試看另一種方法。

Word Definition Used

"there's more than one way to skin a cat" is a term as well as an idiom. When these exact words are used this way, they take on the unique meaning above.

使用的字詞定義

「there's more than one way to skin a cat」是一個詞，也是一個慣用語。當這些字一起使用時，便會有上面提到的獨特意義。

Examples

例 There's more than one way to skin a cat and I know what to do.

要達到目的，方法不只一種，我知道該怎麼做。

例 So what if it didn't work, there's more than one way to skin a cat.

因此，要是行不通的話，還有其他的可行方法。

Background

The "cat" referred to a big cat like the American mountain lion. Skinning is removing the fur and skin from an animal so it can be tanned. A cat's skin is loosely attached, and easily removed. The only firm connection points, that have to be cut away, are the body openings and paws.

With many types of animals, skinning has to be done a certain way, or the hide will be ruined. However, almost anyone who wants to skin a cat can do it. It doesn't really matter where you start because the process is so simple.

背景資料 在這個表達法中的 cat 指的是大型貓科動物，像是美洲豹。表達語中的 skinning 是把動物身上的皮給拔下來，才能做成獸皮。貓科動物的皮很容易拔下來，唯一連的比較緊的是身體上的孔、通道及爪子，所以需要把它們切開。

對許多類型的動物而言，去皮這個動作有一定的做法，要不然皮革會被破壞。但如果去皮的對象是貓科動物，那麼幾乎所有人都做得到。要從哪裡開始著手並不重要，因為這整個過程真的非常簡單。

Business Use

In business, this is usually used when someone reports they were unsuccessful in an attempt to do something. This is used to introduce a different method the speaker feels will be more successful. It's a very old idiom, but it still gets a lot of use.

商業用法 在商業界中，當某人提到他做某件事情失敗時，常常用到這個表達法。用這個表達法來介紹另一種做法，說話者認為這種做法會比較容易成功。這個慣用語歷史悠久，但還是常常被用到。

Alternatives 相關用語

◇ I know a trick   我知道另一個方法

◇ let's try something else   我們試試看別的做法吧

◇ let's try something new   試試看新的做法吧

◇ Let's give it another try   再試試看吧

◇ there's lots of alternatives   還有其他許多方法

◇ if at first you don't succeed, try, try again
如果一開始不成事的話，再試試看

a <u>w</u>in, win situation
雙贏局面

MP3-175

Idiom Definition

This is used to describe a situation where everyone wins something, and no one loses everything. It's sort of a compromise situation where everyone walks away with part of what they wanted, or at least enough so that they're happy.

成語定義 這個表達語用來描述一種情況，在該種情況中，每個人都是贏家，沒有人輸掉一切。該種情況有點像是某個程度的妥協，讓每個人都或多或少得到一些東西，至少每個人都有得到一些東西、都很快樂。

Word Definition Used

"a win, win situation" is a term as well as an idiom. When these exact words are used this way, they take on the unique meaning above.

使用的字詞定義 「a win, win situation」是一個詞，也是一個慣用語。當這些字一起使用時，便會有上面提到的獨特意義。

Examples

例 A win, win situation is always desired and seldom achieved.

一個雙贏局面是大家都想要、卻很少做得到的。

例 We were fortunate, a win, win situation isn't always possible.

我們算幸運的，一個雙贏的結果不是要就有的。

This is a fairly new idiom that quickly became very popular. The tricky part is the word win is repeated, which is highly unusual. It's alright in this case, because one win is used for each party.

背景資料 這個慣用語很新，很快受到大家的歡迎。在這個表達語中，把 win 這個字重複一次，在英文中這種做法並不常見。在這個表達法中可以這樣做，因為雙方各有一個「贏」字。

Business Use

Repeating the word "win" adds emphasis to the fact that everyone won something. In a three party deal with three winners, I have seen it used with three wins, a win, win, win situation. However, with four or more winners, the word win is only repeated once.

商業用法 這個表達語重複 win 這個字，在於強調每個人都是贏家。在交易牽扯三方時，我曾看過 a win, win, win situation 的用法，三方都有一個「贏」字。但若交易牽扯四方以上，win 這個字只會重複一次。

Special Considerations

The situation, context, tone, facial expression and body language should all convey a positive feeling. The speaker should be happy that things worked out so well.

特別留意 用這個表達語的情況、上下文、語氣、面部表情及肢體語言，都應該傳達一個正面的訊息。說話者應該要很高興，因為事情解決的非常順利。

Alternatives 相關用語

◇ everybody wins	每個人都是贏家
◇ no losers	沒有輸家

windfall profit
意外獲利

MP3-176

Idiom Definition

This is used to describe an unexpected and possibly unearned or underserved financial gain.

成語定義 這個表達語描述一個預期之外、不應得的財務獲利。

Word Definition Used

"windfall" unexpected money that comes because of luck

"windfall profit" is a term as well as an idiom. When these exact words are used this way, they take on the unique meaning above.

使用的字詞定義

"windfall" 意外之財

「windfall profit」是一個詞，也是一個慣用語。當這些字一起使用時，便會有上面提到的獨特意義。

Examples

例 The windfall profit was unexpected but very nice.

這些意外獲利是我們沒有預期到的，但我們還是很高興。

例 Their unexpected windfall profit was carefully planned for.

他們這個意外的獲利其實是小心計畫的後果。

Background

Originally, a windfall was used to describe fruit, like an apple fallen from a tree by the wind.

背景資料 意外之財原來是用來描述水果，像是意外被風吹落的蘋果。

Business Use

This describes any unexpected gain that appears to have been blown someone's way by the wind. Use of the word "profit" automatically makes it a business application.

商業用法 這個表達法描述一個人似乎是因為一陣風而得到意外的收穫，用了 profit 這個字，使得這個表達語變得和商業活動有關。

Alternatives 相關用語

◇ we lucked into it	我們幸運碰到的
◇ blind luck	純粹是好運
◇ dumb luck	純粹是好運

work out the details
把細節敲定

MP3-177

Idiom Definition

This is used to describe what is done after a basic agreement is reached by the principals. The matter is then turned over to the staff who negotiate a framework to implement the deal.

成語定義 這個表達法描述在雙方達成基本共識後，下一步要進行的細節。接下來的事要交給那些協商人員，由他們來敲定一個框架，才可把交易落實。

Word Definition Used

"work out" is all by itself a term, meaning come to an agreement.

使用的字詞定義

"work out" 本身就是一個詞，意思是「同意」。

Examples

例 I'm glad that's over; now all we have to do is work out the details.

很高興那件事結束了，現在我們只需要把細節敲定就可以了。

....

例 The people who work out the details need to know what they're doing.

那些敲定細節的人，需要知道他們的角色。

....

The term "work out" means to come to an agreement as stated above. However, it implies that some effort was involved and it wasn't a simple thing.

背景資料 「work out」這個詞的意思如上所述,有著「大家都同意」的意思。但它也暗示需要某個程度的努力,並不是件簡單的事。

Business Use

In a big negotiation where both sides have a staff of professionals, the principals meet and agree to the basic principles of a deal. The matter is then turned over to the staff who will negotiate the details to make the arrangement work.

商業用法 在大型談判中,兩方都會派出專業人士,主要人物在會面時,要先同意一些基本原則。然後其他事就會交給談判人員,去把細節全部敲定。

Alternatives 相關用語

◇ line up the ducks	把東西都排列好
◇ set your house in order	把家裡整理好

work with (me)
和我合作

MP3-178

Idiom Definition

This is used when the speaker is asking for cooperation and maybe some assistance.

成語定義 當說話者要求他人的合作或協助時，會用到這個表達語。

Examples

例 That's the problem, but if you work with me, I think we can solve it.

那就是問題所在，如果你願意協助我，我想我們可以把問題解決的。

例 Work with me and we can go home early.

幫助我，這樣我們都可以早點回家。

Background

This is listed here because it has such a wide range of uses. It's fairly new, very popular and gets a lot of use just about everywhere right now. It has jumped the generation gap, and has applications everywhere people cooperate. If you visit the US or work with Americans in person or on the phone, you're likely to run into it.

背景資料 這個表達法收錄在這裡，因為它有很多不同的用法。這個用法很新，很受到大家的歡迎。現今，這個用法幾乎處處可見。它超越了代溝，幾乎只要有人們合作的場合，就會看到這個詞的用法。如果你造訪美國、和美國人肩並肩工作或利用電話溝通，你很有可能會碰到這個用法。

This is pretty much a universal idiom popular everywhere. It can be used as a plea, an order or a demand. Its use is determined by tone, facial expression, body language and context. Regardless of where, when or why it's used, the meaning is the same.

商業用法 這個表達語大概可稱為是一個處處受歡迎的用語。它適用於懇求、命令或要求。它的用法取決於語調、面部表情、肢體語言及上下文。不管地點、時間或原因為何，其意思都一樣。

Alternatives 相關用語

◇ I need your help	我需要你的幫忙
◇ lend a hand	伸出援手吧
◇ can you pitch in	幫個忙吧
◇ roll up your sleeves	捲起袖子幫忙吧

W the <u>writing</u> is on the wall
結果已經可以預知

MP3-179

Idiom Definition

This is used to describe when a sign or omen foretelling the future is perceived by the speaker.

成語定義 這個表達法用來描述説話者已經看到預測未來的徵象、前兆。

Examples

例 We're going to lose that account; the writing is on the wall.

我們會失去那個客戶，這是無法避免的未來。

例 No one said anything, but the writing is on the wall.

沒有人說任何事，但結果都可預知道了。

Background

This comes from a story in the Jewish Bible, familiar to both Christians and Jews. In the story, writing magically appeared on the palace walls, a Jewish prophet was called in to interpret their meaning and he warned of a drastic event would soon befall the kingdom.

背景資料 這個表達法來自猶太人的聖經，是個基督徒和猶太人都熟之的故事。故事裡提到，在皇宮的牆壁上出現了神奇的訊息，一個猶太先知被宣進宮，去詮釋訊息的意義，他警告大家一個激烈的事件即將臨到他們的國家。

Today, it refers to when there's no overt unmistakable sign something's going to happen but little hints indicate something is up.

商業用法 今日，這個詞意指沒有任何明顯的事預告某事即將發生，但暗示了有事情會發生。

Alternatives 相關用語

◇ read between the lines 你要讀出絃外之音

◇ the signs are there 有跡可循

◇ I smell a rat 我可以聞出有事不對勁

◇ it doesn't add up 這事不對勁

◇ something's rotten in the state of Denmark
丹麥那裡出事了

◇ something's not right 有事情不對勁了

國家圖書館出版品預行編目資料

商務談判英語看這本就夠了 / 湯姆斯, 張瑪麗合著.

-- 增訂1版. -- 新北市：哈福企業有限公司, 2024.05

　　面 ；　公分. --（英語系列 ; 89）

ISBN 978-626-7444-09-2（平裝）

1.CST: 商業英文 2.CST: 會話 3.CST: 商業談判

805.188　　　　　　　　　　　　　113003727

免費下載QR Code音檔
行動學習，即刷即聽

商務談判英語　看這本就夠了
（QR Code版）

作者／湯姆斯，張瑪麗
責任編輯／Judy Chou
封面設計／李秀英
內文排版／林樂娟
出版者／哈福企業有限公司
地址／新北市淡水區民族路 110 巷 38 弄 7 號
電話／(02) 2808-4587　傳真／(02) 2808-6545
郵政劃撥／31598840
戶名／哈福企業有限公司
出版日期／2024 年 5 月
台幣定價／450 元 (附線上 MP3)
港幣定價／150 元 (附線上 MP3)
封面內文圖／取材自 Shutterstock

全球華文國際市場總代理／采舍國際有限公司
地址／新北市中和區中山路 2 段 366 巷 10 號 3 樓
電話／(02) 8245-8786　傳真／(02) 8245-8718
網址／ www.silkbook.com 新絲路華文網

香港澳門總經銷／和平圖書有限公司
地址／香港柴灣嘉業街 12 號百樂門大廈 17 樓
電話／(852) 2804-6687
傳真／(852) 2804-6409

email ／ welike8686@Gmail.com
facebook ／ Haa-net 哈福網路商城

電子書格式：PDF

哈福

哈福